THE DIVIDING SEA

Ruth Elwin ⬚⬚⬚⬚⬚⬚⬚⬚ ⬚⬚⬚⬚⬚⬚ ⬚hen, during the la⬚⬚⬚⬚⬚⬚⬚⬚⬚⬚⬚⬚⬚⬚⬚⬚⬚⬚ ⬚ to stay with thei⬚⬚⬚⬚⬚⬚⬚⬚⬚⬚⬚⬚⬚⬚⬚ set house: "We le⬚⬚⬚⬚⬚⬚⬚⬚⬚⬚⬚ ⬚⬚e says. "Not that we ⬚⬚⬚⬚⬚⬚. We read a lot and made up stories to entertain each other. We both loved the house and were very happy."

It is that house, christened Hillcrest, which plays an important part in the Quantocks Quartet. "My grandfather bought it in the 1930s from three elderly sisters – all of whom had been painters. Their murals still remained on the stable walls. I used to think about those sisters and wonder about life in the village when they were young." From these thoughts came the author's books about the four Purcell sisters. *The Dividing Sea*, the third title in the series, is set mainly in France during the Great War and tells the story of Julia Purcell.

Ruth Elwin Harris lived abroad herself for several years, both before and after her marriage – at one time helping out at an orphanage in India run by Mother Theresa's nuns. She has written stories for magazines and radio and three other novels in the Quantocks Quartet: *The Silent Shore* (shortlisted for The Observer Teenage Fiction Award), *The Beckoning Hills* and *The Secluded Garden* (published by Julia MacRae Books). She lives with her family in North Yorkshire.

Also by Ruth Elwin Harris

The Beckoning Hills
The Secluded Garden
The Silent Shore

The Dividing Sea

Ruth Elwin Harris

WALKER BOOKS
LONDON

First published 1989 by Julia MacRae Books
This edition published 1990 by
Walker Books Ltd, 87 Vauxhall Walk
London SE11 5HJ

© 1989 Ruth Elwin Harris
Cover illustration © 1989 Emma Chichester Clark

Reprinted 1993

Printed in Great Britain by
Cox and Wyman Ltd, Reading, Berkshire

British Library Cataloguing in Publication Data
A catalogue record for this book is
available from the British Library.
ISBN 0-7445-1757-5

Contents

Part One

1910

Chapter One

Julia Purcell sighed as she studied Mrs. Mackenzie's copy of *Household Management. Very economical*, it said of the section headed *Little Dinners for April* – printing the words in italics as if to emphasise the fact. Economy, apparently, meant mutton – mutton roast, mutton cold, mutton hashed ... Julia sat in the Rectory morning-room carefully copying each menu into her notebook and tried to persuade herself that mutton was her favourite meat. Not until she had come to the end of the April menus did she let her eyes linger over the section entitled *Family Dinners*. There was nothing economical about the Family Dinner menus – duck, chicken, ham, fillets of turbot, salmon cutlets, four courses always rather than three, and cream, not cornflour custard, to go with the puddings. Julia sighed again. No point in wondering whether those were the meals Mrs. Mackenzie served at the Rectory in the evenings. The Purcells had never eaten in such style when their mother was alive; they certainly could not afford to do so now they were on their own.

She turned the pages, avoiding the section on *Responsibilities of the Second in Command in the House* which never ceased to frighten her, and was studying the drawing of a skinned rabbit with some surprise – nothing looked less like any rabbit that she had ever seen – when she heard the sound of carriage wheels on the Rectory drive outside.

"Here's Master Geoffrey already," said Bertha's voice in the hall, "and the Mistress not home yet. The poor lad. 'Tis the same every term. Get Mr. Shattock in from the garden, Alice. Quickly now. We'll need help with Master Geoffrey's trunk."

Cold air swirled under the morning-room door. Bertha must have opened the front door. "Whoa, there." That was Mr. Gould. Harnesses jangled. A horse harumphed. Julia looked guiltily at the clock as she returned *Household Management* to its place on the shelf. She hadn't realised it was so late.

"Welcome home, Master Geoffrey." Bertha's voice was indulgent, but changed immediately. "Lord love us, how you've grown! Look at those sleeves. Halfway up your arm, they are. Come in quick, there's a good lad. We don't want the place turned into an ice-house. How was school then?"

"Hateful, as usual. Where is everyone? Where's Mother?"

"Well, now . . ."

Julia went out into the hall.

Geoffrey turned to greet her. The disappointment on his face was unmistakeable. "Oh," he said, "I thought . . ."

Julia said the first thing that came into her head. "You're not a bit like your brothers."

Thick black eyebrows met over the bridge of his nose. "That's what everyone says. Who are you? I don't know you, do I?"

"It's Miss Julia from Hillcrest, Master Geoffrey," Bertha said. "You must know of the Purcells, surely?"

"Your father's our guardian," Julia said. "He's been our guardian since" – her voice quavered – "since January."

"Oh. Yes, of course. Father told me." He blushed and looked away, pushed his hands into his pockets, brought them out again. "I'm sorry," he said. "About, well, your mother. It was rotten luck."

There was a long silence. Bertha had gone outside to supervise the unloading of Geoffrey's school trunk. Geoffrey kicked the hall rug, still avoiding Julia's gaze. His wrists and hands stuck out from the too-short sleeves, stiff and awkward, like those of the scarecrow that was supposed to frighten the birds away from Tinker's Meadow behind Hillcrest.

[4]

"You've got sisters, haven't you?" he said at last, looking about him as if expecting them suddenly to appear. "Four of you, Father said. Are they here too?"

"They're at home."

"Are you the eldest?"

She shook her head. "That's Frances. She's seventeen. I'm fifteen. Just."

"I'm older than you then." He sounded pleased. "I've been fifteen for months and months."

"Now, Master Geoffrey," Bertha said, coming back into the hall, "let's have your coat. Time you was off, Miss Julia. Annie'll be wondering where you've got to."

"Yes, well . . . Goodbye, then."

Geoffrey was not listening. "Where's Mother?" he said to Bertha, as Julia closed the front door behind her. "Why isn't she here?"

Julia hurried along the Rectory drive and up the road to Hillcrest. It was a way she had come to know well in the past three months. Strange to think that during the last school holidays Mrs. Purcell had been alive and Mackenzies and Purcells barely knew each other . . . She mustn't let herself think of such things. Think instead of the warm, snug Hillcrest kitchen, where her sisters and Annie awaited her return.

Sarah and Gwen were busy with their homework, Annie with the mending, when she burst in.

"I've met Geoffrey Mackenzie."

"Well?"

"He's not a bit like I expected."

"What did you expect?" Gwen asked.

Julia paused, picturing Geoffrey's sister and two brothers. "To be like the others, I suppose, but he isn't. He's dark, for one thing. And quiet. He hardly said a word."

"Lucy doesn't say much either," Gwen pointed out. "It's Gabriel and Antony who do all the talking in that family."

"Is he nice?" Sarah asked anxiously. "Do you think he'll

talk to me?"

"I don't know," Julia considered. "I think he's shy."

"Get back to your work now," Annie told the younger Purcells firmly. "You'll be meeting Master Geoffrey soon enough. Give me a hand with this mending, Miss Julia, there's a good girl. You know I can't darn for love nor money." She pushed the stockings across the table to Julia, exclaiming at the sight of Gwen's exercise book as she did so. "Just look at that page, Miss Gwen. Flowers down the margin again. How many times do I have to tell you? It doesn't do, nicely drawn though they may be. What will the Rector say when he sees that lot? Eh?"

Julia smiled as she threaded her needle. Gwen and Annie were always at loggerheads over Gwen's drawings. Gwen insisted that Mr. Mackenzie didn't mind. Julia suspected Mr. Mackenzie had bowed to the inevitable.

Julia's thoughts returned to Geoffrey as she darned. She wished now that she had not made that remark about his brothers, however true it had been. She had realised he did not like it the moment she spoke. He had taken it as criticism, when she had meant it as an observation only. Perhaps when she next saw him she could try to explain ...

Julia might consider Geoffrey to be both shy and quiet but no one could think the youngest Mackenzie was either.

"Eh, Master Antony," Annie said, when he brought Geoffrey over to Hillcrest to meet the rest of the Purcells later that day, "anyone would think you own the place, the way you carry on. Showing off ... Let your brother say a word, do. Pleased to meet you, Master Geoffrey. We've heard all about you."

"You have to be nice to Annie," Antony said, "because she's in charge. She makes wonderful fruitcake. Now ... you say you've met Julia, so you know her. That's Gwen over there. She has lessons with me. She's hopeless. Oh yes, you are – at lessons, anyway. And this is Sarah. Father

[6]

teaches her too, but she's the baby. She's only seven."

Geoffrey stayed in the doorway. "We're not allowed in the kitchen at home," he said.

"I should think not, indeed," Annie said. "Down those nasty basement stairs ... It's different here. We have to watch the pennies in this house. We don't light the fire in t'other room till tea-time. It should be warming nicely enough by now, Miss Julia, if you want to take them in."

"We're not poor, exactly," Gwen was anxious to explain, as Antony led the way to the living-room. "We're not very rich, that's all. We should be renting a house in Taunton, you see, instead of living in a big house like this, but we wanted to stay here after, well, after ... so we're trying it out for a year to see if we can manage. That's what Annie meant when she said about watching the pennies."

"I see," Geoffrey said, though Julia was sure he did not. She tried to look at the living-room with his eyes, as he sat on the edge of the settee. Comfortable, a bit shabby, the fire just beginning to catch and give out some warmth – it was very different from the spacious, elegant Rectory drawing-room.

His eyes came back to the sisters. "Where's ... Frances, is it?"

"She'll be working," Julia said.

"Working?"

"Painting."

"That's not work."

"Of course it's work," Julia and Gwen said together.

"It's not. Lucy paints. She doesn't call it work."

"We do," Gwen said, defiant.

Geoffrey's eyes were curious as he looked from one to the other. Tactfully he changed the subject. "Why's Father your guardian? It isn't as if you've ever had anything to do with us. You don't even come to church."

"We do now," Gwen said. "Every Sunday. Twice sometimes. Sarah has to go to Sunday School too. Your mother

[7]

sees to that."

Geoffrey grinned. "She would. No, but seriously ... about Father?"

Gwen and Sarah looked to Julia. "There wasn't anyone else to look after us," she said. "Only two great-aunts, but they're too old. So ... Are you any good at games? Sarah and Antony like Ludo. Why don't we play?" She had seen Sarah's mouth begin to tremble. Besides, she found it hard herself to talk about what had happened; those dreadful January days were still too close.

Ludo needed four players only. Julia volunteered to sit out; she always preferred to watch and was amused now by the different styles of play. Antony hovered over the board and then swooped, with shrieks of alarm or crows of triumph. Gwen never made a false move, deciding which counter to move before she put out a hand and counting precisely when she had done so. Sarah was young enough to mind losing; she watched every move, deliberated for what seemed hours over which counter to play and then, having chosen, changed her mind. Today she was winning ... until Geoffrey threw a five. Sarah gave a squeak, clutched the table and gazed at him with terror in her eyes. His hand hovered over one counter before picking up another. "One, two, three, four, five. There. Your turn, Sarah."

"You missed it!" she cried. "Silly, silly you. You didn't see me. Five – you could have landed *there* and sent me right back to the beginning."

"So I could," Geoffrey said. "How stupid of me. Well, never mind." He caught Julia's eye and gave her an apologetic, what-else-could-I-do smile. "I'll have to take more care next time, won't I?"

Frances came into the room as the two Mackenzies were leaving. Her greeting was perfunctory. "So you're Geoffrey," was all she said. "Come along, Sarah. Time for bed."

Geoffrey's eyes went from Frances to Julia and back to Frances again. In the hall he watched Frances take Sarah

[8]

upstairs and waited until Antony had departed.

"I think you are very like *your* sister," he told Julia. "Except . . ."

"Except what?"

"Oh . . . it doesn't matter."

It did matter. She had understood his meaning exactly, although she could not have put it into words either. All her life she had been compared to Frances and found wanting; Frances, no beauty in the accepted sense – 'pre-Raphaelite' was how Mrs. Purcell had always described her – but fascinating nevertheless; Frances, lively, imperious . . . and talented. "What do you expect?" had been Mrs. Purcell's invariable reply when Julia expressed disappointment at her own pictures in comparison to those of her sister. "She's two years older than you. Of course her paintings are better." Julia had not been consoled, knowing even then that something other than difference in age separated them.

She thought about Geoffrey after his departure. How little they knew of him. "We've heard all about you," Annie had said, but it was not true. His name had scarcely been mentioned at the Rectory during the term. "Out of sight, out of mind," as Annie herself might have said. Julia remembered how her own mother had always come into Taunton to meet her children at the end of the school term. Mrs. Mackenzie hadn't even been at the Rectory to greet her son when he came home.

Geoffrey often came over to Hillcrest during the Easter holidays, at first with Antony but later, as he became more at ease, on his own. He was quiet but observant, sometimes content to sit in watchful silence, sometimes asking questions. He wanted to know about Commander Purcell's portrait hanging on the wall and was surprised to learn that it had been painted by Mrs. Purcell. "But it's a proper portrait," he said. Gwen and Julia looked at each other but made no comment. "Why the tropical uniform?" was his next question. They explained, reluctantly because of the voyage's end, that Commander Purcell had been about to depart for the Far East with his ship at the time. Presumably Geoffrey sensed something was wrong for he changed the subject quickly, admiring instead the embroidery lying on a nearby chair. "Mother sews a lot," he said, when Julia admitted that it was hers. "You ought to talk to her."

They liked having Geoffrey around. They could ask him questions they felt unable to ask of the other Mackenzies. Why was Antony educated at home, for instance, when his brothers had been sent away to school?

"He did go to school once, but he nearly died during his first term. Scarlet fever, it was. They had to pray for him in church, three Sundays running." Such a necessity was obviously a source of pride. "Father's taught him at home ever since. He's delicate, Mother says." Geoffrey admitted to being envious. "I hate school."

Julia found that hard to understand. She had been sorry to leave hers; she missed it still. Lying awake in bed she would sometimes picture herself returning to the familiar buildings, being greeted by Miranda Cartwright and welcomed by Miss Teasdale, the art mistress. Occasionally she dreamt of the old days, always waking afterwards with an oppressive sense of loss.

Geoffrey was happy at Hillcrest. "It's so comfortable, somehow," he said, as if the Rectory were not. He was toasting muffins at the time, kneeling up on the hearthrug. "Muffins come up on a special plate at home," he said, "with a silver cover like the dome of St. Paul's to keep them hot. They don't taste as nice somehow, if you haven't cooked them yourself. They aren't as hot either." His face was crimson from the heat of the fire. Julia wanted to draw him but was too shy to ask. It was Antony, told in confidence by Sarah, who blurted it out later.

[10]

Geoffrey thought Julia must be joking. "What do you want to draw me for?"

"I like drawing people. I always have. I've only got us now that we've come home. I persuaded Antony to pose once, but he was hopeless." It wasn't so much that Antony couldn't keep still, but that he would play the fool, waggling his fingers in his ears and sticking out his tongue – "Like this, Julia? Like this?" Sometimes she found twelve-year-old boys hard to understand.

"I don't mind you drawing me if you want to," Geoffrey said, "as long as I can see what you've done." He made no comment when she did so, favourable or otherwise. She suspected that he had expected a portrait like that of Commander Purcell and was disappointed.

"You have to look and watch first, and then do lots of sketches," she explained. "I'm not very good yet, so I just do quick drawings. I might try something formal in the summer, when I know you better."

The summer holidays seemed a long way off, with three months of the summer term lying between. When Geoffrey went back to school, Julia was surprised to discover that she missed him.

In the old days – before January – divisions in the Purcell family had been clear cut. Frances was a member of the adult world, Julia and Gwen were children, Sarah was in the nursery. Things had changed since Mrs. Purcell's death. Julia no longer felt herself to be a child, but neither did she feel grown-up. Gwen took it for granted that Julia was her companion still; Frances expected her to be supporter and confidante. She did not know where her place lay. She felt that Geoffrey and she had family position as well as their age in common. She hid her insecurity better than he did, perhaps, but she sensed that they were much alike.

It was Frances who had decreed that Julia and Gwen should no longer share a bedroom. "You're grown-up now," she told Julia. "Or as good as. It's time you had your own room." Julia had been dismayed by the change. She missed Gwen's company, particularly on those nights when sleep was slow to come and memories of Mrs. Purcell too vivid, and had been hurt by Gwen's cheerful acceptance of the new arrangement. Gwen, indeed, had welcomed the extra space Julia's departure gave her, quickly replacing Julia's bed with a table on which she was now busily propagating spider plants. The only advantage Julia could see in having a room of her own was the opportunity it gave her to get to know Frances better. Often Frances would come in in the evenings, wrap her quilt round her and curl up at the bottom of Julia's bed and talk.

On this particular evening, towards the end of the Easter holidays, it was some time before Frances brought up the subject that was the reason for her visit. "How would you feel if I went away?" she said. "You wouldn't mind taking charge, would you?"

Julia's heart missed a beat. "Went away? Where to?"

"The Slade, of course. Why the surprise?"

Although she had known for years of Frances's determination to attend art school, Julia had never taken it seriously. She had certainly never believed it possible. "Mr. and Mrs. Mackenzie would never let you go. You know what they think of art school. 'No respectably brought up young girl', all that sort of thing. You'll never get their permission."

"I might," Frances said. "I've got Gabriel on my side now, and he's been talking to them. He thinks he can persuade them to let me try for an interview. After that . . . well, it's up to me, isn't it? I'm sure I can persuade Mr. Mackenzie, if I do get a place. The parable of the talents . . . it should be quite easy arguing that out with a clergyman, don't you think? It's what I'm hoping, anyway."

So that was the explanation of the many discussions that had taken place between Gabriel and Frances during Gabriel's time at home over Easter. Julia was amazed, as much by her sister's temerity as by her determination. "Wouldn't you be frightened, living in London on your own ...?"

"Oh, *Julia*!" Frances said, as if ridiculing the idea, but after a moment she gave a little shrug. "I expect I shall, but I'll just have to put up with it."

"What about the cost?" Julia said, thinking of all the economies they had had to make since their mother's death. "Surely we couldn't afford it?"

"We'll have to work that out once I've got a place. Mr. Mackenzie's much more cheerful about money now that our allowances have been sorted out with the Navy. I don't care how much I have to scrimp and save in London – I won't eat if I don't have to – so long as I'm learning. It's not the money I'm worried about – well, I am, of course I am – so much as the rest of you. We must make the Mackenzies realise everything will be all right, even with me away. I don't see why you and Annie shouldn't be able to manage. You're more practical than I am, and Annie's been running the place on her own for years, anyway. Ever since Father died really. Besides, you get on so well with Mrs. Mackenzie ... You will say yes, won't you? Please."

"I don't know," Julia said. "I'll have to think about it."

"There's no hurry," Frances said. "I wouldn't be going until September. There's something else you should realise too. If the Mackenzies agree to my going, then they can't object to your doing the same in three years' time."

Such a possibility had never entered Julia's head. "I couldn't ever go to art school," she said. "I'm not good enough."

"Oh, Julia," Frances said. "Don't be so silly. Of course you are."

Julia's first reaction had been to refuse Frances's demand. Not that she could do anything, if Frances were determined; she knew that from experience. It was the responsibility that frightened her. Suppose something went wrong – an accident, illness, financial disaster – and Frances, coming home, blamed her? After a while, however, her thoughts changed. Responsibility would not rest on her alone. There would be the Mackenzies, and Annie. Perhaps it wouldn't be so difficult. She might even enjoy it. She was more practical than Frances, whose thoughts were absorbed by her painting. She did not mind household activities; some she even enjoyed. She still felt pleasure and pride every time she saw the jars of marmalade on the larder shelf that she and Annie had made earlier in the year. It occurred to her – though it seemed treacherous even to think it – that life might be easier with Frances away. Frances could be difficult, particularly where Mrs. Mackenzie was concerned, resenting Mrs. Mackenzie's interference in Purcell affairs and refusing to believe that the Rector's wife was motivated only by kindness and a sense of duty.

Julia was very conscious of the burden that had been placed on the Mackenzies' shoulders. To take on the guardianship of four girls, as Mr. Mackenzie had done, simply because their mother was a parishioner was an act of true Christian charity. If only Frances could be made to appreciate that fact.

Chapter Two

It was the start of the cricket season, strangely enough, that marked the beginning of the Purcells' recovery from their mother's death. They knew nothing of cricket, having played tennis at school, and were incredulous when Antony explained the rules. "You must have got something wrong, Antony," Frances said. "No game could be as complicated as that."

Antony was indignant. "Come and watch on Saturday and you'll see. I know what I'm talking about. I help score."

The Purcells did not even consider the invitation. Mrs. Mackenzie had strict ideas about what could or could not be done; attending cricket matches, they assumed, would come into the latter category. But Mr. Mackenzie announced at lunch the following Saturday that he would be 'wandering down' to see the start of play that afternoon and would take anyone who wished to accompany him. The sisters looked at each other, at the Rector, at Mrs. Mackenzie . . .

"Now you'll see how right I was," Antony said triumphantly.

Mr. Mackenzie's version of the rules was certainly more concise than Antony's but sounded no less strange. It didn't matter. The Purcells might not understand the finer points of the game, nor the terms (byes, wides, leg before – such extraordinary words), nor even something so basic as the scoring, but watching cricket was a pleasant way of spending a summer afternoon. Attending matches became a regular event whenever the Huish Priory team played at home. No one could call them attentive followers of the game, but they clapped when other people clapped and groaned when groaning seemed appropriate. The most enjoyable aspect of watching cricket for the three eldest Purcells was the new opportunities it gave them for drawing and painting. Frances, now gathering a portfolio of work to take to her Slade interview, spent most afternoons at the edge of the cricket field or beyond, painting distant views, while Julia preferred to sketch people – the players on the field, batsmen sitting out, the spectators – delighted to have subjects other than her sisters and Annie. More importantly, though the Purcells did not realise it at the time, watching cricket became the means by which they were drawn into village life. Mrs. Purcell had become a recluse in her widowhood, with the result that her daughters had rarely left Hillcrest, except to attend school. Saturday afternoons helped them put names to the faces they saw around the village every day and in church on Sundays – Bill Roberts, the large, smiling blacksmith, who captained the Huish Priory team, as well as playing solo trumpet in the village band; the Chedzoy brothers, fierce, burly men, of whom the Purcells were secretly afraid; Mr. Cross, owner of the general store, whose umpiring was acknowledged by the village to be grossly partisan; and the church organist, Mr. Podimore, an enthusiastic cricketer with a distressing tendency to get run out. "Had his mind on his latest composition again, instead of the game," Antony would remark in disgust, after yet another premature dismissal.

Jess Hancock, Sarah's friend from Sunday School, was the one who filled in the gaps in their knowledge. Jess knew not only the names of everyone in the village but also their connections, through marriage or blood, and could answer any question they cared to ask. On occasion she even volunteered information. "Bill Roberts's sweet on our Mary," she said once, and Gwen and Julia watched with new interest the way Bill Roberts came over to talk to Mary when the other side was fielding. Julia liked drawing Bill and Mary together for the contrast they made – Mary, fair-haired and dainty, against the swarthy, heavy-muscled blacksmith, his bulk made bulkier by the pads he wore while waiting to go into bat.

Geoffrey played for the village team on his return from school at the end of the summer term, usually batting at number two or three – the most important places, according to Antony. Watching him the Purcells were impressed. Normally clumsy and uncoordinated, particularly so at home under his mother's irritated gaze, Geoffrey on the cricket field appeared both graceful and confident, hitting fours, even off Dunkery St. Michael's fast bowler, with seeming ease.

"You're good, aren't you?" Julia said to him, after a match in which he had distinguished himself by hitting the highest number of runs in any match during the season; and was then cross with herself for allowing surprise to sound in her voice.

He pulled a face. "Not as good as Gabriel. I never am. At anything."

She felt a sudden sense of kinship. "Really?"

Earlier that summer, long before Geoffrey came home for the holidays, Annie had returned from a visit to her invalid mother bearing a hamper of squawking birds. The Purcells, she announced, were going to keep hens.

"Only pullets, these are," she said, opening the hamper on the grass outside the stables. "And not many to start. We'll see how we go. Jack says he can get more if we want them."

After their initial shock, and despite the discovery that hens required a surprising amount of attention, the Purcells realised that Annie had been talking sense. There was space enough at Hillcrest for hens to scratch about, and the stables to keep them in at night. Although family finances were by now more secure, fear of losing Hillcrest still hung over the household and the impending expense of Frances's three years in London meant that every penny mattered. For very little outlay hens would provide a regular supply of eggs, and in time an occasional bird for the pot. Annie's brother supplied extra pullets ("This time next year we'll have our own chicks," Annie said), and by the time Geoffrey came home from school at the end of the summer term the Purcells could scarcely remember when hens had not been running free on the grassy slope by the stables.

To Annie, with the countrywoman's respect for the calendar, summer was the season in which to prepare for the shortages of winter, a time to make jams and jellies, bottle fruit and salt vegetables. And to collect grain for the hens.

"They won't get by on household scraps through the winter," she told the Purcells, "and where's the sense in having birds if we're paying out for their food half the year? You'll have to go out and glean. Mr. Escott's sending the reaper into Tinker's Meadow tomorrow. He says you can glean there. It's a special favour, mind. They won't have raked by then, so it shouldn't be hard."

It had never occurred to the Purcells that gleaning was anything but a Biblical occupation. They were astonished to learn that it was still done; astonished, too, to discover what a sociable occasion harvesting was. All Huish Priory seemed to be gathered in Tinker's Meadow. Not only Mr. Escott's men were working but men from other farms in the area too, while women collected sheaves together into stooks, and the village boys clustered round the steadily diminishing square of uncut barley in the middle of the field, brandishing sticks, whistling and shouting.

"Look," Sarah said suddenly. "There's Antony. And Geoffrey."

Geoffrey saw the Purcells as they saw him and came bounding over, waving a stick of cudgel-like proportions. Earth and straw clung to the old clothes he was wearing. He might have been a village lad himself.

"What are you doing here?" he said. "Does Mother know? What have you got in those baskets?"

[18]

Julia explained about the gleaning.

"Meal's expensive, Annie says," Gwen said. "We have to watch the pennies, you know. We can't afford to spend money on the hens and us too."

Geoffrey was silent. "I didn't realise it was like that," he said at last. "I'll help you, if you like. Not now. Later. When the reaping's done."

He left them to join the crowd gathering round the dwindling square of barley. The horses came up out of the dip in the field, the red arms of the reaper flailing the air behind them. Small grey shapes burst out of the barley and bobbed frantically over the stubble. Boys whooped and shouted, threw sticks and stones ... Julia turned her head quickly. Rabbits were pests. They ate Gwen's vegetables. It didn't do to think about such an end, all the same ... Better get on with the gleaning.

Sarah had tired long ago and gone home to Annie. Frances was painting at the edge of the copse that bordered the field. Only Julia and Gwen were left. How much grain did hens need, Julia wondered, straightening up to ease her aching back, and saw Geoffrey approaching, a smile of triumph on his face.

"I've brought you a present," he announced.

"A present? What sort of present?"

With a theatrical flourish worthy of Antony he produced from behind his back – one large, dead rabbit.

"A rabbit!"

"I thought it might help," he said, and laid the body on the ground by her basket. Traces of blood marked the grey fur on its head. "I fell on it," he said. "I must have suffocated it. Poor thing." He looked down at the corpse. "I suppose I should skin it for you. I'll have to ask Bertha. She might know how."

"Don't worry. Annie will. Or I can borrow your mother's Mrs. Beeton. I remember seeing about rabbits in there. Drawings too."

"It looks a lot smaller, somehow, now it's dead," he said doubtfully. "Will there be enough to feed you all?"

"Of course there will. It is ... you are ..." She tried to find adequate words. "Kind," was all she could say.

"Mr. Escott's reaping High Field on Friday," he said. "He told me so. I'll get you another rabbit then. Two, if you're lucky." He flung his stick into the air and caught it. "You'll see. You'll be able to have rabbit for dinner every week while I'm home."

Oh yes. There was no doubt about it – life was getting better day by day. She was almost sorry to be going away to stay with Miranda Cartwright.

It was *The Tempest* that had brought Julia and Miranda Cartwright together at school, and in particular Miss Dawson's rendering of *Full fathom five*. Until that particular Shakespeare lesson the two girls had scarcely noticed each other. " 'Of his bones are coral made'," Miss Dawson warbled, in her thin reedy voice, " 'Those are pearls that were his eyes ...' " at which point Julia leapt up from her desk and rushed from the room to be followed at once by Miranda, who eventually found her sobbing among the hockey sticks at the far end of the cloakroom. Miranda sat down beside her and patted her knee in silence, before pushing a small, lacy handkerchief, quite inadequate for the purpose intended, into Julia's hand. "I think worms would be much worse," she said. "I've always hated the thought of worms. Whereas this is quite a nice end, really. 'Something rich and strange' – it's beautiful, don't you think?"

Later, when Julia had been condemned to copy four pages from the dictionary as punishment for leaving the class without permission, by a headmistress who might, in a school for naval daughters, have given more thought to the implications of burial at sea, it was Miranda who dictated each page to her at writing speed. "I don't mind. It's only fair. I left the classroom to come after you. They should have punished me too."

After that they naturally became friends and remained so for the rest of Julia's time at school. When Miranda's parents took Miranda out to lunch Julia went too. She discovered that it was Mrs. Cartwright's naval father who had provided Miranda's qualification for a place at the school, for Mr. Cartwright himself worked in a London hospital – running it, Miranda said, though Julia thought she might be exaggerating. Julia got on well with the Cartwrights. They were kind and jolly, treating her as they might have treated a second daughter and when the Purcells had to leave school Julia missed Miranda's parents as well as Miranda herself.

Miranda missed Julia too. She wished Julia could come and stay in the holidays, she said in her letters. Julia wished it too, without thinking it possible – and was incredulous when Mrs. Mackenzie told her that Mrs. Cartwright had issued an invitation through the Rectory. "We have discussed it, Mr. Mackenzie and I, and think that it might be arranged, if you would like to go ..."

Frances was put out. "When I think of all the trouble I've had, getting them to agree to anything I want ..."

Mrs. Mackenzie made the arrangements without consulting Julia. Julia would accompany Mrs. Mackenzie to London when Mrs. Mackenzie visited her sister, newly back from India. The Cartwrights lived south of the river; it would not be difficult for Mrs. Cartwright to come into London to collect Julia. "It would give us an opportunity to meet," Mrs. Mackenzie told the Purcells.

"But suppose Mrs. Mackenzie doesn't approve of Mrs. Cartwright?" Gwen said afterwards, making Julia suddenly nervous. The two women were, after all, very different ... She even wondered whether she and Miranda would have anything in common now that their lives had gone such different ways. But all went well. Mrs. Mackenzie and Mrs. Cartwright spent nearly an hour closeted together, apparently happily, and Miranda was as affectionate and ebullient as ever.

"Oh, Ju," she said, the first moment they were alone together. "You don't know how wonderful it is to see you again. Are you all right? *Really* all right? I've been so worried about you. You think no one could be the same after such an awful thing happening, but you haven't changed a bit."

Julia settled easily into the Cartwright routine, becoming one of the family in no time at all. Mr. Cartwright teased, Mrs. Cartwright fussed. Mrs. Cartwright fussed over Miranda too. "It's because I took so long coming," Miranda told Julia one night, as they lay in bed exchanging confidences in the dark. "Twelve years before I arrived . . . I suppose that's why there's only me. I do envy you, having sisters."

Life had never been so carefree. Julia woke every morning to a world without problems, money worries or household chores. She was not even expected to make her own bed. She and Miranda talked endlessly. They ran occasional errands, took letters to post, picked flowers from the garden for Mrs. Cartwright to arrange; sometimes arranged flowers themselves. They called on friends of Miranda's living nearby, who then called back. When it was not too hot they played tennis.

Mrs. Cartwright took the two girls up to London for the day, together with her sister, Madame Drouin, who was also staying. Madame Drouin – "call me Aunt Amy, dear, like Miranda" – had come over from Paris where she lived with her French husband; she was taking Miranda and Mrs. Cartwright back with her later that month. "Part of Miranda's education, I keep saying," Mr. Cartwright told Julia, mock severe. "I shall expect to be told all about Paris when she gets back, geography, history, art – the lot."

Julia found London overwhelming. Such noise, such dirt, and so many people. She was impressed, however, by Self-ridges' roof garden, where they lunched in the open air beside a flower-entwined pergola, seemingly far from city streets. On their way home Mrs. Cartwright insisted that the taxi driver make a detour by Gower Street to allow Julia a glimpse of the Slade. Julia, looking at the stately buildings of University College, felt her admiration for Frances growing. How did Frances have the courage to contemplate spending three years in such grand surroundings?

It was some time before Julia became restless, and even longer before she realised the cause – she simply didn't have enough to do. She was not used to such a leisurely pace; at Hillcrest there was never enough time for all that needed doing. If she had brought her paints with her, she thought, she could have painted Mr. Cartwright, standing with one foot on the fender, watch-chain stretched across his stomach, exuding well-being as he played with the coins in his pocket; or Mrs. Cartwright, glancing up over her half-moon spectacles in that endearing, rather flustered way she had. Leaving her paints at home had been deliberate; she had not wanted to draw attention to herself, but she realised now she was so much part of the family no one would have minded. Indeed they would probably have been delighted to pose. At least she had brought her embroidery. That gave her something to do.

And then she found herself another occupation. Aunt Amy suggested that Julia should join in the French lessons she was giving Miranda prior to Miranda's visit to Paris. Surprised by the speed with which her French came back and flattered by Aunt Amy's praise – she had a remarkably good ear, Aunt Amy said – Julia became enthusiastic. French provided her with the challenge she needed.

Mrs. Cartwright was ecstatic about Julia's embroidery. "It's the way you use the colours," she said, when Julia protested that really it was nothing compared to Mrs. Mackenzie's beautiful sewing on the church vestments. "So clever. So original." She insisted that Julia should fetch it to show to friends who had come for tea. "You can see the eye of the artist at work," she was saying to them, as Julia went reluctantly up to her room.

She was still talking when Julia came down. Her voice carried with terribly clarity out into the hall. "... tragic, absolutely tragic. Four of them, you know, and none out of school at the time ... Oh, yes. A charming girl. So brave, so very brave ... One doesn't know how best to help ... we're delighted to have her to stay."

Julia gripped the banister. She stood without moving for a moment. Then very slowly she crept back up the stairs to the landing before coming down as noisily as she dared without risking suspicion.

"Ah, there you are, dear," Mrs. Cartwright greeted her. "We were beginning to think you'd got lost. Are you all right? You look very pale."

Her first reaction was to pack her bag and go. She did not want pity. She hated pity. They were not brave. They were behaving as anyone else would have done in the same circumstances. They did not need help. They could manage on their own.

She recovered her equanimity in time. She knew that the Cartwrights were genuinely fond of her. She believed – hoped – that it was as much for Miranda's sake as her own that she had been invited. Had Mrs. Cartwright not said that she was delighted Miranda should have a companion for part of the holidays? More important, she could think of no reason, other than the truth, for a premature departure.

More disturbing was an incident that occurred towards the end of her stay. Miranda was having new clothes made especially for her visit to Paris, and as a special favour – it was not far, there were no roads to cross, and dear Julia was so sensible – Mrs. Cartwright allowed the two girls to go on their own to the dressmaker for Miranda's last fitting.

"I keep on thinking it must be like getting married," Miranda giggled, as she and Julia set off down the road. "Don't you think it must be fun, getting married? First of all

the trousseau, and then the wedding, and last of all, babies
... Have you ever wondered what your husband'll be like?
I do hope mine's handsome."

Julia was amazed. Thoughts of marriage had never entered
her head. She did not know what to say and was thankful
that their arrival at the dressmaker's removed the need for a
reply.

Traces of perfume from previous clients still lingered in
the air of Miss Webber's fitting-room. Half-drawn curtains
protected it from the sunlight outside. Fabric lay over the
table, shapes already cut out on chairs, straw hats perched
on wooden blocks on the floor. Garments in various stages
of completion hung from hooks and rails round the room.
In one corner a dummy stood draped with white gauze, like
a ghost. Julia sat quietly out of the way and watched, admiring both Miranda's dresses and Miranda in them, but abstractedly. Another missed opportunity, she was thinking,
and glanced again round the room. Why, oh why, had she
not brought her sketchbook with her?

Miss Webber stepped back, biting one fingernail as she
studied Miranda. "I *think* what we need is contrast," she
said. "A sash, perhaps. Yes, of course. I have just the thing.
Wait here."

"I do *wish* you were coming to Paris with me," Miranda
said, twisting in front of the cheval-glass while she waited
for Miss Webber to return. "Of course I'll enjoy it with
Mother, but it would have been so much more *fun* if you'd
been allowed to come too." She turned her head to smile
at her reflection. "Particularly when you're so clever about
painting. You could have told me what to say to Daddy
about places like the Louvre. I'm sure I shan't know."

The words took a moment to sink in. "*Allowed* to come?"
Julia said. She could not believe it. There must be some
mistake. "Paris? Me? What do you mean? No one's ever
said anything about Paris."

Miranda's hand went to her mouth. "I'm sorry, I'm sorry.

I shouldn't have – Mother *told* me not to say, in case ..."

"In case what?"

"In case you didn't know. In case you hadn't been told."

"Here we are," Miss Webber said, returning with a length of scarlet silk over her arm. She knelt down beside Miranda and began draping and pinning.

I'm being stupid, Julia thought. Miranda *can't* mean ...

"So striking," Miss Webber murmured. "I'm sure Mrs. Cartwright will approve."

The half-drawn curtains made the fitting-room too warm, airless. Why, then, should she feel so cold? "Didn't know what? *Miranda*! You can't not tell me now. In case I didn't know what?"

"About Paris." Miranda's frightened eyes looked at her over the dressmaker's head. "We wanted you to come. Mother *asked* ..."

Gabriel arrived to escort Julia home. "Mother was called back to the Rectory," he explained. "Some crisis or other – you know what it's like in the village – so I volunteered. I was in London, anyway, at the Settlement." He smiled at Mrs. Cartwright. "I spend my time escorting Purcells round the country these days."

Mrs. Cartwright smiled back. Indeed, she positively fluttered as she gave him coffee and pressed him to stay to lunch, an invitation he declined with apparent regret. "I think we should be leaving. We've a long journey ahead of us."

"Why haven't you mentioned Gabriel before?" Miranda asked, going upstairs with Julia to check that nothing was left behind. "He's very good-looking, isn't he?"

Julia liked Gabriel and trusted him. She knew that Frances relied on him for support in her dealings with his parents, but she herself had never given him special thought and had certainly never considered his looks. Surprised by Miranda's admiration, she studied Gabriel surreptitiously as he sat opposite her in the train down to Taunton. The fair hair, too long for Mrs. Mackenzie's liking, the classical features – strong bone structure, long nose, firm chin – yes, Miranda might be right. What would Miranda think of Geoffrey, she wondered, so different in looks from Gabriel, with heavy eyebrows that made him look bad-tempered though he was not, a face plumper than Gabriel's and brown eyes instead of Gabriel's blue? She thought of other, more subtle differences, in carriage and confidence, and wondered whether they were due to the difference in age between the two brothers or to something else beside. It seemed to her, watching Gabriel now, that the same differences existed between herself and Frances, but those she knew could not be due to age, when less than two years separated them.

Gabriel looked up. "Penny for them," he said.

She blushed.

"Did you have a good time?" he said. "Everything go all right?"

"Yes, thank you." She added, "I'm sorry you had to come and fetch me."

"Don't think I was complaining," he said.

"I didn't think you were really." She hesitated. "What's the Settlement?"

"A place I visit in London."

"Something to do with the Minority Report?"

He frowned. "How do you know about that?"

"Lucy said that was why you've been away such a lot this summer. She mentioned the Settlement too."

"Don't talk about such things at home," he said. "Mother doesn't approve."

His tone was such that she did not like to question him further, despite her curiosity. She watched his gaze return to his book and wondered whether he was aware of the Cart-wrights' invitation to Paris. She knew that it was largely due to his insistence that the Mackenzies were allowing Frances to study at the Slade. They must surely have discussed Paris with him too. She wanted to ask him now, while they were alone, but lacked the courage. By the time the train drew in at Taunton she realised that it would have been a mistake. She must talk to Frances first.

Frances was bewildered. "*Paris*? I don't know anything about Paris. What are you talking about? Sit down and tell me again. Slowly, this time."

Impatience – she had waited until both Sarah and Gwen had gone to bed – and anger repressed for so long had made Julia incoherent. She took a deep breath and began again. "The Cartwrights wanted me to go to France with Miranda. She's going to stay with her aunt, in Paris. Her aunt's Mrs. Cartwright's sister. Mrs. Cartwright's such a dreadful sailor she didn't want to go, so she thought *I* could go instead. To keep Miranda company, you see. And Miranda wanted it, too. She said Mrs. Cartwright would spend all day chattering to Aunt Amy and it would be dreadfully dull for her but if I was there Aunt Amy would take us round Paris and we could have fun . . . And you needn't have worried because it would have been quite proper. Aunt Amy's old and married and respectable. They'd have paid, too, Miranda said, because I'd be doing them a favour. Just think of it, Frances – Paris. I'll never get another chance like that, never. It's not *fair*, really it isn't. No one asked *me* what I wanted."

"So," Frances said. "They wanted you to go to Paris. What happened then? Who said no?"

"Didn't you?"

Frances stood up. "*Of course* I didn't. I didn't know anything about it. I'd have discussed it with you. You should have known that." Her eyes blazed. "It was that woman. It must have been Mrs. Mackenzie. *She* decided. Without a word to me. Oh . . . she makes me so wild." She took a deep breath, as if preparing for battle. "I won't let her get away with it. I'll have it out with her . . . Just wait till I see her."

Too late Julia realised what she had done. "No," she shrieked. "Don't. Come back. You mustn't fight with Mrs. Mackenzie. It won't do any good." She said the one thing she knew would hold Frances back. "She'll stop you going to the Slade."

Frances hesitated at the door, turned and came slowly back. "You're right. I suppose it's too late to do anything, anyway. The Cartwrights will have made other plans. Oh, Julia, I'm so sorry. Really I am. I swear no one said anything to me. I'd have told you. You must believe me."

"Yes, of course I do. I didn't think. And I do know really that I couldn't have gone. We couldn't have afforded it, even with the Cartwrights paying. I'd have needed new clothes, for one thing. You should have seen the wardrobe Miranda was taking. I wouldn't have minded so much, Frances, if only I'd been told. It was the not knowing that made me angry. I felt so stupid, when Miranda said and I didn't know anything. Like a child."

"I can't get over Mrs. Mackenzie," Frances said, bitterly. "I thought she understood by now that we aren't part of her precious family. That I'm the one in charge; not her. No, don't worry, I won't say anything. Though I might have a word with Mr. Mackenzie, to make sure it doesn't happen again. It would be easier for him to say something to her."

Upset as she was, Julia could not bear to be the cause of trouble between Frances and Mrs. Mackenzie. "It's not her fault. I expect she thought it was best. After all Lucy isn't even allowed to go into Taunton on her own, and she's older than you. And I know you don't think so, but it must be difficult, being responsible for someone else's family."

Such a philosophical attitude was easier to say than to maintain, however. Paris continued to occupy her thoughts for days after her return. One night, long after the rest of the household had gone to bed, she crept downstairs and searched the bookshelves in Commander Purcell's study, finding not the guide to France that she had hoped might be there, but a greater treasure, a thin, musty volume of printed watercolour sketches of Paris itself. Its pages, speckled with damp, had to be prised gently apart. 'Laura Ellison,' said the writing on the flyleaf in firm, dark letters, 'Kind regards, Robert Purcell,' and underneath, in a fainter, feminine hand, 'Christmas 1891.'

She shivered as she gazed down at the familiar handwriting. How little she knew about the past. Why had her father chosen to give such a book – because of the paintings alone, or for some other reason? What had Paris meant to her parents? She would never know. It was too late to find out.

The discovery that she had been missed at Hillcrest came as a surprise. Sarah greeted her with a shy smile and followed her round house and garden clutching a book. "No one had time to read to me when you were away," she complained. "'Tis good to have you back," Annie said, and when Julia remarked on the newly made raspberry jam in the larder added, "Aye, I could have done with your help. Miss Gwen did all the picking, 'tis true, but Miss Frances's been busy with her sewing for London. Miss Sarah's willing enough, bless the child, but there's not much she can do. No, love, it's you and me that does the work in this house."

"Thank heavens you're home," Frances said. "That blue dress I'm making – it's not come out right at all. Have a look and see what you think." She needed Julia's opinion on her paintings, too. "I felt quite lost, not knowing what you thought."

Julia was touched as well as gratified. She was surprised by the strength of her pleasure at being home with her sisters. Even her bitterness over the French holiday had been eased by Frances's sympathy and concern.

Mrs. Mackenzie made no reference to Paris. She asked for details of Julia's stay, was interested to hear Julia's opinion of London, said she considered Miranda to be 'a very suitable friend' – and offered Julia an unwanted boxful of embroidery silks she had come across when turning out a drawer.

"That's guilt," Frances said shortly, when Julia showed her the silks, a view Julia, preferring not to think that there might be truth in it, considered uncharitable.

Antony grumbled that Julia's absence had ruined his croquet. "Gwen's been too busy in the garden, Frances is always working and Sarah's too little. I haven't been able to play once since you went away. Thank goodness you're back."

"I missed you," Geoffrey said, blushing. "There wasn't anyone to talk to."

"Don't be silly," Julia said, made awkward by shyness – and was then more awkward because she had sounded rude.

Geoffrey's pleasure in her company was short-lived. The autumn term cast its shadow days before it began.

"You don't know how lucky you are," he said one afternoon, while he and Julia were knocking croquet balls across the lawn. "Three more years I've got at that place." He gave the ball a violent *thwack* that sent it skidding across the lawn into the border under the wall. "I don't know how I can stand it."

Julia searched for some means of consolation. "The autumn term's good for sport. You know you like cross-country running. And rugby."

"It'll probably rain all term, so there won't be any." He gave her a sheepish smile, as if apologising for his bad humour. "I suppose you think I'm stupid. I haven't got much to complain about really, have I? Not like you."

She was surprised. "What have I got?"

"I don't have to go back," he said, as if the realisation had suddenly struck him. "I could hide in your stables. Mother doesn't come into Taunton now that I'm older. She wouldn't know if I didn't get the school train. I could wait until dark and then come back here across the fields.

[31]

There's that room under the roof of the stables. Gwen and Antony took me up there while you were away. No one would know if I hid there. Except you."

He couldn't be serious, surely? "Wouldn't they write to your parents from school and tell them you hadn't arrived?"

For a moment he looked defiant. Then he drooped. "I suppose so." Dispiritedly he went over to the herbaceous border where he trampled among the bushes and plants so carelessly in his hunt for the croquet ball that Gwen screamed at him, threatening dire punishment if he should harm just one of her plants. "I'll *kill* you if you do, don't think that I won't."

Rectory tradition, the Purcells discovered, allowed a departing Mackenzie to choose the menu for the last dinner at home. "On the condemned man principle," Gabriel explained to them over Rectory lunch. The Purcells listened in awe as Geoffrey gave his order. Partridge soup, chicken cream, ribs of beef, marbled jelly, amber pudding ... they had never heard of such a feast.

"And syllabub," Geoffrey finished. He looked across at Julia. "You'd like syllabub, wouldn't you?"

"I don't think I know what syllabub is."

"It's delicious – one of Cook's specialities." He gave a satisfied smile. "That's settled then. You'll all be coming, won't you?" and as Mrs. Mackenzie opened her mouth to protest, "They are family, Mother. As good as, anyway. They should be here. I want them here. It *is* my last evening. If I'm allowed to choose the food, I should be able to choose the guests too."

"Be sensible," Mrs. Mackenzie said. "Frances may come, if you feel so strongly, but the others are far too young. And five puddings, Geoffrey, does seem excessive."

Geoffrey ignored that last comment. He stabbed the tablecloth with his fork. "Julia's as old as me," he said. "If I'm allowed to stay up why can't she?"

[32]

Julia was hot with embarrassment. Why couldn't he wait until she had gone home before making a fuss? He must know how awkward he was making her feel.

"Geoffrey!" Mrs. Mackenzie said sharply. "Leave the tablecloth alone, *please*."

Geoffrey laid down his fork. He glowered. "I want Julia to be here," he said.

Mr. Mackenzie came to his rescue. "We've always made a special occasion of the last evening, have we not, my dear? I think, if Geoffrey wishes and Julia would like it – and Frances, too, of course – we would be delighted to welcome them."

Geoffrey gave Julia a triumphant smile. She wondered then whether he had deliberately introduced the subject in her presence in order to make refusal more difficult.

When the evening arrived, however, she wished that he had not been so insistent. She was quite at home in the Rectory by now, but only during the daytime. Evenings were different. She was shivering while she got dressed. When she looked at herself in the mirror she knew something was wrong.

Frances was sitting at her dressing-table brushing her hair, the whiteness of her camisole accentuating the rich chestnut colour. Julia stood in the doorway, admiring the picture she made and wishing that her own hair was less ordinary.

Frances smiled at Julia's reflection. "You look nice," she said.

"I don't think I do," Julia said. "I've been wondering, in fact ... It is evening ... and I know you didn't put your hair up till you were older than I am now, but Mother was alive then and things were different. I'm almost sixteen, and I am going to be in charge ..."

Frances turned round, her expression a mixture of amusement and mischief. "Of course. Why didn't I think of it myself? Can you manage, or would you like me to do it?"

"I'd rather you did."

She would not have known how to start but Frances divided and twisted and pinned as if she had been dealing with other people's hair all her life. "I can't wait to see Mrs. Mackenzie's face when she sees you. There – how's that?"

Julia moved her head experimentally. "Are you sure it won't come down?"

"Of course it won't. It takes getting used to, that's all." She stood back and studied her sister. "You're still not right though. I know. It's your dress. Short skirts look ridiculous with hair that's up. Why don't you borrow one of mine for the evening?"

Astonishing the difference clothes and hairstyle made. Julia not only looked grown-up, she felt grown-up. Apprehension remained, however. "Aren't you nervous?" she asked Frances.

"Nervous? No. Why should I be? About time we were invited for dinner, I'd say. Good old Geoffrey. Who'd have dreamt he could be so obstinate? With his mother too."

Gabriel was talking to Annie in the hall when they came downstairs. "Mother insisted you should have an escort ..." His mouth curved up when he saw Julia. "Well, well. We do grow up quickly in this household."

Bertha's eyes widened when she opened the Rectory door. "Oh my, Miss Julia, how lovely you look."

The Mackenzies' welcome was more restrained. If Frances had expected protests from Mrs. Mackenzie she was disappointed. Mrs. Mackenzie smiled. "How well that colour suits you, my dear," she said. Mr. Mackenzie made no comment, despite the twinkle in his eye. Geoffrey's eyes never left her. He offered his arm when dinner was announced – "May I?" – holding her back when everyone else moved to the door and bending his head towards hers. "I think you look ..."

She waited. "Yes?"

He stumbled over the word. "N-nice."

Dinner at the Rectory was a much grander, more elabo-
rate meal than lunch. A greater quantity of silver and glass
decorated the table, there were more courses and wine was
served, though not to the Purcells. Julia was surprised that
Antony should be allowed wine, and more than surprised
that he, a whole year younger than Gwen, should be staying
up to dinner. Gwen should be here too, Julia thought, and
was disconcerted to realise that she was glad Gwen had been
left at home. Gwen was a child, after all. It was she and
Frances who were the adults, partners and companions as
well as sisters.

Geoffrey's eyes admired her from across the dining-table.
She smiled back, at ease, happy – and confident, for the first
time, that she would be able to take Frances's place.

Chapter Three

No one expected Geoffrey to be home so early for Christmas. Julia and Gwen gaped when they found him on their doorstep. "We thought term ended next week."

"Yes, well, it does, but I've got flu and Matron said I might as well come home." He shivered. "I think she wanted an excuse to clear the San, really."

"You'd better come in," Julia said. "We're in the kitchen." She eyed him critically. "You look awful. Shouldn't you be in bed?"

"I'd rather be here. The train was hot, that's all, and then it was icy waiting at Dunkery ... Nobody'd thought to tell them at home I was coming, you see, and when I did get back the house was full of clacking women and Mother was busy ... so I thought I'd come over and see you." He gave Julia his rare smile. "Where is everybody? Where's Annie?"

"It's her day off. She's gone home. Sarah's with Antony somewhere."

"And Frances? Is she back yet?"

"She came home yesterday."

"How was the Slade?"

Julia and Gwen exchanged glances. "Well ..." Julia began.

"It's all a bit difficult," Gwen said. "The Slade's given her funny ideas. We can't paint any more. Colour doesn't matter. It's drawing that's important. That's all they do at the Slade, she says. She's going to make us all wear different clothes so we can pose for each other. That's why she's gone into Milverton today, to buy the material."

"Goodness," Geoffrey said. "She sounds more frightening

than ever. What sort of clothes?"

Julia frowned at Gwen, reluctant to criticise Frances outside the family, even to Geoffrey. "Loose and flowing. So that they fall in folds. It's good practice for drawing."

"I'd like to see Mother's face when the four of you come in wearing something loose and flowing," Geoffrey said.

His interest was short-lived, however. He hunched himself up in Annie's chair, and held out his hands towards the glowing range. He had grown during the past term; his legs seemed longer than ever. The dark hair accentuated the pallor of his face.

"You do look ill," Julia said. "What about something to eat? Hot buttered toast?"

He shook his head.

"A cup of tea?"

He made a face. "I don't think I fancy that either."

"I know. Annie gives us blackcurrant cordial when we have colds. I expect it's good for flu too. You'd better have some of that. See if it's in the larder, Gwen."

But the bottle contained less than a glassful. "There must be more somewhere," Gwen said. "Annie made lots and lots last summer."

She went out. They heard her rattling about in the cupboard outside the kitchen. She returned at last, bottle in hand. "Here we are. Let's have your glass." She frowned as she filled it. "It's not as black as the other. It must be redcurrant. Never mind. I expect red is as good as black for flu."

"I don't know," Geoffrey said. "It doesn't taste quite the same. It's all right, though. I don't suppose it matters anyway. I like it." He helped himself to a second glass when he had finished the first. "Are you sure you don't want some?"

The cordial had the desired effect. He sat up. Colour came into his cheeks. He became quite talkative – for Geoffrey, indeed, almost loquacious – as he told them about the school term and his activities on the games field. He recounted in minute detail every movement of his last rugger match. He told them jokes, silly jokes, Gwen and Julia thought, which grew sillier as the evening progressed. His face became flushed. Drops of perspiration appeared on his forehead and on his upper lip.

Julia felt a crushing sense of disappointment. She had missed him after his departure at the end of the summer holidays. She had even been tempted to write to him several times during the past term and had looked forward to his return, believing that he and she had things in common. She realised now that she had been mistaken. In his absence she had turned her remembrance of him into somebody quite different from the real person.

Annie's footsteps sounded on the cobbles outside. "It's a wild night," she said, coming into the kitchen. She stopped. "Why, Master Geoffrey! What are you doing back so early? Next week, Bertha told me."

Geoffrey made to stand up, swayed and sat down hurriedly. "Happy Christmas, Annie."

Annie turned round in the act of removing her coat. "What's going on?" She stared at Geoffrey. "Lord love us. The lad's *drunk*."

"What do you mean?" Gwen said. "He can't be. It's your blackcurrant cordial he's been drinking."

"We thought it would make him feel better," Julia said. "He's got flu. That's why he's home."

"Blackcurrant? *Blackcurrant*?" She grabbed the bottle, held it up to the lamp and then to her nose. "That's your mother's best elderberry wine. I don't know, I'm sure. I can't leave you alone for a minute."

Geofffrey looked up at her, owlishly, as if he had difficulty in focussing. "Not a minute, Annie. Longer than a minute."

She stood over him. "On your feet, lad," she said fiercely. "At once, now."

Geoffrey half rose, grabbed the table and collapsed back

[38]

into his chair. "My legs won't work," he said in a puzzled voice.

"I thought as much," Annie said. "Wait here. And don't you dare move while I'm gone. Not one of you. I'm ashamed of you. I thought I could trust you, but the moment my back's turned . . ."

She went out. Geoffrey gave a sigh and slumped over the table. Gwen and Julia sat in frightened silence, watching him.

Annie was soon back. "Thank the Lord it's dark. Come along, Miss Julia. I need your help. We're taking him back to the Rectory but I can't manage him on my own."

He was not easy to manage. Annie was smaller than Julia; Geoffrey, having grown during the term, taller than both of them. It made for lopsided walking. He was surprisingly heavy, nearly a deadweight. Julia thought his arm round her neck was going to strangle her. Progress was easier once they had negotiated the cobbles and the steps out of the yard and were able to stagger along the lane. Gusts of cold wind blew the rain into their faces. Geoffrey began to revive. "Where am I?" he said. "Where are you taking me?"

"You're going home," Annie said. She stopped in the middle of the Rectory drive, forcing Julia and Geoffrey to stop too. "Listen to me, Master Geoffrey," she said, slowly and deliberately as if to a child. "If your mother finds out you're going to be in trouble. Not just you, either. The girls too. *Real* trouble. So . . . you'll not make a sound. Not one. Do you understand?"

"Not one sound," Geoffrey repeated carefully.

No lights showed in the Rectory. They avoided the front door, skirting round the house until they came to the tradesmen's entrance. The steps leading down to the basement were wet, almost slimy. Julia was terrified of slipping and dragging Geoffrey down with her.

Bertha opened the door the moment Annie tapped. "Oh, Master Geoffrey," she said, giggling. "You are a one."

"We can't dawdle," Annie said urgently. "Miss Frances will be back any minute. It's best she don't know."

Bertha closed the door behind them. "Wait here. I'll get Master Antony to take Miss Sarah home through the churchyard. That will keep them out of the way. The Guild's gone. I've had a word with Miss Lucy. She said she'd play to the Rector and the Mistress in the drawing-room."

The basement smelt of damp and coal dust. Maids' voices sounded from a nearby room, Hilda's above the rest. If Hilda came out now and saw Geoffrey she would tell Mrs. Mackenzie at once. Hilda was the sort of person who would consider it her duty. Please, please, Hilda, stay where you are.

Bertha came back down the stairs. "There. That's done. Now, Master Geoffrey, let's get you up to your bed." There was affection in her voice.

The stairs were cramped, steep, badly lit, with scarcely room for two abreast, let alone three. Julia led the way with the lamp, leaving Bertha and Annie to struggle with Geoffrey. The brief burst of energy out in the lane had subsided; he was muttering nonsense and dragging his feet against the stair edge. Buckets of coal stood by the door into the hall, an obstacle to the unwary; Julia saw them only just in time. A torrent of piano notes came from the direction of the drawing-room. "Miss Lucy promised to play the loudest piece she could find," Bertha whispered. The stairs to the bedroom floor were steeper still. Bertha and Annie began to pant.

"That's the door," Bertha whispered to Julia. Julia pulled it back. Faint bars of light from the hall below came through the banisters onto the landing carpet. A line of bedroom doors led away into the distance.

"Wait here," Annie told her.

Minutes ticked by. She shivered as she waited. If only she could wake up and find that this was no more than a dream.

"There," Bertha said, when she and Annie returned at last. "That's done. Better see you out before I get the lad into his bed. Elderberry wine, was it?" She sounded as if she might burst out laughing any minute. "Ah, well. Boys will be boys. Don't you worry, Annie. Miss Lucy will think up some way to explain things to the Mistress."

Gwen could scarcely contain her mirth when she returned from lessons at the Rectory next morning with the news that Geoffrey was in bed with flu. "Mrs. Mackenzie's *furious* about it. Any fool could see he wasn't fit to travel, she says. She's written to the headmaster asking for Matron's dismissal."

Sarah was wide-eyed with distress. "He's very ill. Hilda says he'll still be in bed at Christmas."

Hilda was wrong, of course. Geoffrey was up within a day or two. He was subdued when he came over to Hillcrest, even for Geoffrey. "Bertha told me to thank you," he said to Annie. "It was all due to you, she said ... Getting me home, I mean. I'm afraid I don't remember much about it. I didn't mean to be a nuisance."

"Eh, lad," Annie said. "Let it be a lesson to you, that's all. And I'd keep off elderberry wine for a while, if I was you. You might find Hillcrest put out of bounds else. You won't want that."

He sat in the living-room with Gwen and Julia, hands hanging limply between his knees, apologising over and over again.

"Good heavens, Geoffrey," Frances said, coming into the room, "whatever's the matter? You do look hangdog," and was gone before he could attempt a reply.

"He didn't drink very much," Julia said later to Annie. "Only a couple of glasses. He had wine when Frances and I were over at the Rectory in the summer. He was all right then."

"I daresay the flu had summat to do with it," Annie said.

[41]

"And elderberry's powerful stuff ... Not that it takes much drink to do it, when all's said and done." She sighed. "They're all the same, men. Remember that, love."

Julia was curious as well as dismayed. A couple of glasses of wine ... was that what it did to people? Made them noisy, silly, not themselves at all? Was it the same with everybody? Mr. Mackenzie? Gabriel? Her own father? She watched Mr. Mackenzie during Rectory lunches, and tried to picture him as she had seen Geoffrey, slumped over the table ...

One afternoon during the Christmas holidays the four Mackenzies arrived at Hillcrest with gramophone and records, and announced that they were going to teach the Purcells to dance. They pushed back the kitchen table and wound up the gramophone. Gabriel took Lucy in his arms. "We'll show you what you're supposed to do first, and then you can all try." Lessons had begun.

"It's one of the things Mother's always gone on about," Geoffrey said, partnering Julia at Gabriel's command, "how important it is to be able to dance well. I can't see why, really. In India perhaps, where she grew up, but round here ...? Still, this is fun, isn't it?"

Frances had had dancing lessons at school. Julia had never had the opportunity and now, overcome by Geoffrey's proximity, was too nervous to find it fun. Geoffrey surprised her, as he had on the cricket field. He knew what he was doing. He was confident. Patient, too, with her. Perhaps dancing wasn't as difficult as it looked.

At the end of each lesson Gabriel and Lucy would entertain everyone with what Gabriel termed 'a turn around the floor'. They foxtrotted or tangoed, or showed off some other currently fashionable dance with an extraordinary name, and left the Purcells gaping with admiration and awe at their fleetness of foot and mastery of intricate steps.

Lucy's involvement with parish affairs – she spent her

time helping Mrs. Mackenzie – made her appear older than her years. In reality she was younger than Gabriel; scarcely a year older than Frances. She was also shy. In the informal atmosphere of dancing lessons and tea afterwards she and the Purcells came to know each other better. Lucy had accomplishments other than dancing. She was an excellent pianist and a good singer, having a pleasant soprano voice which blended well with Gabriel's tenor and her father's baritone.

Until recently the Purcells had assumed that singing meant hymns or Christmas carols. Sing-songs round the Rectory piano introduced them to hitherto unknown delights – folk songs, sea-shanties, madrigals, ballads.

"Oh vision entrancing . . ." Gabriel sang, rolling his eyes at Frances in mock–romantic mood, while Lucy's fingers rippled a waterfall of notes on the piano. The Purcells were often baffled by Gabriel, never quite sure whether he was being serious or merely teasing. Sometimes they suspected him of making up his own words for the songs he sang. "Come into the garden, Gwen," he begged an embarrassed Gwen, one hand pressed to his heart, the other gesturing extravagantly towards the window, "while the black bat night is here . . ."

No one could mistake Gabriel's enthusiasm for theatricals, however. Not even Antony was allowed to fool around when Gabriel was arranging drawing-room performances of Gilbert and Sullivan, or games of charades. Playing charades, the Purcells soon discovered, was a serious business – and apparently much improved by their arrival. "You've doubled our numbers at a stroke," Antony told them. "Worth Father taking you on for charades alone."

The last traces of the reserve they felt in the presence of the Mackenzies disappeared during those Christmas holidays. No one who heard Mr. Mackenzie sing Pooh-Bah, or watched him impersonate the Holy Roman Emperor in a charade, with a huge, striped bathtowel draped over his everyday clothes and a shaky paper halo perched on his silver hair could regard him with quite the same awe again. "Not that the Holy Roman Emperor was holy – or Roman either, for that matter," Antony pointed out. One drawback to playing charades in as erudite a household as the Rectory, the Purcells discovered, was the difficulty they had in recognising not only the classical allusions but sometimes even the solutions to charades and conundrums. Frances was unperturbed by their ignorance. "What if we don't know about the Greeks and Romans? The Mackenzies don't know anything about art. They haven't the faintest idea. They're Philistines, the lot of them."

Julia came to enjoy running the household during Frances's three years at the Slade. She and Annie worked well together and, however reluctant Julia might be to admit it, relationships between Hillcrest and the Rectory were easier with no Frances around to take offence at what she always called Mrs. Mackenzie's interference. Holidays were the highlights of the year even so. Term-time was organised, orderly, uneventful. Frances's return, followed by Geoffrey's and often Gabriel's too, meant that life became busy, stimulating and fun. There was much more to-ing and fro-ing between Hillcrest and the Rectory, games of croquet and tennis, arguments and discussions. Sometimes Frances brought fellow students home to stay, regarded by Gwen and Sarah at least as exotic birds from another planet with their extraordinary clothes and dogmatic views. What Julia and Gwen found of more interest was the different view such visitors gave them of Frances herself. Both sisters knew that there was a gulf between her talent and theirs but assumed it to be due to the difference in age and training. Now comments from Frances's friends led them to think that there was more to it than that.

"Not that anyone actually *says* Frances is exceptional," Julia said, trying to explain to Annie. "It's just ... an

[44]

impression they give, somehow. Gwen's noticed it too."

"Aye," Annie said. "I've thought suchlike for a while now. Ah well, you can't have it all ways. I daresay that's why Miss Frances has her awkward moments." She and Julia smiled at each other in perfect understanding.

Frances herself seemed unaware of the views of her fellow students, and no more satisfied with her work than she had been since her start at the Slade. She devoted much of her time during the holidays to passing on what she had learnt to Julia and Gwen. Though a hard taskmaster, she was – particularly for someone of her character – a surprisingly patient teacher, and her criticism, even if harsh, was always constructive.

It was light and landscape that fascinated Frances, in particular the hills and combes of the Quantocks with which she was beginning to make her name, but she understood Julia's preoccupation with people and encouraged her portraiture. When Frances painted her sisters together it was any sisters she painted. She was more interested in their illumination – lamp or firelight or reflected sunlight on the verandah – than in them as people. When Julia painted the three together it was their different characteristics she made important – bookish Sarah, self-contained Gwen and Frances so confident and self-possessed. Julia had always been intrigued by the differences in the family. "It's odd, isn't it, how the three of us have gone in different directions?" she once said to Gwen. "Frances's landscapes, you with flowers and your pen-and-ink work, and me and my portraits." Gwen didn't think it odd at all. "What else could we have done, Frances being like she is?"

There was no shortage of subjects in the village to paint. The Mackenzies were happy to pose, Bertha too when she came over to see Annie. Then there was Bert Hawkins, Sir James's chauffeur down at the Manor, who sometimes brought Frances back from Taunton station at the end of term, and Bill Roberts at the forge. There were spectators and players during cricket matches in the summer and hockey in the winter. Much to Julia's embarrassment Frances even approached Sir James Donne, who commissioned Julia to portray his wife. Julia would have preferred to paint Sir James himself, whom she both liked and admired, but was too shy to say so. Lady Donne disliked the finished portrait, complaining that it made her look petulant. "Which she is," Frances said. "Patronising too. I don't see how she can complain. Hasn't she ever looked in a mirror?" Sir James considered it an excellent likeness, but did not, as Julia had half-hoped, commission a portrait of either himself or of Hester, his daughter. He did pay the full fee, however, despite Julia's offer to take less because of his wife's dissatisfaction. "Wouldn't hear of it, my dear, wouldn't hear of it."

It was not her first commission – that came from an awkward Bill Roberts stuttering over his request for a miniature of Mary Hancock ("Don't 'ee don't tell none, mind") – but it was the first payment she had received for her work. She was surprised how much her confidence increased as a result.

"I do envy you," Geoffrey said, "knowing what to do." He was home for Easter, his final holiday before leaving school the year that Julia was due to start at the Slade. "What you *want* to do, I mean."

Julia was surprised. "Don't you? I thought you were going to Cambridge."

He pulled a face. "Well, yes, but I don't want to, particularly. I can't see that it'll be any different from school, and you know what I think about that."

"Why go then?"

"It's always been taken for granted that I would. First Gabriel, then me, then Antony. It's Father's old college, you know, which makes it worse somehow. I couldn't refuse. He'd be so hurt if I did."

She could understand that. "What will you do after Cambridge? Try for a fellowship, like Gabriel?"

"Heavens, no. I'm not clever enough for that. Be a schoolmaster, I suppose." He must have sensed her surprise. "What else could I do?"

"I don't know. It seems . . . odd, that's all, particularly when you hate school so much. There must be something else you could do."

"Well, let's see . . . I could go into the Church, like Father. I couldn't, you know. Can you see me standing up in the pulpit? Or the Army. I wouldn't want that, either. They're all boneheads in the Army. You've only got to look at Fergus Donne. Though he is a terrific cricketer, I admit. So . . . the Army's out, and the Church. What is there left but schoolmastering? At least I'd get decent holidays."

"I suppose so." After a moment she said, "They're not boneheads in the Navy."

He gave her an apologetic smile. "Sorry. I didn't mean . . ."

"No, I know." She tried to cheer him up. "It doesn't matter anyway. There's plenty of time. To find something else, I mean. Three whole years at Cambridge. Anything could happen."

"Maybe." He obviously thought it unlikely. "The trouble with Cambridge is that Gabriel's there. I don't know that I'd mind going if it weren't for that. It was bad enough coming after him at school but Cambridge will be worse. Everyone expects so much. I know he only scraped a first, but that was because he didn't work until the last minute. I haven't a hope of even *scraping* a first. You can't imagine what it's like having someone brilliant ahead of you."

"I can."

"Yes," he said slowly. "I suppose you can."

She felt guilty afterwards, for admitting as much. Her close relationship with Frances was nothing like his with Gabriel. There was not the same companionship between the Mackenzie brothers that existed between the four Purcells.

Gabriel treated Geoffrey with casual, almost damning, good humour; Antony with amusement. "Oh, *Geoffrey*!" was Antony's usual mode of address. It was Gabriel and Antony who were close, despite the nine years' difference in age. Julia remembered coming back to the Rectory with Geoffrey one winter afternoon and glimpsing the two brothers through the half-open door of the dining-room. They were sitting at the table amid a clutter of books and papers ... Julia had never seen such absorption on anybody's face before.

"Don't go in," Geoffrey said. "They'll be discussing poetry – Antony's poetry, probably. Gabriel gives him advice. Helps him. Not just about poetry either. Work, ideas, that sort of thing." There were undertones in his voice that disturbed Julia. She sensed traces of envy, a feeling of exclusion, even rejection, and was upset by them, both then and for long after.

Later, she wondered how much the conversation with Geoffrey about his future had affected her decision about her own. Suddenly – overnight it seemed – she knew that she could not go to the Slade. Her future had been planned for so long, had become so familiar through Frances's experience, that she had given little thought to its reality – that it would mean leaving home, her sisters and the life she knew, living in lonely digs, mixing with people she knew nothing about ... She thought of the Slade pupils Frances had brought home in the holidays, girls both confident and talented, and remembered how depressed Frances had been in her first term at her lack of ability compared to others – Frances, whose talent was so much greater than Julia's own ...

Gwen was unexpectedly pleased at Julia's change of mind. "It'll make it much easier for me. I've never had any intention of going to that place, if you must know, but I always knew it would mean terrible fights with Frances. Now you'll be the one having the fights."

Julia stared. "But I always took it for granted you'd go."

"You should have known I wouldn't," Gwen said. "Can you see me in London? Away from the garden? I'd hate every minute. And I'd like to see you lot coping with the vegetable garden without me. Besides, Frances can teach me all I need to know."

At least the fights Gwen had envisaged were carried out on paper rather than face to face. In letters from London Frances alternately threatened and cajoled. She tried, but vainly, to persuade Julia to go through the Slade interview, apparently assuming that once in London Julia would realise her mistake. On her return at the end of her final term she argued face to face with Julia, and when that failed tried to enlist the Mackenzies' support.

"She's distressed," Mr. Mackenzie told Julia. "Such wasted talent, she says ..." He smiled. "I could scarcely have imagined, three years ago, that I would now be advocating art school ... It does seem a pity not to take the opportunity, my dear, but it's up to you. You may well be right. The Slade has obviously been excellent for Frances. That doesn't mean that it would be the best place for you."

Her refusal had Geoffrey's approval. "Provided you're sure you're doing the right thing, of course. I wish I had the courage. I think you're tremendous, really I do."

Julia knew that she was not. She had surprised herself both by her temerity and by the strength of her determination. When at last Frances conceded defeat it was that surprise that remained, rather than triumph or relief.

Chapter Four

The walk over the Quantocks in the summer of 1913 marked the end of an era. They all felt it, Purcells and Mackenzies alike. Frances had left the Slade that July. Geoffrey had finished with school. Life would never be quite the same again.

They had never been on a walk of such length before, not all eight of them together. Sarah had been too young (and still was, according to Annie), Lucy too busy, Gwen always reluctant to leave the garden. It was Gabriel and Frances who were the keen walkers in the two families, and Gabriel who suggested this particular expedition, along the Quantock ridge to the sea – "We always said we'd get up early and see how much of the Quantocks we could explore in a day."

It was still cool when they set out. Dew outlined the spiders' webs in the hedges. Mist hung over the lanes. By the time they had walked through the village and left the common behind them, the sun was beginning to break through, warming their backs as they began to climb. The day promised to be one of the hottest in an already hot summer.

Geoffrey was whistling as he led the way up Bagborough Hill. Julia had never seen him in such high spirits. "How *slow* you are," he called back to her. "Do you need me to pull you up?"

She was panting as she caught up with him. "I don't do all the cross-country running you do, remember. And do consider poor Sarah. She's only ten. She's not used to long walks like this."

He grinned as he watched the others toil up the hill

towards them. "Happy?" he said.

She nodded. "And you?" As though she need ask.

"I can't believe I've finished with that place for ever."

"You've still got Cambridge to do."

"I won't think about that till later."

Gabriel's determination to show Sarah the sea turned the one-day expedition into two. The Purcells were apprehensive, fearing Mrs. Mackenzie's wrath on their return, but Gabriel was unperturbed. "We'll send her a telegram – Annie too. They can't make a fuss if we sleep under shelter. We'll spend the night in a barn. I've done it before often. Farmers don't mind if you ask them first."

Gabriel could still surprise Julia. "He hasn't really slept in barns, has he?" she asked Geoffrey.

"Oh yes. Lots of times, I think, when he was campaigning with the Fabians. Antony and I slept out in the garden once, for a lark. You can't imagine how splendid it is to wake up with the sun on your face. Mother was furious, of course. We've never dared do it again, though I've often wanted to."

Gabriel took them to a barn he remembered from previous walks in the area, below the Quantocks ridge not far from St. Audries. "It won't take us long to get to the coast in the morning," he said, as he and Frances departed to send telegrams and find the barn's owner, leaving Julia and Lucy to make the straw in the barn comfortable for sleeping. Sarah's eyes were already closing; she made little protest at being put to bed so early and was asleep within minutes. Lucy smiled at Julia. "She's very good, isn't she? I hope we haven't worn her out."

Outside the barn Gwen and Antony had removed their shoes and stockings and were paddling in the stream that ran through the field to the road. "Do come, Ju," Gwen called. "It's *freezing*. It makes your feet feel wonderful after all that walking."

Geoffrey was peering down into the water. "Do you

think it's deep enough for fish? Do stop splashing, you two. If we make a dam we might be able to trap something for supper ... there's plenty of wood for a fire. No, seriously. Help me make a dam."

Julia was amused. He was like a small boy, she thought. His disappointment, when told that there was no need for dams or fish, was as intense as any boy's whose plans had been thwarted. Annie's picnics were always generous; there was more than enough left over from midday to satisfy them now, together with the milk that Frances and Gabriel had brought back from the farm.

Replete, Antony stretched his arms above his head and yawned. "'*The Bridegroom's doors are open'd wide,*'" he began, "'*And I –*'"

"That's enough, Antony," Gabriel said sharply. "Off to bed. At once."

To Julia's astonishment Antony went without another word. Geoffrey gave a sigh of relief. "We've had nothing but *The Ancient Mariner* all day. I can't understand what he sees in that poem. I think it's horrible."

"There are nice bits," Julia said, who had been entertained rather than irritated by Antony's delight in recitation while walking.

"Everyone thinks he'll become a don, you know," Geoffrey said. "Like Gabriel. Only cleverer. *He* says he's going to be a poet. I think he'll end up on the stage, myself. He can't stop playacting."

There was a moon that night. It came slowly out of the trees and rose up into the sky, transforming the clearing around them into the magical world of Victorian etchings. They remained in the doorway of the barn for a long time, reluctant to bring such a day to a close. Julia had never been so aware of Geoffrey's physical presence as he sat beside her, close but not touching, and when at last they went to bed that awareness kept her awake, listening to his slow, even breathing long after everyone else slept.

Next morning they went down to the beach. Julia felt a childish longing to splash through the waves but Geoffrey persuaded her to walk with him through the woods instead. "If we go beyond that point over there we'll be able to see for miles up the Channel. Flatholm, Steepholm, all sorts of places. Do come."

After the brilliance of the sun in the bay the woods seemed dark and mysterious. An occasional shaft of light fell across the path. Voices faded. The seagulls' cries sounded thin in the air above. A bee darted through the sunlight with a faint buzz. It seemed to be taking them a very long time to reach the point. Suddenly Geoffrey stopped, turned, and grabbed her.

She did not resist. She remained limp in his arms, not knowing what else to do. His skin felt rough against hers, his lips soft and warm. Their teeth touched. When he let her go she did not know what to do or say.

"Hadn't we better get back to the others?" she said at last.

He followed. She heard the occasional twig crack under his feet behind her. She could feel his eyes on her back. As they came out of the trees he drew level. "Julia – I'm sorry."

She felt colour flood up into her face. "It's all right."

Lucy waved up to them from the beach. "Lend me your handkerchief, Geoffrey. I want to take these shells back for Sunday School."

Julia avoided Geoffrey's gaze as she helped Lucy sort out perfect shells from the imperfect. Stupid to have been so awkward. It hadn't been unpleasant, after all. It had been the shock more than anything else ... She glanced across to Geoffrey, sitting on a rock anxiously watching her, and tried to smile. Relief spread over his face.

Sarah was tired, too tired to walk home from the coast. They caught the train at Watchet instead, planning to walk home from Dunkery St. Michael. It was in the train that Julia noticed for the first time the expression on the faces of both Frances and Gabriel. She felt panic surge through her.

[53]

They had always been such good friends, the eight of them. Life was all right as it was; she did not want it to change. She remembered Geoffrey's behaviour in the woods. Looking out of the train window she saw not the Quantocks passing by but the reflection of Frances and Gabriel smiling at each other across the carriage.

"Lord, yes," Geoffrey said. "Have you only just noticed? He's been smitten for months. Years, almost, I'd say."

Julia had avoided Geoffrey after the walk, taking care not to be alone with him, out of embarrassment more than any other emotion. Then one afternoon when she was gathering plums on her own he came to the orchard. "Please let me help," he said. Nothing was said about the incident in the woods. There was no need. They were at ease in each other's company once more, so much so that she felt able to mention Frances and Gabriel, hoping that he would laugh at her and tell her she had too vivid an imagination. She was disconcerted to discover that he took for granted what she had only just begun to suspect.

"What do you think will happen?" she said.

He shrugged. "I don't know. Gabriel doesn't say anything to me. I'm sure he's serious, though. Not that I can see Mother agreeing . . ." He began to laugh. "*That* explains all the tennis parties we've had this summer. Mother's been lining up suitable girls for inspection . . . Frances is crazy about him too, isn't she?"

"I think 'crazy' is exaggerating it a bit," Julia said stiffly.

But was it? During that autumn Frances visited Gabriel in Cambridge, met him in London, wrote to him. Almost every day it seemed a letter from Cambridge plopped down on the Hillcrest mat. Two days before Christmas Gabriel came back to Huish Priory and asked Frances to marry him.

Neither Julia nor Gwen were surprised. As autumn had progressed into winter they had discussed the possibility more than once.

[54]

"What do you think'll happen if Frances says yes?"

"They'll get married," Julia said.

"And then?"

"She'll have to go and live with him in Cambridge."

"She won't like that," Gwen said. "She needs the Quantocks for her painting."

"She'll have to find something else to paint."

Gwen was silent. "What's it like round Cambridge?" she said at last. "The landscape, I mean."

"Flat, I think. Good cloud effects. And sunsets."

"That wouldn't make up for the Quantocks. Not for Frances."

"No," Julia agreed. I'm lucky, she thought. It doesn't matter where I go. There are people everywhere.

"What would happen to us if she does ... you know?" Gwen said. "We'd still stay here, wouldn't we?"

"I don't know. Let's not worry about it, Gwen. Not until it happens."

Which turned out to be sensible advice, for Frances turned Gabriel down. Brutally, as far as her sisters could make out.

Julia and Gwen might have expected Gabriel's proposal; Frances apparently did not. She was astonished, hurt – and angry. "How *could* he?" she demanded of her sisters. "He knows how I feel about marriage. I've always *told* him that it's my work that matters. Didn't he ever listen?" Her rage was made worse by the discovery that Julia and Gwen sympathised with Gabriel rather than with Frances herself.

Julia was exasperated by her sister's behaviour. "Why couldn't you treat him better? At least you could have been kind about it." She was apprehensive, as well as exasperated. Christmas imminent, comings and goings between the two houses, joint festivities – a quarrel between Frances and Gabriel could not have come at a worse time. Mrs. Mackenzie would be upset. Gabriel was her favourite; she would never forgive Frances for hurting him. "You'll have to go over to the Rectory. Be nice to him. Make friends."

Frances refused. "How could I? *You* go if you feel so strongly about it."

Geoffrey grinned when he saw Julia in the Rectory hall. "If you're wanting Gabriel he's gone into Taunton. He won't be back till this afternoon."

"Behold," Antony said, appearing at the door of Mr. Mackenzie's study, "Julia, the peacemaker!"

"Don't be silly," Julia said, more sharply than she had intended, taken aback to discover that the affair was common knowledge. "I just wanted to have a word with Gabriel. If you could ask him to come over when he gets back . . ."

"I'll ask him," Geoffrey said, "but I don't expect he will. Not to Hillcrest. Not at the moment."

It was not possible to talk to Geoffrey with Antony standing there agog. "I'm helping decorate the church later this afternoon," she said. "Do you think he might meet me there?"

He came, rather to her surprise, and sat beside her in a pew at the back of the church, hands thrust deep into his pockets, glowering down at his knees. "Some girls would feel honoured," he said bitterly. "A chap prepared to spend the rest of his life with them – it's quite something, after all."

"She was upset," Julia said. "She wouldn't have said . . . whatever she did say . . . if she hadn't been upset. And you did know, Gabriel. She's always made it quite clear that marriage wasn't for her."

"But it's different now. You know how she's been, ever since that day at St. Audries. Didn't *you* think . . . ?"

Yes, she had. That was the trouble. "It's not because she's not fond of you" – or love; should she have said love? – "it's just that she's ambitious. Not for money, or fame, or anything like that. Just to paint as well as she possibly can."

"And that allows her to go round trampling on other

people's feelings, does it? What does she think I'm made of? Stone? I'm a man, Julia. Flesh and blood."

"I know, I know. I'm sorry." She did not know what to say or how to placate him. Such emotion ... and all the time the knowledge that tomorrow was Christmas Day. "It's just, well, if you could ... apologise. Or something. It'll ruin Christmas, having an atmosphere between the two of you, and it is special this year, with Sarah staying up for the first time. You don't want to spoil it for her, do you?"

"I don't see why I should apologise." But the mention of Sarah had softened him, as she had hoped it might. "All right, Julia. Don't look so worried. I'll behave myself."

He certainly behaved better than Frances did on Christmas Day. There were times, Julia thought as she watched her sister during the evening at the Rectory, when she could gladly have strangled her. At least Sarah was too young to sense the undercurrents that seethed below the surface. Sarah's Christmas had not been spoilt.

No one knew what happened or which of the two made the first approach, but by the end of the year Frances and Gabriel were reconciled. Indeed, to see them dancing together during the New Year's Eve dance at the Manor no one would have believed there had ever been any differences between them.

"I can't understand Frances," Geoffrey said, watching her perform a flamboyant tango with Gabriel on the dance floor. "Really I can't. To turn down *Gabriel*, of all people ... And anyway, I thought every girl wanted to get married."

"Not Frances. It's because of her painting. At the Slade they say that girls are as good as the men until they get married. You know what Frances is. She doesn't want that to happen. Her work's the most important thing in her life."

"Well, it seems very odd to me. I'm glad you're not like that."

My painting's important to me, Julia thought, but she

knew that it was not, or at least not in the way Frances's was to her. She watched Geoffrey make his tentative way through the crush in search of drinks and wondered how she would have felt had it been Geoffrey proposing to her ... Ridiculous even to contemplate. It would be years before Geoffrey was in a position to marry.

The dance at the Manor was Julia's first experience of a grand occasion, and enjoyable because Geoffrey was with her. The many evenings spent practising in the kitchen at Hillcrest meant that they danced well together. She was at ease in his arms, could follow his steps, knew exactly what he was going to do next – and was astonished, therefore, when he waltzed her into the conservatory in mid-dance and kissed her behind an orange tree. It was a much more satisfactory affair than the kiss at St. Audries. There was less fumbling. He held her both longer and closer. To her surprise she realised that she liked it. This time she kissed him back.

Frances took Julia with her on her first visit to Cambridge in the new year, making Geoffrey's presence there the excuse. "You know how much he'd like to see you," she said. Julia suspected the reason was simpler, that Frances was reluctant to be on her own with Gabriel. Frances herself insisted that she and Gabriel had sorted things out between them. "He understands how I feel now," she told Julia. "He didn't before. And as for that business at Christmas, well, he's forgotten all about it." The expression Julia sometimes glimpsed on Gabriel's face when he thought he was watching Frances unobserved, an expression both bewildered and hurt, contradicted that belief.

Geoffrey was happier at Cambridge than he had been at school, less oppressed by Gabriel's example before him. He had taken up rowing, no doubt choosing that particular sport because Gabriel had never been interested. "I'm hoping to get picked for the college boat," he told Julia. "Father would be very tickled if I were. He rowed for the college himself, you know."

Frances took Julia to London as well as to Cambridge. She was concerned about Julia's painting. "Just because you aren't going to the Slade doesn't mean that you can slack off."

Frances herself never slacked. Every morning she spent working alone, either in her studio up in the stables or outside in the grounds of Hillcrest. Because her interest lay more in landscape than other forms of painting her studies and practice were almost always devoted to that end. She painted the sky at the same time each morning, making a note of the wind direction and its strength as well as the day's temperature. She drew the same trees three or four times a week, watching the different way in which each variety stood, grew, lost its leaves in the autumn. Julia was both impressed by her self-discipline and dedication and cast down, knowing that Frances would never let herself be distracted, as Julia so easily was, by things unimportant or trivial.

In London they stayed with one of Frances's friends from the Slade, Katherine Jamieson, referred to always only as Jamieson in the Slade tradition. Her exotic clothes and dramatic behaviour had overawed the younger Purcells on her first appearance at Hillcrest, but during later visits she had become a good friend and was delighted now to have the two girls to stay when Frances brought Julia up to go round the galleries, or spend time in the Kensington museums.

Occasionally Gabriel came down from Cambridge and took them out to the theatre or the ballet. On one visit he offered, rather diffidently, to introduce Julia to the Settlement in the East End.

Gabriel's membership of the socialist Fabians, while acknowledged, was rarely discussed in Huish Priory. Mrs. Mackenzie disapproved of his political leanings, and the

Purcells, though curious, did not want to cause trouble by raising the subject. Julia knew by now that the Settlement was supported by Gabriel's Cambridge college and that he visited it to help and occasionally to teach, but she had not realised before the strength of his feelings or his commitment, not merely to the Settlement but to political change in the country as a whole. She was both impressed and interested.

"Come and help whenever you want," Gabriel said, when she tried to express something of her feelings on the tram back to Jamieson's flat.

"It probably sounds very selfish, but what I'd really like to do would be to sit in a corner and draw. There were some fascinating faces there."

"Why don't you? You're never obtrusive when you're drawing. I don't suppose anyone would mind, anyway."

Frances showed no interest in the Fabians or the Settlement. "He gets so carried away by it all," she complained to Julia.

Julia never heard Gabriel criticise, though in an unguarded moment he did once admit that he would have liked Frances to visit, if only to see what it was all about. "Not that I don't understand why she doesn't," he added quickly. "It's a matter of time. Her work's more important."

Visiting London gave Julia the opportunity to see Miranda again. They had written frequently to each other since Julia's visit, though Julia had refused every invitation to stay again, for reasons that seemed ridiculous now they were reunited. Mrs. Cartwright took the two girls out to tea at Gunter's, allowing them to order whatever they wanted. "It's Miranda's birthday in three weeks. We'll pretend this is a birthday party."

Miranda had left school the previous summer and was now living at home. "And it's so lucky we can meet," she told Julia, "because I've been dying to tell you all about my plans, only I didn't quite like to, not knowing how you'd feel." She was going to Paris in the autumn to be 'finished'. "I shall be staying with Aunt Amy – do you remember Aunt Amy? She remembers you. 'Such a lovely girl,' she's always saying, 'and such *bee-autiful* embroidery.' I don't know which impressed her the most – you or your sewing!"

"So ridiculous," Julia said. "It wasn't anything special. You must give her my regards. I always wish I'd kept up my French."

"*Well*," Miranda said. Her eyes sparkled. "Now we come to the exciting bit." She turned to Mrs. Cartwright. "You tell her, Mother."

Mrs. Cartwright leant forward, putting her hand on Julia's. "Miranda's father and I think it would be sensible if Miranda went over to France a little early. To get the feel of things, you know. Help her with the language. She's very *naughty*, is Miranda. Her French is no better than it was when you came to stay, and think how long ago that was. *Now*. We did wonder whether things have changed for you? Do you think you'd be able to go with her this time? Just until the beginning of term?"

"Do say yes, Ju," Miranda begged. "I wouldn't be nearly so nervous if you were with me and we'd have such fun together. Aunt Amy would love to see you again."

Julia could scarcely believe her ears. "I – I don't know. Oh, but it would be wonderful. Only, I'm sure they wouldn't . . . I shall have to ask."

"It does seem to us that you're allowed a great deal of freedom these days," Mrs. Cartwright said. "Staying in London on your own, for instance. I don't know that Mr. Cartwright and I . . . But that's beside the point. Let's get back to Paris. Would you like us to write to your guardian?"

Would she! But it would need more than a letter from the Cartwrights to persuade Mrs. Mackenzie. Julia laid her plans as if for a military campaign. She had Frances's support, as she'd known she would. Together they asked Gabriel for help in approaching his parents.

Gabriel groaned. "You Purcells will send me grey before my time. *I* wasn't allowed to go to Paris when I was your age, let me tell you. Mother always considered France decadent and immoral. All right, Julia, all right. No need to look so down. I'll do my best. Tell Mrs. Cartwright to write with all the details."

Julia, prepared for a long battle, was almost disappointed by the ease with which the Mackenzies were persuaded to give permission.

"I won't say that we're enthusiastic," Mr. Mackenzie told her, "but Mrs. Cartwright assures us you'll be well looked after and perfectly safe. If Madame Drouin is prepared to act as chaperon, as I understand she is, Mrs. Mackenzie and I agree that it would be wrong for us to stand in your way. Frances has made quite clear the benefits of such a visit for someone like you." He smiled. "I believe she hopes you will spend your time in the galleries copying the Old Masters."

Afterwards Julia thought that it must have been those words that sowed the seed in her mind.

She had never regretted her refusal to go to the Slade. She was certain that she had been right. But now, thinking of Paris, the wildest ideas came into her head. Not an art school, but a studio ... She knew, from Frances's friends, that it was possible to join an artist's *atelier* for lessons and training. Suppose, just suppose, she could find one prepared to take her. For a term – two terms – all winter even. For as long as her money held out.

Her body sat on the verandah at Hillcrest, podding the first peas of the summer but her mind was far away across the English Channel. Aunt Amy still remembered her – with affection, if Miranda spoke the truth. Suppose Aunt Amy could be persuaded to let Julia stay on, as lodger instead of guest. Expensive, yes, but one winter in Paris must surely cost less than three years at the Slade?

[62]

The Mackenzies would be appalled. Julia suspected that even Frances might have doubts. So ... she would have to wait until she reached Paris before making arrangements. Then, when everything was settled, she would write home to tell them her plans. There would be nothing anyone in England could do then, so far away, with the Channel between.

She felt a desperate need to confide, to talk to someone who could give disinterested advice, someone knowledgeable ... During her next visit to London she refused an invitation to accompany Frances to her old teacher's Cheyne Walk home, pleading a headache, and instead spent the evening at home with Jamieson.

"An *atelier*?" Jamieson said. "I can't think of one off-hand. I expect I could find out, though. Nina Hamnett went over to Paris a couple of months ago. Montparnasse, I think – I've got her address. Shall I write and ask her what she'd suggest?"

"Would you?" Julia said gratefully. "I'll only have a couple of weeks there to fix everything up. It'd make things much easier if I had some introductions to start with. And, Jamieson, *please*. Don't tell Frances. The Mackenzies are bound to be difficult. I don't want them to blame her. If she can truthfully say she didn't have the faintest idea ..."

It seemed madness to trust Jamieson, whom Julia knew from Jamieson's visits to Hillcrest to be wildly indiscreet, but trust her she did. Besides, she had no choice.

"I won't say a word," Jamieson promised. She started to laugh. "You are an amazing family. What do you think Gwen and Sarah will get up to in a couple of years' time?"

Julia did not know. Or care. She was going to see Paris at last – the Paris of her parents' watercolours, the city she had longed to visit for years. She would be able to draw, paint, breathe in the French atmosphere. This time her luck would hold. This time everything would work out. She knew it.

She returned to Hillcrest treading on air.

Part Two

1914

Chapter Five

It never occurred to Julia during those first heady days following the outbreak of war that events on the continent would prevent her visit to Paris. Not until Mr. Mackenzie said, "My dear, I am so sorry. I know how much you'd been looking forward to your time away," did the truth dawn. Even then she hoped. The war would be over by Christmas – everyone said so. Perhaps it might finish earlier, by October.

Mrs. Cartwright wrote, a letter full of sympathy and regrets. Aunt Amy was living with the Cartwrights now, having fled from Paris when Uncle Henri was taken prisoner-of-war.

Julia was inconsolable. She could not believe that something so stupid as a war should spoil her plans. She knew that everyone thought she was making a great fuss. She did not care. Her life was ruined, her future destroyed ...

Geoffrey did his best to cheer her. "I know it's a shame, and I'm sorry, but it can't be as bad as you make out. I think it's tremendous to be living in such exciting times. Besides, the Cartwrights sound a jolly family – I'm sure they'll arrange something later on."

"It's not the Cartwrights I care about," Julia raged. "It's Paris ... work ... my painting ... I'll never, ever get a chance like that again."

"Your *painting*? What are you talking about?"

Too late she realised. "You mustn't tell anyone. Not your parents. Not even Gwen, and certainly not Frances. Promise?"

He stared open-mouthed when she told him. "You were

[67]

planning to find somewhere to study – not knowing anyone, not speaking the language . . . ?"

"I do speak it a bit."

He began to laugh. "Oh, Julia! You are wonderful! I'd have been scared out of my wits, but there you are, planning it all . . . You haven't told anyone? Not even Miranda?"

"I was waiting till we got there."

"Well, look. This thing's going to be over by Christmas. Provided I've got over to the other side by then – and I'll be very cross if I haven't – I'll see if I can wangle a trip to Paris and send for you. We'll see Paris together. That will be more fun than seeing it with Miranda, won't it?"

"Yes. Yes, of course, but . . ."

"And we'll go round and look at . . . whatever it is you call studios, and see what we can fix up. I don't think it's a good idea your doing it on your own. You need a man with you. All right? Feel better?"

She tried to smile. "Yes."

"And now will you test me on the Field Regulations?"

He and Gabriel had been among the first in the village to enlist, though others had followed quickly on, Bill Roberts among them two weeks after his wedding to Mary Hancock. Even Antony had followed his brothers later that autumn, fibbing about his age in order to get taken on.

Geoffrey was enjoying his life in Kitchener's Army, finding it infinitely preferable to university life. Rugger matches on Saturday afternoons, cross-country running, shooting for his platoon – he was able to indulge in all the activities he enjoyed most. The food was good, the company in the mess congenial. Even marching was fun, and night-time exercises best of all. "It doesn't matter how dirty we get," he told Julia. "Mother would have a fit if she could see me sometimes." He was happier than Julia had ever known him. When he came home on leave he seemed to have grown inches taller in a matter of weeks.

Christmas 1914 came and went, with no sign of the war's

end and Geoffrey still in England. Not until March, after Antony had sailed with the Royal Naval Division to the Mediterranean, did Geoffrey come home for his last leave before embarking for France. At his suggestion, and not caring what his parents thought, Julia went up to London with him the day before he sailed.

London was full of recruiting posters, the parks of drilling men, the streets of khaki. They went to a tea dance which they spent in each other's arms and then on to *The Three Musketeers* at the Lyceum, which contained exactly the right proportion of romance to excitement. All day they had been buoyed up by the exhilaration of being alone together, but in the taxi taking them back to Jamieson's flat silence came between them. She sensed apprehension for the first time underlying his excitement, apprehension not so much about injury or death, as hers was, but as to how he would perform under fire.

"You don't know if you've been trained correctly, that's the trouble. It's all wrong what the text books say. Digging in with a good view of the enemy, for instance – chaps back from the front say that's fatal. If you can see the Hun he can see you. The middle of a ploughed field's supposed to be the safest place."

It didn't sound safe to Julia.

He was adamant that he did not want her at the station the following morning. Their farewells were said in the privacy of the hall below Jamieson's flat, clinging together in the dim light that filtered through the fanlight from the street outside, delaying for as long as possible the moment of parting.

Miranda was envious when she met Julia for coffee next morning. "You are lucky, having someone at the front. I haven't got anyone. Well ... I do have a cousin, but he's in the Medical Corps. That's not very romantic, is it? And anyway, he's married. Quite old, too. He won't do at all."

Julia barely listened, preoccupied as she was with thoughts of Geoffrey. Was he thinking of her, as she was of him ... had he reached Folkestone yet ... would the Channel be rough ... where would he sleep tonight?

Miranda felt she wasn't doing enough to help the war effort, she told Julia. Her mother had vetoed her suggestion of joining the Voluntary Aid Department. "She says nursing isn't a suitable occupation for young girls. I'm having to work on Daddy. He thinks he might be able to arrange something for me at the hospital."

"I'd wondered about nursing, too," Julia said. "I'd hoped to be able to nurse at the Manor. The Donnes were going to turn it into a hospital but then Lady Donne decided their London house was more suitable. There's more entertainment for convalescent officers in London, she said."

Julia remembered Miranda's words in the train back to Somerset. She felt the same dissatisfaction as Miranda, but had less idea what to do about it. She was not idle – life had always been busy and was now even more so, with war work to be fitted in between the usual domestic activities and her painting – but hemming nightshirts, knitting socks and practising bandaging seemed an ineffectual use of time when one considered that men were fighting and dying across the Channel. Anyone – everyone – could sew and knit. What else could she do?

Everyone had done their best to make the last leaves of both Geoffrey and Antony cheerful, memorable occasions. Nothing could have made Gabriel's last leave happy. On the very morning that he was expected home, to the astonishment and horror of the Purcells, Frances left Huish Priory to visit friends from the Slade.

Julia tried persuasion; she tried argument. She begged Frances to stay; she ordered her. She lost her temper and shouted. Frances was adamant. That Frances loved Gabriel, Julia did not doubt; but how she could behave so monstrously to anyone, let alone someone she loved, was beyond Julia's comprehension. Mixed with the anger she felt on Gabriel's behalf was anger she felt on her own, for Frances did not have the decency to tell the Mackenzies herself; she left that to Julia. On every occasion during the Purcells' years with the Mackenzies it had always been Frances who behaved badly and Julia who had to make the peace. Not, Julia suspected, that Mrs. Mackenzie would be altogether displeased by Frances's absence. Frances's attitudes and what Mrs. Mackenzie considered her Bohemian behaviour made her the last person Mrs. Mackenzie would want for one of her sons. But any hurt caused to Gabriel Mrs. Mackenzie would deem unforgivable.

The Purcells went over to the Rectory once Gabriel was home; and Gabriel came over to Hillcrest. Nothing was said about Frances; her name was not mentioned. They discussed the progress of the war, local events and attempts at fundraising. Gwen asked Gabriel's opinion about the usefulness of future activities in the garden. What did he think about beekeeping, she wondered? Would rearing pigs be more sensible? They talked about Antony, now serving with the Royal Naval Division, and Geoffrey, with whom Gabriel had corresponded.

"Well, of course I have," he said, seeing Julia's surprise. "One does like to know what to expect. Nothing to worry about, according to Geoffrey. He's having a very jolly time by the sound of it."

'Like a first-class picnic,' Geoffrey had described his life to Julia. She had not believed him, thinking he was doing his best to allay her fears. There was no reason why Geoffrey should lie to his brother, however. Perhaps she could breathe easily after all.

Gabriel searched her out on the last morning of his leave. "Come up to the Quantocks with me, Julia. I don't want to go on my own."

They walked fast and in silence, taking the quick, steep way through Combe Florey and up over Will's Neck. The April day was grey and cold, the wind bitter. Cloud obscured distant views. She had brought bread and cheese from Hillcrest and some apples; they picnicked in the fold of a combe, out of the wind.

"I'm sorry," he said. "I'm not very good company, I'm afraid."

"It doesn't matter."

He sat looking out over the combe to the valley beyond. "I saw a painting of Frances's once in the Mayfield Gallery," he said. "You know how there's always a painting sitting on an easel in the window . . . It was an autumnal one – the beechwoods above Cothelstone. I could tell it was hers from the end of the street, and not just because of the setting. More the effect of light, I think, the way the scene burst out of the canvas. I stood at the window for hours, trying to work out how she does it. If you try to analyse – a touch here, a colour there that no one in their senses would choose, and yet it's the only one that's right. What makes her see that? Does she know what she's doing when she does it? Is it instinct? Or training? What is it? Do *you* know?"

Julia shook her head. "I wonder myself sometimes. Not only about that, but about the difference between people and their talent. If I worked twice as hard as Frances I still wouldn't . . . We can paint the same scene, you know, and her canvas is – outstanding, I suppose, whereas mine's only, well, mediocre. She is exceptional, Gabriel. Really. I know that doesn't help you but it's true."

There was a long silence.

"I've never been able to understand," Gabriel said, "why if you're outstanding in one way you should be able to behave so outrageously in others."

She said nothing.

"You paint too," he said. "You don't behave like that."

"No, but . . . I'm just one of thousands. I wish it weren't so, but it is."

"I don't believe it," he said. "I think your portraits are terrific."

"Frances didn't think much of the one I gave you. And Lady Donne wouldn't even hang the one I did of her."

He smiled for the first time. "They were too true. Both of them. Weren't they?"

"I don't know. I paint what I see as best I can, that's all."

He did not look at her as he busied himself pushing apple cores into the undergrowth. "Mother thinks Frances is possessed."

"Don't think Frances wanted to walk out like that, Gabriel. She hated doing it. If you'd seen her you'd have known . . ."

He stood up suddenly and brushed down his trousers. "Don't let's talk about Frances any more. If we sit here much longer you'll catch a chill and then Annie will never forgive me. What a rotten day for one's last view of Somerset. Even the Brendons are in cloud. Do you remember that walk we did? All the way to St. Audries. And that night out, in the barn. When I look back it seems like another world – and yet it was less than two years ago."

She remembered the shadowed wood, the seagulls' cries, the feel of Geoffrey's fingers gripping her arms. "It was the first time I'd been kissed," she said.

"Really?" He sounded amused, delighted. "But not the last, I trust. It's the only time we've all been out walking together – do you realise that? We must do it again, all of us, as soon as the war's over."

A dream only. Less than a month later Lucy stood in the hall at Hillcrest, clutching onto the newel post at the bottom of the stairs for support as she tried to say the words, "Antony's dead."

[73]

Had it been Geoffrey, or Gabriel, they might have been better prepared. It had occurred to no one that Antony was in danger. Cruising through the Mediterranean far from German forces, sightseeing in Egypt, sending home almost daily accounts of his travels – descriptions of Cairo and the pyramids, Greek islands and the coast of Troy – he had been envied rather than considered a cause for anxiety.

"The waste of it," Annie sobbed, rocking to and fro in her kitchen chair. "They shouldn't have taken him. He were only a lad. The Rector should have stopped them."

"How can I write to Gabriel?" Frances asked Julia. "What can I say? He hasn't forgiven me for that last leave."

Julia, remembering the picture she had glimpsed, years ago, of Gabriel and Antony bent over their books in the lamplight of the Rectory dining-room, had little sympathy for Frances's difficulties. "I don't know," she said. "But you're going to have to say something. And quickly. He's going to be hard hit. He'll need all the help he can get."

Out in the empty vegetable garden Gwen turned over the ground, digging furiously every day, whatever the weather. "Go away," she shouted, as Julia drew near.

"Leave me alone," she said, when Julia persisted. Tears rolled down her cheeks. "I don't want your . . . it's the wind that's doing it . . ."

"Oh, Gwen," Julia said helplessly.

"Don't you come oh Gwenning me."

"There must be *something* I can do."

Gwen lifted her spade and rammed the blade down into the red earth. "One letter," she said. "One letter – that was all I got after he'd gone. And a . . . a *trinket* from Alexandria. He was writing letters to Sarah all the time, hundreds of them."

"Not hundreds. Oh, all right, then. A lot. But can't you see why? Everything was play-acting to Antony, even the war. He's always dragged Sarah into his play-acting, ever since she started lessons with Mr. Mackenzie. They lived in a make-believe world. You know they did. He thought he was fighting the Trojan War all over again. She understood that. You didn't. You'd never been interested in that sort of thing. That was why he wrote to her."

"What good would she have been to him?" Gwen said, as if she had not heard. "It wouldn't have helped him, her knowing about Achilles and that lot. I'd have looked after him. He needed someone like me, you know he did. Someone sensible, who could manage things and leave him to write his poetry and do all that clever stuff. He needed me. Didn't he need me?"

"I don't know," Julia said wearily. "I suppose so. Yes, of course he did. What does it matter? It's too late now." She did not know what comfort to give, confronted with such emotion. It seemed absurd – two children, barely seventeen . . .

She felt emotionally drained as well as frustrated. She wanted to do something more definite to help the war effort but did not know what. Miranda's letter gave her the answer.

She felt worse about leaving Lucy than she did leaving her sisters and Annie. Everyone took it for granted that Lucy would take over all the duties in the parish until Mr. and Mrs. Mackenzie recovered from the shock of Antony's death. No one wondered how Lucy felt at losing her youngest brother. It was Julia who let her talk about Antony, who helped with the parish visiting and the Girls' Friendly Society, who took over the village Coal Club and insisted that the Sewing Circle should meet at Hillcrest for the time being.

"I wish I didn't have to leave you," she said, when she told Lucy that she intended joining the Voluntary Aid Department, "but I feel I can't stay here doing nothing, particularly now Geoffrey and Gabriel have gone over to France. The Cartwrights won't let Miranda join on her own, but they say if I join too . . . and I think I'll be all right as a nurse."

Lucy nodded. "You'll be very good. Don't worry about me. I'll manage, and anyway, Mother's beginning to get back into the way of things again. I'd go with you, you know, if I could."

Frances behaved as if she regarded Julia's departure as a personal betrayal.

"Don't be so stupid, Frances," Julia said. "All these reasons why I can't leave ... You were happy to let me go to the Slade. What's the difference now? Nothing – except this time I shall be helping other people instead of myself. You ought to be pleased."

It would be dreadfully sordid, Frances told her. She'd ruin her hands. She wouldn't have time to paint. And why on earth did she want to go to France? What was wrong with nursing in Taunton? "I suppose you've got some ridiculous notion of nursing Geoffrey on the battlefield," she said, a supposition so stupid that Julia could scarcely bring herself to reply.

Frances was right in most of her predictions. Julia did ruin her hands. She didn't have time to paint, and wouldn't have had the energy if she had. Frances said nothing about home-sickness, which was strange when she had suffered so much herself during her time at the Slade, or exhaustion, both of which Julia had to endure. Worse was the disappointment. She had joined to nurse but soon discovered that lowly V.A.D.s were looked down on by the nursing staff and regarded as no more than maids of all work. At least I'm doing *something*, Julia told herself as she washed mountains of dishes, scrubbed and polished, ran errands and laid out trays, served up meals and rolled bandages. I'm not entirely useless. I shall be able to look Geoffrey in the face next time we meet.

There was always the fear that she might not survive the probationary period, an unnecessary fear as it turned out, for both she and Miranda were asked to sign on. Now at last they were allowed near the patients. Only routine tasks at first, washing, massaging with methylated spirits against pressure sores, the simpler bandaging, but gradually they progressed to sterner duties. Though she would never have admitted so to Frances, Julia had been apprehensive before coming up to London, wondering how she would react. Surprisingly she found she could face the sights, however horrific. Perhaps the detachment of an artist helped. It was the smells that brought on dizziness and caused sudden nausea. She never fainted, though she came near to it more than once. In time and with greater experience she learned to cope.

She returned to Somerset whenever she had sufficient time off. Her half-days she spent with the Cartwrights, who had begged her to make their house her London home. At the Cartwrights she met Aunt Amy once more, looking much older than Julia remembered. She had taken to wearing widow's weeds and had a disconcerting tendency to burst into tears without warning, although Uncle Henri was still alive, as far as anyone knew.

"And do you know?" Mrs. Cartwright confided to Julia. "She's become so *French* since all this happened. She used to pine for England before the war, but now she can't think of anything but that apartment of hers. She keeps saying she must go back to make sure everything's all right. It's impossible, of course. She could never manage without Henri. We tell her so, but she won't believe it."

Determined to improve her French, Julia monopolised Aunt Amy unashamedly during her visits to the Cartwrights. Aunt Amy suggested that Julia should arrange to nurse in Paris so that she could look after Aunt Amy's apartment, even live in it perhaps. In vain Julia told her that she had to go where she was sent and no one had ever been sent to Paris that she knew of; Aunt Amy continued to talk as if Julia's stay there was a *fait accompli*.

News of Bert Hawkins's death came in a letter from Frances. Frances, by now resigned to Julia's departure, wrote often, for which Julia was grateful – cheerful, gossipy letters to keep Julia in touch, passing on news not only from the village but from further afield. She mentioned the names of men from the cricket team and the village band, both disbanded now that their players were scattered over the world. Bill Roberts had been put forward for the Military Medal; Jimmy Watchet had sailed for France; Billy Gould had been wounded in Mesopotamia. And then, casually as if it were no more important than the rest, Bert Hawkins ... killed in France.

Julia sat in her cubicle with Frances's letter on her lap and remembered Bert Hawkins. Jolly, tubby Bert Hawkins, Sir James's chauffeur down at the Manor who always had a twinkle in his eye and was ever ready to help. When one or other of the Purcells returned from a London visit more often than not Bert would be waiting at Taunton station with Sir James's car. "Seeing as how I was in Taunton anyways, on an errand for her Ladyship," he would say, "*and* a little bird having told me ..." or, "Just seen Sir James off on the London train, miss, so's I thought I'd wait and see ..." Back at Hillcrest he would deliver them to Annie – "Everything all right, Miss Sampford?" – and Annie would smile as she lifted the kettle from the hob. "Right as rain, Mr. Hawkins. Now then, how about a nice pot of tea?"

Once, a long time ago, Julia had caught sight of Annie through the window on the back stairs, talking to Bert Hawkins in Tinker's Lane below. There was something about the way they stood together, apart but close, and the way they talked, that made Julia pause ... If she shut her eyes she could see them now.

She went home as soon as she could. There was no way of telling anything from Annie's greeting but when Julia went out into the kitchen later that evening she found Annie sitting in front of the range, hands lying idle in her lap, gazing into space. Julia made tea for them both and pulled up a chair.

"I'm sorry about Bert Hawkins," she said.

Annie glanced across. "Ay," she said.

"What happened, do you know?"

"'Twas a sniper, they said. One moment they was all joking together, next moment Bert were dead. That's what his officer wrote."

At least it had been quick, Julia thought. Instant death. No pain, no disfigurement, unlike the men she dealt with. "He wasn't local, was he? Where did he come from? Was there a family?"

"There's his mother, lives over Frome way."

"Were you and he . . .? I don't want to pry."

"I know, love. We talked about it. It meant waiting – we knew that. Until Miss Sarah'd settled down at Oxford, I reckoned. Bert said Sir James would find us a cottage then. I could have carried on here, coming in days . . ." She sighed. "It doesn't do to make plans."

"Does anyone else know?"

Annie shook her head. "Only Bertha. She's known all along."

Of course, Julia thought. Bertha had always been a good friend, and not only to Annie. It had been years before Julia realised how much the Purcells owed to Bertha over at the Rectory, particularly during the early years when Bertha's willingness to pass on details of Rectory discussions, overheard in the course of her duties, had kept Annie aware of Mr. and Mrs. Mackenzies' thinking and warned her of problems likely to arise.

"She's been kind, Bertha has," Annie said. She gave Julia a bleak smile. "Don't fret over me, love. There's no knowing how things would have turned out. He was ambitious, Bert was. That's why he enlisted. More scope for the likes of him in the Army, he said, than tinkering about with Squire's car. Even without this old war he'd have finished up in some grand London house, like as not, and how would I have done then? I'm a country girl, love. Can't see myself living in a town." She stared down at the mug in her hands, her face in shadow. "I daresay it's all for the best," she said.

Perhaps she was right. Perhaps it was. It seemed bleak comfort, all the same.

Chapter Six

Miranda and Julia had applied to join the V.A.D. together, they had trained side by side, appeared in front of the Selection Board on the same day and were members of the same Detachment. It had never occurred to either that they would not go abroad together – until Miranda returned swollen-eyed from a day off and told Julia that her parents had forbidden her to leave England.

"I can't help being the only one," she said, sitting on Julia's bed and bursting into tears all over again. "It's not my fault. It's so unfair. They always *knew* I wanted to go abroad. *You* go and talk to them, Julia. They think you're such a good influence ... you'll be able to persuade them."

Good influence she might be but Julia was no more successful at persuasion than Miranda.

"Please try to understand," Mrs. Cartwright begged. "She is our only child. It's different for you. You don't have parents to worry. I know we haven't said anything against foreign service before. Perhaps we should have. To tell you the truth, Julia dear, we didn't think Miranda would stick the training. She's led such a *sheltered* life, we expected her to give up long ago. In which case, you see, the question of foreign service would never have arisen. And we do feel we are doing our bit for the war effort already. My nephew's been in France for almost a year now."

The Cartwrights obviously did not appreciate their daughter's true worth. Beneath the surface froth there was dogged determination. The training had been far harder for Miranda than for Julia. Julia was used to physical work. She had scrubbed floors at Hillcrest, though not often, had suffered discomfort, been both cold and frightened. Miranda had always been cosseted and indulged, but never once, so far as Julia knew, had she even considered giving up, though she did acknowledge Julia's support. "I'd never have done it without you. And it does help, doesn't it, thinking of the boys over there. Their suffering must be so dreadful."

Frances had wondered whether Julia would stay with Miranda in England, but did not try further persuasion herself, having at last accepted Julia's decision to join the V.A.D. "I do admire you," she said, when Julia went home for the last time before sailing for France. "I could never do what you're doing. You will keep up your painting while you're away, won't you? There shouldn't be any shortage of people to draw, I imagine." Sometimes Julia wondered whether Frances had any idea what was happening in the outside world.

The strangeness of her own world never left her during her time at home. She walked round the garden with Gwen, admiring the new plantings while listening to Gwen's future plans, she looked at and discussed Frances's latest work and tried to show an intelligent interest in Sarah's study. Hillcrest had never looked lovelier, and her sisters never been more dear, but all the time she felt remote. Could this really be the same world as the one she had just left, the world of the crowded hospital ward where gramophones ground out the everlasting sound of popular songs to drown the groans of wounded men, and no number of lavender bags could make the air smell sweet?

The Mackenzies gave her a small gold cross in farewell, which Mr. Mackenzie fastened round her neck himself. "Send me your address when you know it," he said. "I shall ask Gabriel to keep an eye on you while you're in France."

The Cartwrights went with her to Charing Cross. "You will write, won't you?" Miranda said. There were tears in her eyes – tears of disappointment. "As often as you can. I'll be thinking of you all the time."

Aunt Amy insisted on giving her a carefully wrapped package. "Please, *chérie*, take it. It's the key to my apartment. If you are ever in Paris you must go and see ..."

"But I shan't ... I can't. I don't want it. I might lose it. Oh, very well ... but I can't promise."

Mr. Cartwright pressed a sovereign into her hand. "I don't know what the Froggies do about English money over there," he said, clearing his throat, "but anyway ... You might be able to find a use for that."

She was touched. Only the presence of her fellow V.A.D.s stopped her shedding tears as the train rattled on its way towards Folkestone and the Channel. That, and the knowledge that every moment was drawing her nearer to Geoffrey.

She could laugh at her naïvety later. She had been so pleased with her home nursing and first aid certificates, so proud to be selected to serve abroad. It had never occurred to her that the base hospitals in France were desperate for anyone with a modicum of common sense to help cope with the casualties that were pouring in from the front line. That heady feeling, standing on the quay in Boulogne, breathing in French air, exhilarated by the fact that she was on the continent at last, did not remain with her for long. She had not felt the panic in London that she did here, confronted by men arriving straight from the trenches, filthy, foul-smelling and bloody, working under professional nurses who expected her to know what to do without explanation.

She gained confidence over the weeks. The Sister, so frightening at first, stiff and disapproving – "I can't think what they're doing, sending out girls with no proper training" – began to unbend, to treat her as an adult and allow her some responsibility. In time Julia began to feel that she might make a nurse after all.

She panicked all the same when summoned to Matron's office. What had she done wrong? Nothing in the ward presumably, for Sister was as baffled as she. She paused

[83]

outside Matron's office, smoothed down her apron, checked that her cap was straight and went in.

Matron wasted no time in coming to the point. "Ah, Nurse Purcell. I've had a letter from your guardian, delivered to me this morning by his son. Mr. Mackenzie wondered whether he might be allowed to see you, in order to report back to his father." She smiled faintly. "Parents aren't the only ones to worry, apparently. Guardians do too. I told Mr. Mackenzie he could meet you at the Nurses' Club when you come off duty this afternoon."

Julia was too dazed to do more than stammer a thank you. It had never occurred to her that anything might come of Mr. Mackenzie's suggestion that Gabriel should keep an eye on her. Indeed, she remembered – with guilt now – that at the time she had been amused by the proposal. She wondered what Gabriel was doing in Étaples, whether he had made a special journey to see her, and what news he would be able to give her of Geoffrey.

But when she rushed into the Nurses' Club it was Geoffrey who unfolded himself out of an armchair and stood up to face her. "Hello," he said.

She could not believe her eyes. "*Geoffrey*! What are you doing here? Where's Gabriel?"

"You weren't expecting Gabriel, were you?"

"Of course I was –" She stopped abruptly as he came towards her. "You're limping."

He grimaced. "That's why I'm here. I've done my knee in. Something's slipped out of place. I've been sent back to the Base on light duties. They say if it's not better in a couple of weeks I'll have to go back to Blighty for an operation."

She watched him walk. "Does it hurt?"

"It's better than it was. I'm supposed to exercise it, anyway. I'll come over here every day. That'll be good exercise."

Her smile was tremulous. Ridiculous, when she was so

[84]

happy ... "How long can you stay? Shall I make tea? There's a tea-room beyond."

"Why not?" He looked round the room. "It's nice, isn't it? Easy chairs, magazines, newspapers. Books too. Everything you could wish for. I've been reading the war news in the *Daily Mirror*. That's a laugh, if you like. Are you able to spend much time here?"

She shook her head. "We're very busy at the moment. Besides, when I am free I'd rather go out walking. There are splendid woods behind the camp – they're beautiful."

"You haven't said anything about your work. I had to hang around the casualty clearing station waiting for transport, so I did see ... Does it upset you? Do you mind?"

"You get used to it. I never thought you would but you do. We've got terrible burn cases at the moment, from Hooge. It's the Hun's new weapon – liquid fire, they call it. Have you heard about that?"

He had heard rumours, that was all. "Don't let's talk about it. So long as you're not thinking of giving up and going home ... You'd be surprised what a difference it makes, knowing you're here."

She was touched. "I couldn't go home now, even if I wanted to. I signed on for the duration. Frances was furious when she heard. She said I should have only signed on for six months. And I suppose it does sound strange, but I am enjoying it here. It's very satisfying. I know I've got a lot to learn, and I don't want to sound conceited, but I think I could make quite a good nurse in time."

"I could have told you that years ago," he said.

He came up behind her as she made the tea and put his arms round her. His lips brushed her hair. "We'd better be discreet. Brother and sister stuff. I expect they're pretty fierce about that sort of thing round here, and I am supposed to be *in loco parentis*."

She leant up against him. "You're not being very discreet at this moment."

[85]

"No, well ... I'm only human."

They were not alone long. The Club, used by nursing staff from all the hospitals in the area, began to fill with probationers and V.A.D.s coming off duty. To Julia's amazement Geoffrey was not in the least embarrassed at being surrounded by so many women; he sat quietly in an armchair, watching all that was going on and talking to anyone who talked to him. Later he suggested to Julia that they might go out for a walk in the woods.

"You seem to know everyone," he said admiringly.

"It's much friendlier here than it was in London," she said. "We have supper parties in our huts, all mixed up – the Queen Alexandra probationers, V.A.D.s, Red Cross, everyone. It's fun." She smiled. "Do you remember how you and Gabriel and Antony used to complain at the way we talked about painting all the time? It's the same here, only now the talk's medical."

She was more interested in finding out about his life than talking about hers. He had not yet been in action, though he had seen those who had. "They look different when they come back," he said. "Wild-eyed, somehow." He expected the day to come soon. Meanwhile he was taking advantage of every opportunity offered for sport. He had been picked to shoot for his battalion in brigade competitions and was doing surprisingly well. "It's not that our team's so good," he admitted, "just that the rest are so bad." He considered that the comradeship of army life did much to compensate for those aspects of it that he disliked. Recently he had discovered that he and Patterson, his closest friend in the army, had met years before. "We both played for our schools," he said. "Strange, isn't it? Not that we can remember each other."

The visit to Matron had been his own idea, and nothing to do with Mr. Mackenzie's letter to Gabriel. "I wrote to Father the moment I knew I was being sent back to the Base and got him to send me a suitable letter to give her. You didn't think I'd throw away a chance like this, did you?" He was indignant at the thought. "I think it might be a good idea if I went and saw her again. Thanked her for letting us meet, said I'd report favourably to Father — that sort of thing. We want to keep her on our side if we're going to go on seeing each other."

Julia smiled, scarcely recognising this new, forceful Geoffrey. She was still smiling when she climbed into bed that night. If this was what the army had done for him ... She blew out the candle and lay in the dark. An animal scratched under the floorboards of the hut; something, moth or bat, blundered against the glass of the window. A door banged in the distance. She thought of Geoffrey, sleeping safely only a mile or two away. I'm happy, she marvelled, really happy.

What was said during Geoffrey's second interview with Matron Julia never found out, but it had an unexpected sequel: he was invited to dine at the Home Mess.

Julia was late the evening he came, arriving breathless after a frantic day on the ward, to find Geoffrey sitting next to Matron, discussing India with her as if he knew it personally instead of secondhand through his mother. He greeted Julia almost distantly. "I thought I should be sort of avuncular," he said, when Julia protested later. "I am acting in place of your guardian, don't forget."

Sister Forrest, the sister in charge of the Home Mess, thought Geoffrey was wonderful. She brought out the best china for his second visit, and the cutlery kept for special occasions. She was quite in love with him, she told Julia afterwards, a statement that did not worry Julia, who guessed Sister Forrest to be forty at least.

"I remind her of her little brother," Geoffrey said complacently. "She brought him up, more or less, so she told me. He was killed at Le Cateau last year. I think she needs someone to mother."

It was a miraculous couple of weeks. Not all their

attempts to meet during the following days were successful –
an afternoon off was changed at the last moment to the
morning, a time when light duties kept Geoffrey at the Base
– but they managed to spend a surprising amount of time
together. In the Nurses' Club and the Mess, brief periods
coming off duty, an illicit meal in the little fish restaurant in
Étaples, half hours gleaned here and there – minutes added
to minutes, making half hours and then hours, time frozen
for ever.

It could not be perfect. She knew that Geoffrey was
ashamed. To be sent back to the Base for any reason other
than a battle wound was deeply dishonourable. She prayed
nightly that he would need an operation, knowing as she did
so that he would be mortified by such an outcome. It was
the first time she could remember that they had not been in
accord.

The idyll came to an end at last, as they had known it
must. He arrived outside the ward one morning. "I've come
to say goodbye. I'm on my way back to the battalion."

"But your knee ..."

"I persuaded them it'd be all right. I kept telling them it
slipped back by itself last time. Anyway, no one's being sent
back to Blighty at the moment. So ... well ... it's goodbye."

Perhaps it was easier like this, too sudden to think of
the right words to say, too short for anything but a quick
embrace, and no privacy at all. One of the men in the ward
began to whistle 'Who's your lady friend?' An orderly clat-
tered enamel dishes together onto an enamel tray. Sister
called from the other end of the ward, "Nurse Purcell.
Where's Purcell? Find her for me, somebody, quick."

There was not even time to watch him go.

Geoffrey's remark, that men were being kept in France,
surprised Julia. In the wards the wounded were being
marked down for England with a readiness she found aston-

ishing after the reluctance she had noticed up until now. Blighty, convalescent camp or back to their units. Soon they would have no patients left to nurse.

She was never so innocent again. After the battle of Loos she knew only too well what empty-bedded wards foretold – another attack, hospital trains following so rapidly on each other that patients from one had not been dealt with before the next arrived, when time off was unknown and fatigue so extreme that it was difficult to stay awake even when standing, and always, when Geoffrey might be involved, the nagging fear that not even exhaustion could stifle.

It seemed weeks before she heard that Geoffrey was safe, although it was only days. Battles weren't what he had been led to expect, he told her. This one had been chaotic. No one knew what was happening, what they should be doing, where to go. Everything had gone wrong. Still, he supposed it could have been worse. He hadn't done anything stupid. He was all right. She wasn't to worry. She took his letter out with her into the woods behind the camp and read and reread it, shedding tears of relief.

The cold, wet autumn of 1915 was succeeded by a colder, wetter winter. The authorities talked of putting up more huts, of building a covered way from the nurses' block to the bath hut. "I'll believe that when I see it," Matron said grimly. Meanwhile the nurses continued to stagger to and fro in the rain, wellington boots pulled on over bare, chilblained feet, macintoshes covering their nightclothes, as they battled against winds that blew salt and sand over the dunes from the direction of the sea.

If only Mrs. Mackenzie and Annie could see her now, Julia thought, remembering with wry amusement past lectures on the dangers of draughts, wet feet, unaired clothes and, worst of all, unaired beds. Surprisingly, she could not remember having felt better. She was happy – helping the war, supporting Geoffrey, doing her bit. She would have been miserable, she knew, carrying on her old life at home.

Her sisters and the Mackenzies took it in turns to write to her from Hillcrest and the Rectory, sending parcels almost every week, of things she had asked for and things she had not, bits and pieces to help make her hut more homely – cretonne for curtains, a decent pillow for her bed (she hated the straw ones handed out) and matting for the floor – as well as food to help her keep going. They sent practical items – a leather jacket for the winter, a Boots cooker to air her clothes (Mrs. Mackenzie's suggestion, that), lavender bags and Keatings powder – as well as Woodbines and chocolates for the boys and presents to go into their Christmas stockings.

Julia found her own letters increasingly difficult to write. She did not know what to say. The life she led was beyond the imagining of anyone in Huish Priory. She would have found it unimaginable herself, a year ago.

Geoffrey arrived unheralded on Shrove Tuesday. Julia was coping with a convoy at the time and knew nothing of his visit until it was too late.

"He waited around for a bit," Crawford told her, "and then said he'd go off to the Mess. That was the last I saw of him."

"He *is* a nice lad," Sister Forrest said, when Julia arrived at the Mess to find that Geoffrey had already departed. "He insisted on helping me with the pancakes. We did have fun." She giggled like a schoolgirl. "He only tossed two onto the floor – wasn't that good? He'd been on a course at Hardelot, he said. Such a pity you missed him."

Hardelot was only a couple of miles down the road. Julia had walked there once on a day off. To have had Geoffrey so near ... she could have wept with disappointment.

Geoffrey had enjoyed his time with Sister Forrest. He extolled his pancake skill in his next letter to Julia, promising a demonstration some time in the future. He hadn't mentioned the possibility of a visit, not knowing until the last minute whether he could get away. It was a pity he had missed her.

The battalion's winter billets were in a deserted village – 'tray cushy, my men call it. It is, too. Whenever it gets cold I send my servant into the house next door for a bit more of the woodwork.' He had set about clearing the garden of rubbish and was thinking of growing vegetables – Gwen had promised to send both seeds and instructions. Patterson thought he might be able to borrow a motorbicycle from his Service Corps brother stationed nearby, in which case he and Geoffrey would come over. 'I'd like you to meet Patterson. Would you be able to find a girl for him, do you think?'

Crawford was Julia's hutmate, a practical, north-country girl who had expressed amazement on her arrival at the paintings tacked onto the wall above Julia's bed. "Your sister did them? Gracious, Purcell, they're the sort of pictures people buy." Initial wariness became friendship in time. It was Crawford whom Julia invited to make the fourth when Geoffrey and Patterson arrived, dusty, oil-smeared and tired on their borrowed motorbike, and Crawford who suggested meeting the boys in the woods beyond Étaples – "Of course we can't ride pillion. We'd be on the next boat to England if anyone saw us" – and walking on to Paris-Plage from there.

Julia sat crushed next to Crawford in the crowded charabanc that ran between the camp and Étaples. She felt light-headed with relief. Geoffrey had survived the winter. They were together again. The long winter had ended, spring come at last. There was warmth in the sun for the first time. The woods were thick with flowers underfoot – wild daffodils, periwinkles and hyacinths. She was happy.

Patterson was a sandy-haired young man, with freckles and a fierce moustache that went oddly with his peaceable expression, quiet but with a nice sense of humour. Much like Geoffrey himself, Julia suspected, thinking at the same time that he had an interesting face to draw. He was more loquacious than Geoffrey, however, about their experiences. It was the chaos and mess of the battlefield that seemed to have impressed itself on him, and on Geoffrey too. "It was different when my brother and I played soldiers," Patterson said. He sounded aggrieved. "Tin soldiers do what you tell them."

"It's like Frances's landscapes," Geoffrey said. "Everything is so neat and tidy when Frances paints. Nothing like nature at all, really."

"I don't know that you're right," Julia said uncomfortably, reluctant to discuss Frances's work in front of almost strangers.

Crawford had obviously been more adventurous with her time off than Julia, for she knew Paris-Plage well and took them to a restaurant where they were ushered to a table at the back, hidden from the front window and those who might disapprove of nurses and subalterns sitting together. "Though no one really objects as long as there are four of you," Crawford said, with the voice of experience. "It's couples the high-ups are afraid of."

Geoffrey looked at Julia across the table. "With reason, no doubt."

It was the first time she had had time to study him since his experiences at Loos. He had been in and out of the front line frequently during the months in between and it told, though she found it difficult to pinpoint the change. He was thinner. His face had lost flesh, making the bone structure stronger. He looked much older, nearer thirty than twenty. Always quiet, he seemed now almost withdrawn, content to let Crawford and Patterson do the talking, but the smile he gave Julia across the table was the same as it had always been, transforming the solemnity of his usual expression into a look of such happiness that she felt her heart stop.

She learnt more about Geoffrey's garden from Patterson than she had from Geoffrey himself. "You should have seen it when we moved in," Patterson said. "Waist high with the rubbish the Germans had left. Mackenzie nearly did for us all when he cleared it."

Geoffrey looked sheepish. "It seemed the quickest way, to have a bonfire," he said. "It would have been, too, if it hadn't been for the ammunition left lying around."

"Quite lively, it was," Patterson said. "It fizzed like anything. Had us jumping about like firecrackers too. Still, it did the trick. It looks a proper garden now. I keep telling him, he missed his vocation. He should have been a corporation gardener."

Geoffrey grinned. "Thank you. I've got one in my platoon and he's useless. Can't see beyond salvias and geraniums."

Julia was amused by his enthusiasm, as well as relieved, believing that such an interest must do much to make life tolerable. It was the battles she had feared on his behalf when she first arrived in France; only gradually had she come to realise that long spells under frequent shellfire in a hot sector of the line were much more debilitating and often more dangerous than formal attacks. Geoffrey himself dreaded the night raiding parties more. "I wouldn't mind if there was some point to them," he told her. "Well, I would, but not as much. They're murder. Or suicide, whichever way you like to look at it. It's not as if we get useful information from them, because we don't, hardly ever."

They wandered through the town after leaving the café, gazing at the expensive goods in the shop windows and marvelling at the quantities of food on display at a time when food shortages were supposed to be widespread, and then, braving the wind coming off the Channel, walked along the sea-front.

"Do you remember that day at St. Audries?" Geoffrey said suddenly.

Ridiculously, she blushed. "Yes."

They parted finally on the bridge over the river at Étaples. Patterson had been trying to hurry Geoffrey for the past half hour. "If we don't get the bike back in time ..."

"I've been thinking," Geoffrey said, as he mounted the pillion. "I might put in for a spot of local leave."

She was incredulous. "You wouldn't get it, would you?"

"I don't know. Patterson's brother went to Paris on local leave." He grinned at her from under his goggles. "I know how you feel about Paris, but personally I'd rather come to Étaples. We'll have to see. Don't count on it."

Count on it! She scarcely dared consider the possibility. "What about your mother? Shouldn't you go home?"

"There wouldn't be time. Besides, it's Gabriel Mother would want to have back, not me."

Local leave was something to dream about: she never thought Geoffrey would get it. And when he did arrive her happiness was diluted, for he came at the worst possible time when she was working in the Home Mess.

Most V.A.D.s hated their time in the Mess, having come to France to nurse the wounded rather than look after the nursing staff, and were thankful that they had to spend only two months helping Sister Forrest, the permanent sister in charge. Though dismayed at first at having to leave the ward, Julia soon found she was enjoying the work. She got on well with Sister Forrest, who put her in charge of the catering. It was not difficult, catering for sixty rather than for the six at home being more a matter of multiplication than skill and she had batmen to help with the routine work, but shopping and cooking and feeding so many took all the hours available, and she greeted Geoffrey's smug, here-I-am expression when he arrived with a long face. "Why do you have to come now, of all times? I shan't be able to see you. We never have time off."

She had forgotten Sister Forrest's fondness for Geoffrey.

"We don't want to draw attention to the fact that you're here," Sister Forrest told him, "but so long as you don't get in the way ..." She was on Christian name terms with him now, which made the difference in his surname and Julia's less noticeable, though both he and Julia were finding it increasingly difficult to behave like brother and sister.

"Half-brother, actually," Julia said, when a curious V.A.D. brought up the subject, shocking herself by the ease with which she lied. "His father's my guardian."

Sister Forrest was like putty in Geoffrey's hands. She put pancakes on the menu twice during his visit, because he enjoyed tossing them, and at his suggestion sent Julia down to the market to buy the provisions in person, thinking Julia's knowledge of French would save money and never suspecting an ulterior motive. Even Sister Forrest might have had second thoughts had she known what Geoffrey intended to do.

"If we should be seen together ..." Julia said, when he stepped out from behind a delapidated cart of squealing piglets.

He nodded at the two batmen who accompanied her to carry the provisions back to the camp. "You're properly chaperoned," he said, and then did his best to lose those chaperons while he and she wandered through the crowds, giggling over the sickly sentimental cards on the postcard stall, eating brioches in the refreshment booths and drinking red wine warmed with hot water.

Julia worried about him, despite his good spirits. "It's a rotten way to spend your leave, helping me. You ought to be having fun. Relaxing."

"I am having fun. And relaxing. It's very relaxing being with you. And anyway I shan't be here tomorrow afternoon. Guess who I'm meeting for tea."

"I can't. Who?"

"Hester Donne. I bumped into her in Le Touquet this morning. I nearly didn't recognise her. She's quite thin these days. Very attractive, in fact."

"Oh," Julia said, not altogether pleased. "What's she doing in Le Touquet?"

"Nursing at the Duchess of Westminster's hospital. Why don't you come too? I don't know that I'll be able to carry on a conversation with her for all that time on my own."

"I couldn't possibly ask for time off."

"I'll ask then."

There were times these days when she scarcely recognised Geoffrey. Of course Sister Forrest agreed. "Though you must finish the baking before you go," she told Julia. "You'll have to do extra, you know. We've run out twice this week. Another couple of dozen scones should do. They're too good, your scones. People get greedy."

Hester had indeed lost weight. She had also had her hair bobbed. It suited her, as did her uniform, which was infinitely better cut than the regulation one. Julia reckoned it must have cost a great deal of money. No money could do anything about a nurse's hands, however; Hester's were in no better condition than Julia's own.

She had not changed altogether. She still giggled. She giggled as she described how Her Grace and Her Grace's friends put on evening dress and tiaras to welcome each convoy. "Even at nine in the morning. Really. It's the least they can do for the boys, they say. The boys think they've arrived in heaven when they see all the diamonds glittering over them. Such a disappointment when they realise they haven't."

The life Hester led sounded more leisurely than Julia's – the Duchess's V.A.D.s even had time to paint. "Not me, of course, you know I can't do anything like that, but some of them do. We had an exhibition not long ago. I'd have asked you over if I'd known you were here. Are you painting now?" And when Julia shook her head, "Why ever not? I always thought it a shame you never painted Father."

"Your mother wouldn't let me," Julia pointed out.

"I know. So stupid. She didn't like the one you did of her, that's why. Father and I thought you'd got her exactly. You ought to come here some time and do Her Grace ... What about you, Geoffrey? What are you doing all day?"

Geoffrey, who had been saying little but watching the two girls with an air of amusement, sat up. "Me? Oh, I'm learning new things every day. How to improve rissoles, for instance. You sieve tinned tomatoes and mix in some flour – it makes a delicious sauce. Don't tell me you didn't know that. I'm going to give the battalion cooks lessons when I get back. Then, let's see ... Oh, yes ... I spent this morning writing field cards. To everyone I could think of, all over the world. Aunts, uncles, cousins, chaps I knew at school – everybody."

The two girls stared in disbelief. *"Field cards?"*

"That's right. Greatest invention since the wheel, field cards. No thought needed. No effort. You could fill them in in your sleep if you wanted. Cross out everything except 'I am quite well' and 'I haven't had a letter for a long time' and with luck you'll get letters pouring back by return." He leant back in his chair and smiled. "Cast your bread over the waters and it'll come back in mailbags. As Father might say."

"Oh Geoffrey," Hester giggled. "You are awful."

"Good old Hester," Geoffrey said later, walking slowly back with Julia through the woods in the dusk. "I like her, I must say. Did you notice how she asked after Gabriel? As if she wasn't in the least bit interested?"

"We all thought she rather fancied him," Julia said. "Your mother would have liked that, wouldn't she – Gabriel marrying a baronet's daughter?"

Geoffrey considered. "I don't think that would matter to her. She wants Gabriel to be happy. She'd probably say Hester isn't clever enough for him. Which she isn't."

"Would she think Frances clever enough?"

"Frances is different. Frances doesn't appreciate him.

[97]

That's what Mother doesn't like."

"She does, you know. Appreciate him, I mean. It's just that her work's more important."

"Yes, well. That's the whole trouble between them, isn't it?"

Mrs. Mackenzie wanted Gabriel to be happy, Geoffrey said. What did Mrs. Mackenzie want for Geoffrey himself, Julia wondered? She said nothing. There were still subjects she was too shy to discuss.

On the last evening of Geoffrey's leave Sister Forrest sent Julia off duty early. "We'll manage without you this once. Go and say goodbye to your young man."

They did not talk much. He expected the battalion to move out of billets shortly and march south to the Somme. His only regret was the loss of his garden and the vegetables in it. "I'd like to have been there to eat them, but I suppose I didn't expect it really, and, anyway, as long as the next lot enjoy them . . ."

She felt sick with apprehension. Everyone knew the big push was coming. She did not know whether to believe him when he said he wouldn't be involved and found his disappointment hard to understand, knowing his loathing of the trenches.

"You must see," he said patiently. "It's the biggest thing that's ever happened. It'll go down in the history books. We'll slaughter Fritz; everyone says so. It'll mean the end of the war. Of *course* I don't want to miss it. And even if we do get into it before it's all over it's not the same thing. Besides, it's my birthday soon. Wouldn't it be tremendous to go over the top in the greatest battle of all time on one's birthday?"

She tried to match her enthusiasm to his and failed.

"Gabriel's going to be in it," he said. There was envy in his voice. "It's been the same, ever since I can remember. He's always had all the luck." He added, as an afterthought, "You'd better not let on to Mother. I don't think he's told

[98]

her yet. He says there's plenty of time."

Time there was not, in the Base hospitals. When Julia returned from her two months in the Mess she found frantic preparations for the coming battle already under way. Wards were being emptied, delighted men sent back to England, disappointed ones to local convalescent camps or returned to their battalions. Orderlies went round the camp with dogs, flushing rats out from under the floorboards. V.A.D.s scrubbed every possible surface with cresolis and water while the sisters checked incoming supplies of medicines, lotions, and dressings. Trestle beds and straw palliasses were placed between beds already lining the wards. Every possible space was requisitioned – the church tent, the stores, the Y.M.C.A. hut. All the time, night and day, the muffled roar of guns provided a constant accompaniment. So loud, yet so distant – what must it be like close to, Julia wondered.

They were woken early on July 1st. Larks sang in the sky as they walked slowly over the dew-soaked grass to the empty wards. The sun came through the trees in glowing shafts of light. The air smelt fresh, clean. A summer's day, full of promise ...

Exhaustion blurred memories of the week that followed. It was not the dreadful scenes in the ward that remained in her memory, but vignettes, like miniatures painted onto a black canvas screen. A padre, ladling out soup, hour after hour. "You can tell I was in soup kitchens when I was a curate, can't you, nurse?" The orderly, swaying asleep as he tried to hold the hurricane lamp still above an impossible dressing. The commanding colonel, helping cut bread in the few minutes' wait for the arrival of the next ambulance train – the thick, jagged slices of one who has never cut bread before – and the medical major buttering. But it was the faces that would haunt Julia in after years, the mud-caked, dust-covered faces of men and boys as day and night they came, a never-ending procession. "Dear God," Sister said, as the bugle announced the arrival of yet another train, "can there be anyone left at the front?"

For the first time fear crept into Julia's mind. It had never occurred to her before; it wouldn't happen, couldn't happen; it was impossible, inconceivable; and yet ... might England after all *lose* the war?

There were other, more immediate, fears. What had happened to Gabriel? How was he? Unhurt, wounded ... or dead? And the most insidious fear of all ... who had replaced the thousands of men sent back to England, the hundreds lying in the base hospitals at this moment?

Who was standing in the front line now?

Chapter Seven

"We might have known," Geoffrey said, "that Gabriel would get a decoration sooner or later. You can't imagine him not, can you? He only got it because he lost his temper, did you know? Saw red, he said in his letter, and didn't stop to think."

"I didn't know Gabriel had a temper," Julia said.

"Lord, yes. I can remember when we were small ... I felt quite sorry for the poor old Fritzes, I can tell you, when he told me what had happened."

He sounded full of admiration, as well as amusement, talking about Gabriel's Military Cross. Julia had been surprised to discover how closely the two had kept in touch, and to learn of the efforts they made to meet. By giving them something in common the war had brought them closer together.

Geoffrey had written to her in late November, promising a visit should he be able to escape from the course he was attending, but she had scarcely dared hope he would succeed. He arrived late when she was already getting ready for bed. He was cold, hungry and exhausted, after a train journey that had taken almost nine hours.

"I can't think why it should be so tiring, sitting in a train," he complained. "Particularly a train that doesn't move. I kept wondering whether I'd do better lorry-hopping, but as soon as I decided I would the train would lurch off again. I should have got out at Abbeville, looking back. I kept thinking – all those hours wasted when I could have been with you ..."

"You're here now," she said. "That's all that matters."

She took him to the Mess, not knowing where else to go so late in the evening. Sister Forrest was sitting at the far end, struggling with plans for Christmas, but she pushed her lists aside when she saw Geoffrey, and set about cooking what she called 'a decent meal for the lad'.

"She's a good old stick, isn't she?" Geoffrey said, after she had dished up, made sure he had everything he could possibly need and then left, murmuring that it might be nice if they could clear up after he had finished. "Tactful, too."

Julia watched him as he ate, noting the black marks under his eyes, the slight unsteadiness in his hands. He had been in some of the fiercest fighting on the Somme since they last met, though he had said little about it in his letters, beyond remarking that being sent on a course was regarded as no more than a consolation prize for having suffered a rough time. She knew enough, however, and had gathered more from men she nursed, to be able to surmise what he must have gone through. He glanced up as if sensing her gaze. "Don't look so solemn, old thing. I'm here. That's all that matters."

She had an overpowering urge to burst into tears, to tell him that she could not bear the waiting and constant anxiety any longer. She wanted to confess that even the delirious happiness of unexpected reunions such as this could not compensate for the terror she felt on his behalf all the time they were apart. She managed to say nothing, ashamed of herself when she remembered how much easier her life was than his.

"I suppose you heard Gabriel did Mother out of her trip to the Palace?" he said. "He had the M.C. sent to the Rectory – didn't want to waste a day of his leave, he told me. Mother was furious. Lucy's afraid he'll try for another, to make up to her ..."

"As long as *you* don't try ..." Julia said.

"You know me." He looked sheepish. "I'm no hero. I keep my head down. Do what I'm told. You don't need to worry about me."

Perhaps he was right. Yet she had watched him play rugby at Cambridge, seen him in the local hockey team at home. She knew what a moment's foolhardiness could do . . .

He cleaned his plate with a piece of bread, made a face as he swallowed the last of the tea – "tastes worse than ours in the trenches" – sat back and sighed with pleasure. "That's better. I feel a new man."

"You don't look very new."

He gave her a quick smile. "No, well. Don't let's talk about it. Let's talk about us – you and me. I'll try and come again at the end of the course. Quicker next time, with a bit of luck. And then . . ."

"Yes?"

"Do you think we could wangle some time together somehow? I find it very frustrating, meeting like this. I nearly went mad, sitting in that train, watching the minutes go by. You must be due for leave, surely – you haven't had any since you came out."

"You know what it's like. There only has to be a bit of extra activity, and leave gets cancelled for weeks on end. I was at the top of the list earlier this year, but then I gave my place up to a girl who had to get back for a wedding. I don't know that I'd want winter leave, anyway. I'd much rather be home in the spring."

"You'd go home, would you?"

"Where else would I go?"

"We talked about Paris once," he said.

She stared. "I'd forgotten about that."

"You were always desperate to see Paris. I wouldn't mind either. Patterson's brother said he'd been there for a weekend. It made me think. If we could arrange something . . . though I suppose timing would be tricky. And you might feel you have to – I mean, I'd quite understand if you wanted to go home. Frances would probably think it odd if you didn't."

Julia considered. "We don't *have* to tell Frances," she said.

"No." He grinned at her. "Or Mother either."

"Would you be able to get away?"

"I might. If we were out on rest at the time. If I knew you were going to be there."

She remembered Aunt Amy, for the first time for months. "I know somewhere I could stay in Paris. An apartment. Miranda Cartwright – you remember? It's her aunt's. I've got the key. At least I hope I still have."

His smile was triumphant. "I always knew you were wonderful. Well, then. Let me have the dates as soon as you've got something fixed. I'll do my damnedest but you mustn't count on it. Even twenty-four hours would be better than nothing."

Anything was better than nothing, as far as she was concerned, but when he dragged himself reluctantly away after only a couple of hours – "I shall be in real trouble if I take as long getting back as I did coming" – she couldn't help wondering whether he considered such a short time in her company had been worth the long hours spent in travel.

The happiness she gained from his visit buoyed her up for days. She sang as she went round the ward. "It's surprising what the thought of Christmas does for some people," Sister remarked, to no one in particular.

Last Christmas Julia had been working in a ward of recent amputees, far too frightened of sudden haemorrhage and uncertain of her own capabilities to enjoy the festivities. This year she had an efficiency stripe on her sleeve and her patients were less seriously wounded: she could enjoy Christmas to the full. The prospect of meeting Geoffrey in Paris added zest to her enjoyment. Aunt Amy sent a long list of instructions for Julia's visit, enclosed a purse for Julia to pass on to Madame Vialet, the concierge, and told Julia exactly what and what not to say. Julia got the impression that Aunt Amy was afraid of Madame Vialet.

On Christmas Eve the V.A.D.s went from ward to ward, singing carols:

> *"We bring tidings of comfort and joy*
> *Comfort and joy ..."*

It was a perfect night, quiet, clear and mild. Every star was visible in the sky. Julia looked eastwards to where Geoffrey must be and prayed that this time next year he and she would be singing carols together in the church at home.

Paris was a city cold and dark. At night only glimmers of light showed in the streets. The atmosphere was sombre. Mutilated men crept along the pavement. Women wore deep mourning. And it was cold. Frost remained all day between the paper strips that protected the windows against air raids. "Twenty degrees we had last night," Madame Vialet told Julia, adding with ghoulish pleasure, "People freeze to death in the streets every night." There was no coal to be had. In the Rue de la Paix Julia saw a lump of coal set in a jeweller's window above the diamonds and precious stones on display. Madame Vialet blamed striking miners in England for the shortage. Julia suspected that a purse similar to the one she had handed over from Aunt Amy might have a miraculous effect on the supply of coal to the apartment, but she had no idea how much money was required and preferred to do without. Instead she put all the blankets she could find on her bed and during the day walked vigorously wherever she went.

Until leaving Étaples she had not known how exhausted she was, nor understood the strain of the last eighteen months. For the first two days in Paris she did nothing but sleep, and only the realisation that she was in danger of returning to Etaples knowing no more of Paris than the streets lying between Aunt Amy's apartment and the station got her up and out.

She was perfectly content with her own company after

living a communal life for so long, though she still hoped –
without expecting – that Geoffrey might join her. She did
some sightseeing but spent most of her time in the art
galleries. Frances had spent hours in London museums and
galleries copying Old Masters. Lack of opportunity to do
the same was one of her reasons for deploring Julia's refusal
to go to the Slade. Studying the Old Masters in Paris Julia
began to understand how Frances had felt and wondered for
the first time whether her decision not to go to London had
been the right one.

Returning to the apartment one evening towards the end of
her leave she saw an English subaltern coming towards her,
a piece of paper in his hand, obviously searching for an
address. She saw him far off, thought the distance must be
deceiving her, watched him draw near and knew the miracle
had happened.

"*Geoffrey!*"

"Darling!"

The relief of it, the unbelievable relief – to feel his arms
round her, his lips on hers, his hair brushing her skin. How
ridiculous that she should weep . . . They stood in the street,
smiling at each other, almost stupid with happiness.

"I didn't see – I thought you'd be in uniform," he said.

"I couldn't wear uniform, in Paris of all places. I got
Frances to send me over some clothes – though I'll be in
trouble at Étaples if they find out. Oh, Geoffrey. I don't
think I ever believed you'd come."

"I'd have gone absent without leave if need be – no, don't
look so scared. Of course I haven't. Only I was so cross at
not being able to see you at the end of that course. I've only
got forty-eight hours now, but never mind – I'm here." He
looked round. "Well? Where's this apartment? Is it all
right?"

"We've got to get you past Madame Vialet first."

Everyone, resident and visitor alike, had to pass the concierge who sat at the divided door of her loge, noting the comings and goings and examining minutely all those who passed by. Did she believe that Geoffrey and she were brother and sister, Julia wondered. She would hate to make life difficult for Aunt Amy after the war. But Madame Vialet said nothing, though they could feel her eyes following them as they crossed the courtyard and went into the building.

"I say," Geoffrey said, standing at last in the stuffy little salon of Aunt Amy's apartment. "This is jolly. Aren't you clever, finding us a place like this!"

"Not clever. Lucky. I feel sad, though. It'd mean so much to Aunt Amy to be here. It doesn't seem fair, somehow, that it's me instead."

He smiled. "Poor Aunt Amy."

"What do you want to do?" she said. "Have you eaten? I haven't tried cooking – it's enough coping with the water-heater and I can't get coal, anyway – but there's a bistro round the corner which is quite good. Shall we go there?"

"I'm not hungry. Let's stay in. I'm happy just being with you."

He looked out of place, sitting under the red flocked wallpaper of Aunt Amy's salon, his body too large for the spiky gilt furniture, his uniform coarse and dull among so much red plush. Julia would have been amused by the picture he presented had not concern begun to seep in. He sat so still, watching her, apparently not wishing even to talk . . .

They had never been entirely on their own. There had always been others nearby, liable to come in, to interrupt. Now they were quite alone for the first time . . . and she could think of nothing to say. She wondered with a sudden stab of fear how they would occupy themselves over the next two days, what they could possibly find to talk about for so long. Panic threatened. Would this visit prove to be a mistake?

"You know Frances is having an exhibition this summer?"

she said. Her voice sounded nervous, unnatural even to her ears.

"Someone did mention it. Father, I think. How do you feel about that? Do you mind?"

She was surprised. "Why should I mind? I'm pleased. It's time she had an exhibition of her own. She's always hated showing her work, you know. I'm sure she's only doing it now because of her agent. Denis is a determined sort of person. I think he insisted it was time. I am disappointed, though, for myself. She always wants to know what I think – heaven knows why, when she's so much better than I am. I feel I'm letting her down by not being there to help."

He smiled faintly. "You're too conscientious."

"I'm curious too," she admitted. "It's almost two years since I saw her work. I'd like to see what she's doing now. It's bound to have changed."

"Will she ...?" He jumped at the sound of a knock. "What's that?"

"Someone at the door. It'll be Madame Vialet."

The concierge stood on the landing, holding a pile of linen in her arms. "You will need extra sheets, mademoiselle, for monsieur votre frère." Her eyes darted to and fro as she peered over Julia's shoulder. "They are well aired, I assure you."

Geoffrey's fingers dug into Julia's arm as he stood behind her in the doorway. "Thank her," he murmured in her ear.

It had never occurred to Julia that Geoffrey might stay in the apartment with her. She swallowed. "Thank you, Madame," she said, and took the proffered linen. "You are very kind."

"Je vous en prie," the concierge said. Her smile revealed gaps in her teeth. They gave her the air of a witch. "I ..."

"Thank you," Julia said again, and shut the door.

Geoffrey waited for her to speak. "Do you mind?" he said at last.

"No ... No, of course not. I hadn't thought, that's all.

You're quite right. It would be silly, your paying for a hotel when you can stay here."

"Silly to be parted, too, when time's so short." After a moment he said, "It might be sensible not to mention it to Mother, all the same."

"I suppose so."

They made up the bed together. The spareroom was small, little more than a box-room, and very cold.

"Will you be all right?" she said. "It's very cramped. Though I suppose anything's better than the trenches."

He followed her into the bedroom and stood in the doorway she sat down at the dressing-table. Her hair was in disarray as a result of their first – their only – embrace. What must Madame Vialet have thought, seeing it? "We'd better go out soon," she said, picking up her brush. "You can't not eat. When was your last meal?"

"I don't remember. It doesn't matter. I'm not hungry."

"All the same . . ."

He watched her from the door. "It's icy in that room," he said.

"It's cold in here too."

"Not as bad."

She was silent.

"If we were together . . ." – his eyes pleaded with hers in the mirror – "we could keep each other warm. Couldn't we?"

She began to tremble.

"Please," he said.

Still she said nothing.

He came up to her and began to undo the fastenings of her clothes, very slowly, one by one. When he pulled her to her feet her skirt slid down to her knees and then on to the floor. He kissed her gently. "I love you," he said. "I've loved you for years and years." He undid the buttons of her blouse, slipped his hands inside. His fingers were cold, cold against her warm flesh. "Darling, darling Julia."

She shivered uncontrollably.

"Come to bed," he said.

They were there, wherever one looked, all over Paris. Lovers. In the metro, in gardens, in churches and museums, heads touching, arms entwined, gazing into each other's eyes. Their own mirror image. She had thought Paris grey and drab, but behind the closed doors and darkened windows of the bistros, the little cafés where no other English went, Paris was alight with love and happiness. They sat holding hands over marble-topped tables, danced to mechanical pianos jangling out American jazz, and spent the night lying in each other's arms in the candlelit plush and gilt splendour of Aunt Amy's apartment.

Julia went with him to the Gare du Nord when he returned to the front. The fear she had felt in the past was nothing to the fear which gripped her now as she stood on the platform, one anonymous figure among hundreds, and watched the train slowly carry him away through swirls of steam and smoke into the darkness beyond.

Aunt Amy's apartment that night was cold and empty indeed.

At Boulogne the Transport Sister's eyes went immediately to the efficiency stripe on Julia's sleeve. "I suppose you wouldn't consider going to Rouen?" she said.

Julia's mind went blank. She had taken it for granted that she would return to Étaples.

"They're in desperate need of a red striper in Rouen," the Sister said.

She thought of the friends she had made ... Crawford and Gordon, Sister Forrest, the ward sister whose moods she knew, whose orders she could anticipate ... She thought of Rouen, so much nearer to Paris than Étaples.

"I believe it's a lovely old town," Sister said.

She pictured the apartment in Paris, empty, waiting. Geoffrey would say yes. Wouldn't he? "All right," Julia said.

"I'll go to Rouen."

So she went back, almost to Paris itself it seemed, through a landscape made bleak by winter, past the empty sand-dunes of the coastline and the camp at Étaples that she knew so well, past the cemetery with its rows of wooden crosses and across the empty landscape of France fast disappearing behind a curtain of falling snow. The train stopped, started and stopped again. Every so often it rattled and clanked into a siding to allow a hospital train to go by, with its tiers of stretchers and white figures glimpsed through the lighted windows ...

The hospital lay outside the town at the edge of a forest. Ghostly shapes of tents and huts in front of a silent wall of frosted trees made a study in browns and whites, greys and blacks. In the half-light of a late January afternoon it looked more like an Arthur Rackham illustration than a living scene.

They said it was the coldest winter within memory. For weeks on end the temperature never rose above freezing. Liquids became solid: milk, medicines, ink in fountain pens, even mercury in thermometers froze. Bread had to be thawed before it could be cut, lemons boiled before use. Stiffened boots were agony to pull on; frozen laces excruciating to tie. No amount of glycerine rubbed in could ease the pain of cracked chilblains on hands and feets.

In those first weeks Julia regretted her hastily made decision. Geoffrey was far away to the north. Friends took time to make. The ward sister was one of the old school, worse than any she had encountered in England, who regarded V.A.D.s as hindrances rather than helps. Tasks that Julia had undertaken as a matter of course in Étaples were regarded as beyond her capabilities here. Sometimes she wondered why a red striper had ever been requested.

Returning to the ward after lunch one day she found an unknown medical officer talking to the sister.

"Nurse Purcell." Amazing how much disapproval could be put into those two words. "Major Miller would like a word with you."

"It's all right," the major said quickly. "Purely a social visit. I understand we have friends in common." He smiled. "The Cartwrights. I believe you were at school with Miranda."

She stared. "Yes, but how ...?"

"Mrs. Cartwright is my mother's sister. My aunt, in other words. She asked me to make sure you were all right."

"Oh." She did not know what to say, intimidated as she was by Sister's glare. He must have sensed as much. "Why don't we meet for tea in town some time?" he said. "We can't talk here. I'd be interested to discover what Miranda's up to these days. It's years since we met. Besides, I'm expected to report back to my aunt."

He suggested meeting in a Rouen hotel. She was apprehensive. Medical officers were superior beings in the hospital hierarchy, even more so than at Étaples; ward rounds here had the air of a royal progress. But her fears were unnecessary. He was easy to talk to, and they had, after all, the Cartwrights in common. She was surprised to notice grey hairs in a cousin of Miranda's; he explained that the generations had overlapped.

"My mother was twenty when I was born, my aunt much older when Miranda arrived," he said. "Miranda's nearer to my children in age than she is to me."

She was entertained by the new insights he gave into the Cartwright family. According to Major Miller it was his mother who had insisted that Miranda should go away to school – "She said Miranda would be coddled to death if she was kept at home." When Julia told him that she and Miranda had hoped to come to France together, he laughed. "I could have told you that wouldn't happen. Mother was amazed that she was allowed to nurse at all."

He wanted to know how Julia had settled, and because

he was on the staff of the hospital next door, rather than of hers, she could confess her disappointment. "I'm not allowed to do a thing on my own. Oh, I know it was the same when I arrived at Étaples but I really was new then. It's different now. I'm experienced. I've got an efficiency stripe. Here it's the look of the thing that matters. Everything has to be shining, all the blankets tucked in tightly. It doesn't matter if it's a leg wound underneath in agony."

"Rouen's very brass hat," he said. "Look around you when you leave here and you'll see what I mean. It's the same with the nursing staff. They're getting on a bit. You'd be amazed how many of the sisters served in South Africa. Don't worry. It's quiet now but once the fighting starts up again there won't be time to check on the niceties. You'll have plenty to do then."

He astonished her after tea by suggesting that he should book her a room upstairs for a couple of hours so that she could have a bath. "Knowing the water situation in the camp ... My sister-in-law works for the Y.M.C.A. in Boulogne and regularly takes a room at the local hotel, I understand. She says it's only the baths that keep her sane!"

"Well ..." Julia said doubtfully, "if you're sure it's all right."

"Wait here," he said. He was smiling when he returned. "There you are. There's nothing to pay. Will you be able to get back to the camp on your own? It's probably sensible if we don't go together." He brushed aside her thanks. "Let me know if there's ever anything I can do."

She was both amused and touched by his thoughtfulness. Baths were no longer possible at the camp, frost having disrupted the hospital water supply weeks before. Half a bucket of water had to suffice each ward until the watercarts arrived mid-morning. Steam rose up as she turned on the tap. Such unexpected pleasure, to be able to soak in as much water as one wanted, really hot water ... She lay in the bath, watching her flesh colour under the water, and remem-

[113]

bered Geoffrey and Paris. The fear that had gripped her for days afterwards had disappeared, been forgotten. Now she only recognised the inevitability of their coming together.

At their next meeting Major Miller regaled her with stories of his three daughters, talked of his wife and brought out photographs for Julia to see. His gaze returned to the prints as they lay face uppermost on the table during tea. She was touched by the discovery that even majors could be homesick.

Easter brought renewed fighting in the north. Leave was cancelled; time off no longer existed. Life was nothing more than working and sleeping. But Major Miller had been correct. Divisions between V.A.D.s and Q.A.s no longer existed in the aftermath of a push, even in Rouen.

News came that Gabriel had been wounded at Arras and was now back in Huish Priory, Sir James having arranged for him to be nursed at the Rectory. Julia smiled ruefully when she read Mr. Mackenzie's letter. Had Geoffrey not said that Gabriel always had the luck? There was little else for her to smile about. Though Geoffrey said little in his letters she could tell that he had had a bad time at Arras. She consoled herself with the knowledge that his battalion was resting while it waited – hopefully for some time – for new men to replace those lost.

His next letter mentioned the possibility of wangling some leave. He couldn't give her much warning, he said, but if she were ready could they meet . . . go away together . . . walk?

She detected desperation and was in despair herself. How could he expect her to get leave so soon after Paris? Rereading his letter she realised that he was past thinking of such detail. If they were to go away together it was she who would have to arrange it.

She came off duty one afternoon to find Major Miller waiting to invite her out for a walk. She was tired, worried about

Geoffrey and in no mood for exercise, but did not like to refuse.

They walked in silence along the grass by the side of the road until the hospitals had been left behind. She sensed suppressed emotion. At last he stopped, turned to her and said, "There's something I wanted to tell you."

She thought it must concern the Cartwrights and was apprehensive. "What is it?"

The words burst out. "I've got a son!"

"*A son?*"

"A son."

She scarcely knew what to say. She had thought him long past the age of having children. Besides he had three already. "You never said anything . . ."

"I know, I know. I preferred not to talk about it. I was sure it would be another girl, to tell you the truth. You can imagine how I felt when the telegram came. I wanted to tell you earlier but you weren't around, and then, well, you know what it's been like since the last push."

"Well. Congratulations." Congratulations seemed inadequate somehow. "When did it happen?"

"The first of the month. He's four weeks old already."

She laughed at the pride in his voice. His smile was rueful. "One only has the chance to celebrate the arrival of an heir once in a lifetime, Miss Purcell. I insist we drink his health together."

The infant's health was drunk in raspberry wine accompanied by strange flat cakes at a country inn, whose Madame, on hearing the news, lined up her own offspring for inspection – "You see, Monsieur, *four* sons!"

"I know what you must be thinking," Major Miller said, when Madame had shooed her offspring away and departed herself. "How ridiculous – at my age, with three daughters already at school. And yes, of course, we'd called a halt years ago. If it hadn't been for . . . My wife came over last year, you know, when I had leave. We spent a week at

Honfleur together. I suppose the effect of the war, and not having seen each other for so long ... and it's a very romantic place, Honfleur. We couldn't bring ourselves to ... so ... the upshot is ... I have a son." He pulled a photograph from his wallet and laid it on the table. "There."

The shock of black hair emerging from the folds of the shawl was scarcely recognisable as a child. Julia looked down at the blurred image and felt a strange feeling of regret. "He's ..." – she searched for words – "beautiful."

Even parental pride could not accept that. "I'm afraid I'm being a bore," he said apologetically. "My colleagues accuse me of going on. No doubt I'll get used to the idea of a son, given time, but at the moment ... I promise I won't mention him again." Carefully he replaced the photograph in his wallet. "Let's talk about you. How are you? You look tired."

"I'm not tired, just ..." She realised that she had not thought of Major Miller when worrying about Geoffrey. Could she ask his advice? There was no one else she could turn to, and he had proved sympathetic before. She swallowed. She would have to ask him, for Geoffrey's sake. "I've got a bit of a problem, that's all."

"Can I help?"

"I don't know. I don't see how, really." She gripped her hands under the table. "It's to do with a friend of mine. The son of my guardian, in fact. He's had a bad time at Arras and now he's hoping to wangle some leave. He wants me to go away with him. On leave, I mean. He ... we ... sort of ... grew up together."

"Well?"

"I don't know how to arrange it. Rouen's so far for him to come. If he does get leave it'll be at the last minute. It might take all his time getting here ... and then he's got to get back." If only I'd stayed at Étaples, she thought wretchedly, it would have been so much easier. "I'm not due for leave, either," she added, "though they may not know that here."

Major Miller sat back in his chair. She met his gaze without flinching. "Where is he now, your friend?" he said.

"Near Albert."

He considered for a moment, then smiled. "Simple. He can get a lift on a hospital train from Albert itself. There's no shortage of space from that area at the moment. It's the trains from the north that are overloaded. Going back, of course, they're empty. Give me his name and battalion. I'll phone the Medical Officer up the line, and have a word. Then all your friend has to do is get in touch with him when he knows the date of his leave."

She could not believe that a problem that had worried her for so long could be so easily solved. It seemed ungrateful to mention the second. "There's still my leave. I don't know what to do about that. I daren't mention it to Sister."

"No. That's likely to prove more awkward. Not impossible, though, I'm sure. Cheer up, Miss Purcell. Leave it with me; I'll sort something out."

His confidence was infectious; she felt hopeful for the first time. When he said on parting, "Don't worry. Everything'll work out all right," she believed him.

He left her, turned round and came back. "Miss Purcell. Don't think . . . I'd hate you to think I didn't care for my daughters. I love them dearly. But a son – you must realise that a son is something quite different."

Later that night she remembered his words and wondered for the first time whether her father too had longed for a son.

Chapter Eight

'*Noon tomorrow*,' said Major Miller's note. '*Suggest you meet in the cathedral by the west door.*'

Julia thanked the orderly who had brought it, took a deep breath and went to the ward sister.

"There's not much I can say, is there?" said the Sister "If Major Miller says you've got to go, who am I to say no? I don't know what they're thinking of in England, sending out nurses with weak chests . . . Not that I'd have said there was anything wrong with yours, had I been asked."

The dressings next morning took twice as long as usual: Julia was sure Sister was being deliberately slow out of spite. When at last she was given leave to go she decided to take a tram as being quicker than walking, but soon regretted it. She had to wait for what seemed like hours and when one came it dawdled intolerably. She began to panic. Two hours late already – suppose Geoffrey had given her up and gone away. In desperation she got out at the bridge over the river and ran up towards the city centre, searching for him among the hundreds of Allied soldiers milling through the narrow streets surrounding the cathedral. She dodged a column of bedraggled German prisoners being roughly marched across the square, slipped into the cathedral through the west door and stood still, temporarily blinded by the darkness after the sunlight outside.

"Hello," said Geoffrey's voice.

Her heart jumped. She turned round. Relief overwhelmed her. "You're all right."

"Of course I'm all right." He sounded surprised. "Though I was beginning to get into a bit of a state, I admit.

I was afraid you'd had second thoughts about the whole thing."

She shook her head. "Never."

"No," he said. "Well, thank goodness for that."

They stood smiling at each other in the gloom. She felt herself blushing at the memory of their last time together and wondered whether he was remembering it too.

"Well," he said again. "Do you want to see round now you're here? I've been improving my education while I waited. Father will be pleased about that. Did you know they've got Richard the Lionheart up at the other end? It seems funny to me, an English king being buried in France, but it's him all right. Come and see."

She glanced sideways at him as they walked down the aisle, looking for signs of nerves. There were none. What ever effect the fighting had had he was still the Geoffrey she knew.

The stone effigy of the king of England lay stretched out behind the high altar, its feet resting not on the heraldic lion that might have been expected but the carved figure of a small dog. She could not take her eyes off that dog. It seemed so domestic a detail in the cathedral setting.

"It must be nice to be known as the Lionheart," Geoffrey said.

She felt her heart jump. "Not everyone can be like that."

"I know. All the same." After a moment he said, "It's waiting that's worst. Being frightened of being frightened. And of showing it – that's worst of all."

"I know." She had never managed to subdue her own fear when she knew convoys were due, fear not so much of what might confront her but of her own incompetence, of letting everyone else down; worst of all, fear that Sister might suspect how she felt.

"It doesn't matter once we get going," Geoffrey said. "There isn't time to be frightened. It's even exhilarating, in an odd sort of way."

Exhilarating wasn't the word she would have chosen but she knew what he meant. Her panic went too, the moment there was work to do. She had no doubts about her ability when she was rushed off her feet.

They walked slowly back towards the west door, Geoffrey translating the Latin inscriptions as they went. "What a good combination we make, you with your French, me and my Latin. Though I can't help thinking that Latin's precious little use outside a cathedral. It's what I've always said. You girls had a much more sensible education than any of us. Even poor old Antony. Though I suppose the thought of all his favourite Greeks and Trojans must have made his journey more fun."

For a while they sat in a dark corner at the back, while worshippers and sightseers murmured and moved around them and boys' voices sang an anthem near the altar.

"I don't know anything about music," Geoffrey said. "That's something else ... There's so much to learn still, isn't there, and do and see ..."

He suggested staying in Rouen for the night. "We'll go and look for somewhere now. Somewhere quiet, where no one goes. It'll be perfectly safe. I can't wait much longer to be alone with you."

She was reluctant. It was too risky. She thought they should get away from the city as soon as possible, for Major Miller's sake as much as for her own. In the end, and only because of Major Miller, Geoffrey agreed.

"It was lucky you knew him," he said. "Getting here couldn't have been easier. Going back shouldn't be difficult either. I telephone the Transport Officer and he'll tell me what time I have to be at the station."

He had not thought what they might do during his leave; it was enough to be with her. "I'll go wherever you want."

"All right then. We'll walk to the coast. We'll go to Honfleur. Major Miller didn't think we'd have any difficulty finding places to stay. He's lent me some maps."

On the crowded deck of the ferry, surrounded by black-clad women returning from market, with Geoffrey's the only uniform in sight, Julia let him hold her close. They kissed. His skin was rough against hers. He rubbed his chin ruefully. "It's been a long day."

The sun warmed her face. A breeze touched her cheeks. Far down the river white cliffs hung above the plain and beckoned them on. Eight days. A week, more than a week, together. She could scarcely believe it.

"I've brought you a present," Geoffrey said. "I wanted to give it to you somewhere romantic but this will have to do." He put his hand in his pocket. "Shut your eyes. Are they properly shut? Hold out your hand then."

Something light, barely felt, touched her skin.

"You can open them now."

She looked down. A gold ring lay on her palm.

"I was afraid country people might not be as easy-going as your concierge," he said. "And anyway, we will, won't we, when all this is over? Get married, I mean." He lifted her hand and pushed the ring gently over the knuckle of her third finger, twisting it experimentally as he did so. "It's not too big, is it? I didn't realise fingers came in sizes ... I had to guess."

She tried to smile. "It's wonderful." Her voice shook. Such fragile happiness, mingled with ... what? The longing for benediction on their union, no matter from whom – priest or padre, or country curé.

They spent their first night at a country inn not far from the Seine, in a room filled with the scent of the lilac tree growing outside their window. They shared the long narrow table in the downstairs room with their fellow travellers for the evening meal but spoke little, Geoffrey's French insufficient to contribute much to the conversation and Julia too pre-occupied. She was very conscious of the shining newness of the ring on her finger, and of Geoffrey's gaze. His dark eyes watched her every move, his mouth curving up in a smile of pure happiness. Their knees touched under the table. His hands shook. She was trembling herself, though whether from nervousness, remembering the diffidence and awkwardness of inexperience in Paris, or whether from anticipation she could not tell.

As soon as the meal ended, the first to leave and not caring what other diners thought, they went upstairs. Strangely it was laughter that overcame them then, laughter from sheer relief of being alone together, laughter at the absurdity of their haste to rid themselves of their clothes and Geoffrey's impatience as he tugged at his puttees, which twisted and tangled as if having life of their own, and finally laughter of triumph and thankfulness as they fell into bed in each other's arms at last.

But later that night he thrashed about and woke her with his shouting. In the morning he remembered nothing – "You're making it up. I slept like a top. I can't remember when I slept better" – and became so offended that she had to agree with him that it was she who had been dreaming.

He had said nothing about the reasons for his leave. She gathered it was unofficial, assumed that the battalion's rough handling at Arras had something to do with it and wondered aloud whether time in a quiet sector of the line was likely. Geoffrey was quick to put down such hopes.

"You don't understand the way things work in the Army," he said. "The better you do, the more likely you are to be thrown back in." He saw her disbelief. "It's true. Talk to Gabriel if you don't believe me. The battalion that let his down at Loos has never been in a major attack since, and when it has been sent up the line it's always been put opposite somebody like the Saxons. Whereas you know what's happened to Gabriel's battalion since then."

"But they can't *do* that," she protested. "It's not fair."

He gave her an affectionate smile. "You're very naïve, my love."

But the war was far away and almost forgotten in the peaceful countryside through which they walked. Only the absence of men reminded them of the fighting. A small boy bringing in the cow to be milked, a grandfather driving a high-wheeled cart along the road, an occasional old man smoking a pipe and sunning himself outside one of the black-beamed farmhouses – these were the only males they saw. It was women and children who worked in the fields, and solitary wives who ran the farms, welcoming passing strangers as if members of the family and feeding them with cream-thickened soups, chicken stews and omelettes, salads and strange cheeses.

During the day they walked slowly westwards, through undulating farmland of lush meadows and cider orchards of pink and white blossomed trees, and at night slept in small-windowed bedrooms, swallowed up in soft feather mattresses, to be woken in the half-light of dawn by the local cock crowing under their window.

They came into Honfleur one morning while the sun was still shining on the tall, thin, slate-covered houses that rose above the quay and were reflected in the water below it. A shopkeeper directed them to a fisherman's widow living on one of the steep, narrow streets that climbed the hill away from the harbour who willingly took them in, bursting into tears when Julia told her they were newly married. "Les pauvres, les pauvres."

They spent their first day exploring the town and the hillside above it. Paintings by Boudin in the museum by the quay reminded Julia of Frances. "Before the war she used to talk of coming to the Seine estuary to paint," she said. "Someone – Steer, I think it was – said the light was wonderful here for painters."

"Why don't we stay then for the rest of my leave and let you paint?" Geoffrey said. "We don't have to walk back. There's always the train."

"But you said you wanted to walk."

"We have walked. We walked all the way here. I enjoyed it, of course I did, but it's not like, well, the Quantocks, is it? It's too big here. The scenery's too much the same. I like this place; I'd rather stay. I shall buy you some watercolours and then you can paint lots of pictures so that when we're old and grey we can look at them and remember what it was like to be young."

She tried to smile. "I couldn't possibly leave you alone while I'm painting. What would you do?"

"Me? Oh, I'm happy just wandering around, practising my French and watching what's going on."

In the end she believed him. He seemed content, and she thought that doing nothing was probably as good a way as any to recover from the strain of the April fighting. So in the mornings she painted, quick watercolour sketches of the town and its quays, the dark narrow alleyways, the market place and the wooden church beside it. She painted the fishing boats landing their catch, the fishermen spreading their nets out to dry. She painted Geoffrey trying out his French on the fisherwomen and the black-smocked children, and reliving old battles in sign language with Belgian soldiers from a nearby training camp. He watched over Julia as she worked, brought her coffee and brioches, and sometimes sat with her while she painted.

"Come and translate something for me when you've finished," he said. "It's on the wall over there. Something to do with Canada."

She had never heard of Samuel de Champlain, whom the plaque commemorated. "It says he set sail from here in 1608 to explore Canada," she read. "He founded the town of Quebec. 1608 – think of that. Over three hundred years ago." She looked round and tried to imagine what it must have felt like then, leaving a town probably not much different from Honfleur now and sailing off into the unknown. She had been frightened just crossing the Channel.

In the afternoons they left Honfleur, sometimes going up

to the orchards above the town and lying in each other's arms under the apple blossom, sometimes walking further afield. One afternoon they set off for Trouville, but were diverted by a village perfectly arranged for a painter, with manor house, thatched cottages and an ivy-clad church reflected in the still waters of a lake.

Geoffrey lay on the grass beside her. "Do you mind my watching you work?"

"I expect I'd hate it if you were anybody else, but as you're not, no, I don't."

"You ought to have gone to the Slade, you know," he said, after a while. "I do feel very badly about that."

"I don't see why."

"Because it's my fault you didn't. As much as anyone's anyway. Frances asked me to persuade you to go. Didn't she ever tell you? She thought you might listen to me when you wouldn't to her. I was flattered she should think that, I must admit."

"I don't remember your trying."

"Because I didn't. I told Frances it was up to you. I regret it now."

She was curious. "Why didn't you try?"

"Because I understood about you and Frances, I suppose."

"What was there to understand?"

"Your not wanting to be compared to Frances at the Slade."

She could not believe her ears. "You thought that? What an extraordinary – what a *ridiculous* – what made you think such a thing?"

"I'm sorry," he said. "It seemed obvious at the time ... I admired you, you know, for standing up to her and refusing to go. I used to wish I had the courage to do the same with my parents over Cambridge."

It upset her to think that he could so misunderstand her relationship with Frances. "I don't know how you could have possibly had such a notion."

"All right," he said. "You tell me then. Why didn't you go?"

She hesitated. "I wasn't good enough."

"Don't be silly. The Slade doesn't offer places to people unless they're good enough."

"Well, then ... I wanted to study in Paris. That was it. And I'd have gone, too, if it hadn't been for the war."

There was triumph in his smile, as if she had unwittingly confirmed his supposition. "Yes, of course." He rolled over in the grass and buried his head in his arms. His voice was muffled. "All the same, I do wish you wouldn't compare yourself unfavourably to Frances all the time."

A sailors' chapel stood at the top of the hill between town and sea. Model ships hung from its ceiling. Paintings of three-masted vessels battling against stormy seas decorated the walls, together with tablets recording thanks for life preserved and answered prayers.

They wandered round the dark interior in silence. A faint aroma of hot wax and stale incense hung in the air.

"There's another memorial to Champlain here," Geoffrey said. "Look." He shivered. "It's too dark. Spooky somehow. I'm going. I don't like all this superstition."

Julia stopped on the way out. The statue of the Madonna looked down on her with a gaze kindly but remote, the arms of the child she held raised as if in blessing. Pinpoints of light from the flickering candles cast shadows upwards, hiding the expression in the statue's eyes. Thoughts jostled in Julia's mind, prayers and hopes intermingled. Superstitious it might be, but at that moment she was tempted to light a candle herself.

She joined Geoffrey outside. Across the mouth of the Seine Le Havre was little more than a shadow in the heat haze, the church tower on the horizon no darker than a pencil mark against the sky.

"Funny the way Canada keeps cropping up," Geoffrey said after a while. "In Honfleur itself, and now up here. Have you ever thought about Canada?"

"No. Why? Should I have done?"

"I suppose not. It's just that ... I've been thinking about the place a lot lately. And the future – our future, yours and mine. We used to meet up with the Canadians in Béthune last winter. They were grand fellows. They used to talk about life back home, and ever since then I've wondered ..."

She waited. "Wondered what?"

He turned to her. "About living in Canada. Would you ... I mean, I wouldn't go without you ... Could you consider it, do you think?"

For a moment her mind went blank. "You mean, after the war?"

"Yes."

"For ever?"

"Yes," he said, and then, "I'm sorry. I shouldn't have sprung it on you like that. Think about it though. I couldn't go back to Cambridge when all this is over, you must see that. I shall be so old, for one thing. And you were quite right, what you said once, about my being a schoolmaster. I'd hate it, and I don't suppose I'd be any good at it. My brain's gone to pot already. Whereas Canada ... it sounds a splendid life. Really it does. Open air. Plenty of opportunities, provided you're not afraid of hard work, which I'm not."

She knew he was right. But Canada, so far away ...

"Don't say anything now," he said. "If you don't want to go, all right then, we won't. It's just that ... we make a good team, you and I. You probably haven't thought about it like that, but it's true. You build a chap up so. And I, well, I think I'm good for you too. At least I've got you drawing again – Frances would thank me for that. You could become the first well-known artist from Canada. I've never heard of a Canadian artist, have you?" He smiled faintly. "I'm talking too much. You wouldn't want to leave Hillcrest and the others. That's it, isn't it?"

She shook her head. "I don't think so. It's just ... so unexpected. I feel ..." What? Dismay, certainly, and apprehension. Yet if it came to choosing between Geoffrey and her sisters, she knew who would win.

"There's no hurry," Geoffrey said. "The war won't finish tomorrow, unfortunately. Let's not talk about it any more. Get used to the idea before you make up your mind."

He must have continued to think about it himself, however, for he brought the subject up again when they were taking their evening walk round the harbour.

"It's a funny thing," he said, sounding surprised. "I've just realised that I'd miss Hillcrest quite as much as I'd miss home. If not more."

Water lapped against the harbour wall. The air was damp, cool in the dusk. They were the only people on the quay. Fenders creaked between the boats tied up, sheets rattled quietly against masts. Julia tried to banish the picture of her sisters sitting without her on the Hillcrest verandah.

"I'd even miss Frances," Geoffrey said.

They went up to the chapel again on their last day and stood in the shade of the elms, watching the traffic in the estuary – a ship that could be a hospital ship heading for England, an official looking packet boat coming in towards Honfleur itself, fishing boats bobbing on the tide – and then left the coast and took refuge in one of the apple orchards on the long way back into the town.

"Do you remember that walk over the Quantocks?" Geoffrey said. "How innocent we were then."

She felt a pang at the regret in his voice. "Do you mind, our not being innocent any longer?"

"Of course not. I often think of that walk. It was the first time I realised you and I might finish up together."

"We must go back after the war, make a pilgrimage."

"It won't be the same without Antony. Do you remember how he went on about the Ancient Mariner?"

"And the stately pleasure dome. I've always liked that one."

"I read that a lot now. Father sent me a collected Coleridge last Christmas."

She was surprised. "I didn't think you liked poetry."

"Oh, well. You know what it was like at home with the other two around. I kept quiet. I don't know that I was interested, anyway. But then, last autumn, I came across one of the chap's in 'C' company learning a sonnet. He said he made a point of learning something by heart every day, even when he was in the front line – *particularly* when he was in the front line. It kept him sane, he said. It seemed a good idea to me. That's when I asked Father for the Coleridge. He didn't make a fuss about it, this chap; I don't suppose anyone else knew. I only found out myself because I happened to come along at the time I did. He said it was important to choose something long enough to be a challenge, but not so long it couldn't be done. Like a sonnet. He was learning Shakespeare's sonnets, one by one." After a moment he said, "A sniper got him in the end. I've often wondered whether he'd managed to learn the lot."

She shivered. "So ... you do the same? Every day?"

"Not every day." He smiled at her. "Not when I have better things to do."

"Say something to me now," she said. "Something you've learnt."

He sat looking down at her as she lay beside him in the grass, his body silhouetted against the sun. After a moment he said,

"'All thoughts, all passions, all delights,
    Whatever stirs this mortal frame,
    All are but ministers of Love,
    And feed his sacred flame.'"

[129]

She swallowed. "Is that ... did Coleridge write that?"

"*Love*, he called it. Just that. *Love*."

All that night they lay awake in each other's arms. When at last he drifted into an exhausted sleep she remained open-eyed, watching the room slowly lighten, listening to the town come to life beyond the window, trying to imprint every detail on her memory – the dampness of his skin against hers, the weight of his arm across her hip, the faint warmth of his breath on her face – knowing that the memory of such moments as this would be all she had to sustain her in the days and weeks to come.

He muttered and flung himself away, leaving her skin cold where his had touched. She waited until his breathing became regular once more before slipping cautiously from the bed.

The market stalls were already in position outside St. Catherine's. Inside the church black-shawled women told their rosaries, lips silently moving, heads bowed, eyes shut. She stood looking up at the statue of the Virgin, before taking a candle from the open box and lighting it from one already lit. The flame warmed her face. She pushed the candle down onto a spike of the wrought iron stand. She wanted to pray but words would not come. She thought of the hundreds of wards of wounded men, the hospital tents and huts. She thought of the thousands of crosses scattered over the French landscape. Why should God listen to her prayers when he had failed to hear the prayers of so many others? She let her mind go blank and in the end gained a frail kind of peace.

When she turned to leave she saw Geoffrey leaning against a wooden pillar by the door. He came forward and took her arm. "All right?"

"What are you doing here?"

"I followed you."

"I thought you were asleep."

"I think I heard the door close."

She tried to smile at the sight of his unbuttoned jacket and open-necked shirt.

"It's a good thing the army isn't around or you'd be court-martialled for looking like that."

He smiled back. "Yes, well . . . I was in a hurry. I was afraid I might lose you."

They packed in silence. "What will you do with those?" he said, as she gathered up her paintings and drawings. "You won't throw them away, will you?"

"Of course not. You only throw things away if they're no good."

"You'd better be careful," he warned. "Drawings of half-naked men, lying about in bed . . . your matron'll have you shipped back to Blighty at once if she sees them."

"I'll make sure she doesn't," Julia said.

They left the train before Rouen, reluctant to spend their last hours in the company of others. Desperate to prolong their time together Julia suggested searching out caves in the area that she had once heard a padre mention.

"I think I shall have to go home for my next leave," Geoffrey said, as they walked slowly through the beech forest towards the river east of the city. "Gabriel's been back twice already – three, if you count being wounded this summer. They'll begin to think it a bit odd if I don't. I suppose you couldn't break your contract and come too? We could go to London – I'd much rather paint the town red with you than with Patterson. It's all right," he said, seeing her expression. "I don't mean it. I know you can't. I wish you could, that's all."

She felt a pang at the thought of his visiting Hillcrest without her. Would he mention this leave at the Rectory, she wondered. Would she herself say anything in letters home? She did not know.

The caves were grander than she had imagined, like high-ceilinged rooms cut out of the cliff face, the black-stained chimney through the roof of one showing signs of former habitation. Geoffrey clambered over the fallen piles of lime-stone like a delighted small boy, and tried to haul himself up the cliff face. "I've always wanted to have a go at mountaineering. Perhaps we'll get a chance to go over to the Rockies."

He came back to her at last, brushing crumbs of stone off hands and uniform. "It's a pity I've got to get back, or we could have spent the night here. That would have been fun – even better than the barn at St. Audries!"

They emerged from the trees into a clearing high above the Seine and looked out over the river towards the plain that stretched to the horizon, bathed now in the soft light of evening. Below them, in the shadow of the cliffs, a tug was slowly towing a chain of hospital barges round the loop of the river.

"Reminds me of Coleridge," Geoffrey said. "'Five miles meandering with a mazy motion' – I always liked that bit." His voice was scarcely louder than the muffled sound they both knew must be distant artillery:

"'And mid this tumult Kubla heard from far
        Ancestral voices prophesying war.'"

Birds twittered in the trees behind them. A dog barked a long way off. He said, "There's something I have to tell you."

She felt suddenly cold, as if the sun had disappeared behind a cloud.

"I didn't intend to tell you now. I was going to write when I got back, but it seems cowardly doing that, some-how."

She could see the walking wounded moving about on the decks of the barges below, hear faint sounds of laughter floating up from the water. By tomorrow those men would be aboard a hospital ship in Rouen, in less than a week back in England. Fortunate, fortunate few.

He said, "We've been ordered up the Salient. Soon. Within a couple of days of my getting back."

Her first reaction was to hide him here, in one of the limestone caves where people had sheltered in the past. A hint of amusement showed beneath his concern for her. "Damned cold in winter," he said.

"Well, then ... We'll run away. Go south ... anywhere ..."

He held her in his arms. "Come on, love. It's not a death sentence. You should be grateful – it was the only reason I got leave in the first place."

Realisation came like a physical blow. "You knew," she said. "You knew all along." She could not bear it. To have kept the knowledge to himself for the past week, when she had thought they were so happy, so carefree ... She wanted to weep. "You should have told me. Why didn't you tell me?"

"It would have ruined everything. I could push it to the back of my mind, but you wouldn't have been able to forget for a moment. You know you wouldn't. Whereas now ... It's been all right, hasn't it, this week? It's been as good for you as it's been for me?"

She had always believed herself to be the stronger of the two. She knew now that that was no longer so.

Chapter Nine

Sister welcomed Julia's return to the ward with surprising affability. "At least I know I can rely on you," she said, and later admitted that Major Miller might have been right to prescribe rest. "You've been a different person since you came back."

Julia felt quite different from the Julia of ten days ago. The happiness that had enveloped her during her time away buoyed her up now. Her fears were banished temporarily. Both Geoffrey and Gabriel were safe for the time being. She could hope for a miracle, pray that peace might be agreed before either returned to the front. In her present state of euphoria miracles did not seem impossible.

Geoffrey wrote at length about Canada. While realising that Julia would be able to use her French in Montreal he himself favoured settling in Ontario. He was sure neither of them would like the prairies, and the West Coast seemed remote, though Patterson, who had an aunt in Vancouver, said British Columbia was not very different from England. Patterson had been enthusiastic about Geoffrey's plans. What would Julia think if Patterson came with them, Geoffrey wondered? The two of them had been together for over two years, they worked well together and understood each other. Though they had no idea yet what they might do in Canada a partnership seemed sensible, Geoffrey thought, provided of course that Julia agreed ...

Julia thought it sensible, too. She had liked Patterson, and was certain that he and Geoffrey would do well together. A partnership must surely be a more sensible and safer way to start in a strange country than on one's own.

Amazing how quickly life could change. For months, years, there had seemed to be nothing ahead but the fighting. Now, suddenly, and despite the war showing no sign of coming to an end, light appeared on the horizon. There was a future after all. Plans were worth making. Julia searched out Canadians among the patients, nurses and orderlies, talked to them and asked questions, determined to find out all she could about the country. When she discovered that a V.A.D.'s service in France would be counted as part training towards a hospital certificate after the war, she put her name down on the list of those interested. Nursing must be a more certain way of earning money in Canada than painting. Painting would have to wait until they were established, whatever Geoffrey said.

The blossom dropped from the trees in the cider orchards beyond the fence. Fruit began to swell on the branches. The summer days became hot and heavy. The canvas walls of the hospital marquees were rolled up to increase the circulation of air in the wards, making the tents look from a distance like pavilions surrounding a medieval tournament.

In the long, light summer evenings nurses lay on the grass outside their huts, waiting for darkness to bring cooler temperatures before going to bed. One sister had brought out a collection of classical records from England. Mozart piano concertos and Beethoven sonatas made a refreshing change from the sentimental songs and ragtime played day after day in the wards. Listening in the twilight, Julia was taken back to those early days at the Rectory, sewing with Mrs. Mackenzie while Lucy played, waiting, as she was waiting now, for Geoffrey to return.

She missed him desperately; missed his quiet sense of humour and his understanding. She missed his encouragement. More than anything else she longed for his physical presence – his touch, the way he looked at her, the sight of his smile. His letters, though irregular – several arriving together and then none for a week or more – helped her, conjuring up as they did both love and passion. Hers to him were restrained by necessity. Nurses' letters were censored by their matron; Julia knew she would be on the next boat home, contract terminated, should Matron suspect what had happened during that week in Honfleur. Letters sent in the regulation green envelopes provided by the army went uncensored but the supply of such envelopes was intermittent; there were none available now. So Julia had to be guarded in what she wrote, trusting Geoffrey would realise that any constraint in her letters was due to circumstance rather than inclination.

New orders came through. Within days the older, more experienced sisters had departed for casualty clearing stations up the line. Fighting resumed round Ypres. And it began to rain.

Geoffrey wrote telling Julia not to worry if she received no letter for a while. Useless words, when she knew only too well what they foretold.

The wait seemed interminable.

His letter, when it came, fell out of the envelope like confetti onto the floor. She gathered up the scraps of paper, with difficulty sorted them into order and struggled to decipher the faint pencil scrawl, reading his incoherent ramblings with increasing dismay.

The attack should never have been ordered, he said. It had been suicide – everyone knew from the start that the pillboxes were impregnable. It was not his description of the fighting that disturbed her, but of its aftermath, when wounded men marooned out in No Man's Land had been left to drown slowly through the night in the rising water of flooded shell holes. Running like an undercurrent through it was a sense of guilt at his own survival, as well as despair at the impotence of those who had reached safety to rescue those who had not.

She did not know how to comfort him. Letters were hopelessly inadequate. Days went by. She was frantic at her inability to help. Then came a field card. She stared down at the sentence he had ticked. 'I am quite well.' What did he mean? Why a field card rather than a letter? Was he about to go into action again ... or had he just come out? Another card followed a week later. This time he had ticked the line that thanked her for her letter. Bewilderment mingled with fear. She knew what he thought of field cards – a form of communication for the idle or the uncaring. How could he send her such things?

The Purcells told her that Geoffrey was expected home any day. Julia was hurt that she heard the news from her sisters and not from Geoffrey himself. She learnt of plans for his leave in letters from Hillcrest: Gwen was looking out the best elderberry wine (she had underlined the word elderberry), Hillcrest peaches had been bartered for dried fruit so that Annie could bake Geoffrey a fruitcake, Mrs. Mackenzie was drawing up lists of girls to entertain him during his stay. 'Girls like Jane Lynch,' Frances wrote. 'You can imagine how delighted Geoffrey will be with *that*.'

Strangely, the Purcells never mentioned Geoffrey after his arrival at the Rectory. Julia had a letter from him at last, however – a scrappy, disjointed letter, it was true, but better than a field card. England was horrible, he said. His mother was driving him mad. The only favourable comment concerned Sarah, whom he described as 'a grand kid.' Nothing else. Had he mentioned Canada to his parents, Julia wondered, or told them how he felt about her? He did not say. She could not tell. She did not even know whether he loved her still. It was November, now; the last time he had written of love was before the August fighting.

For what seemed like weeks she had pushed the thought away. She could no longer do so. It was recurring ever more frequently, the thought, suspicion, fear, growing stronger and stronger ... Had Geoffrey's feelings towards her changed since their time in Honfleur? She remembered village gossip, whispers overheard in the past. Going too far, that was what people called it. Going too far was the certain way to lose a man's respect. But not Geoffrey's. Surely not Geoffrey's.

Green envelopes were reported to be available once more in Matron's office. Now she could write without fear of censoring eyes. She could tell him how much she still loved him and was looking forward to their future together in Canada. More important, she could seek reassurance, for very slowly, and against her will, she was beginning to believe that Geoffrey no longer cared.

It was often difficult in France to tell how the war was going. Victories reported from England often seemed more like disasters to those coping with casualties in the base hospitals. But when Sarah wrote that church bells had been rung throughout England to celebrate the victory at Cambrai, it did sound as if the end of the war might be in sight. Church bells had been silenced by law for years; to ring them now must surely be a good omen. Julia, exhausted by long hours of work, hoping daily for a reply from Geoffrey to her letter but dreading what it might say, tried to sound enthusiastic when replying to Sarah, but could think only of Bill Roberts, wounded at Sanctuary Wood, who would never ring a church bell again.

Fisher came into the common room waving a bundle of letters. She dealt them out, one by one, like a pack of cards, calling out the names as she did so. Not for the first time Julia regretted being so far down the alphabet. "Owen. Packer. Purcell. Lucky you, Purcell. You've got four."

Julia's hand shook as she took them. Would there be one from Geoffrey, and if so what would he say? That he cared for her no longer? It was impossible, surely? Yet what other reason could there be for not writing to her? She started to go through. A letter from Mr. Mackenzie. One from

[138]

Frances. A thick one from Miranda. And at the bottom a green envelope. She felt her heart thud as she pulled it out and recognised her own writing – her letter to Geoffrey, pleading for an explanation. Unopened, unread, with one word pencilled in an unknown hand across the envelope.

"Are you all right, Purcell?" someone said. "You look awful."

She shook her head, got up and went out of the room, out of the hut, out of the camp, into the forest. Winter mist hung between the trees. Nothing moved. Not a bird sang. The single word reverberated in her head like a tolling bell. Killed, killed, *killed*.

She had nothing to distract her thoughts in the days that followed. She had left the teasing camaraderie of the lightly wounded weeks before. The head wounds in her present ward were barely conscious of the world about them, past discerning the numb misery of their V.A.D. The major she was specialling, failing fast, no longer recognised her voice. His wife had returned to England long ago. "Preparing herself for widowhood," Sister said caustically. "I've seen her type before."

No mention of Geoffrey was made in letters from Huish Priory. Presumably they had not yet heard. It might be weeks before details came through. She needed to know the details now.

The Red Cross probationer gestured to her from the ward entrance. "I can't stop. Was it you looking for a Somerset? We've got one from the Fourteenth in my ward. He was at Bourlon Wood. Was that the place?"

Julia shook her head. "I don't know where it happened."

"Well, you can come and talk to him if you want, but it'll have to be when Sister's out. She usually goes off to lunch about one-thirty."

Julia spent a sleepless night. Should she see this man? Why not wait until the news was official? The Mackenzies would tell her all they knew. Geoffrey was dead. Wasn't that all that mattered?

"You'd better be quick," the probationer greeted her next day. "Sister went to lunch early. Wouldn't she? Come with me."

The ward smelt of stale vegetables. A gramophone ground out a jerky, ragtime tune. Men were playing Slippery Jack in a nearby corner. Those confined to bed watched Julia walk down the ward with the probationer.

"His name's Burrows. He's not bad. Shellshock, more than anything. Sister thinks he's malingering."

Burrows avoided Julia's eyes. His fingers plucked at the red blanket. He made excuses. He was 'D' company, he said. Mr. Mackenzie had been 'B'. He couldn't help her. He didn't know. Yes, he had been in the same action, but . . .

In the past Julia had protested about Red Cross officials who came to interview patients in their efforts to trace missing men. Their questions upset the wounded, brought back memories best forgotten, often caused nightmares and sometimes delayed recovery. Julia thought such interviews cruel, and queried their necessity. Now she found herself being more persistent, more callous than any official. She did not care how much she upset Burrows, disturbed his rest, aggravated the pain of his wounds by mental pressure. She would get the information from him whether he wished to reveal it or not.

In the end there was not much to discover. At least she knew now that Geoffrey had not had to suffer. There had been no lingering death, alone, in the moribund tent of a casualty clearing station. Though Burrows had not seen Geoffrey fall he had seen his body minutes later. "There were a bunch of them all together, like."

She stood in silence by his bed, recognising then that she had hoped for a miracle. The ragtime tune ground to a halt, changed to 'Somewhere a voice is calling.' The record was scratchy from overuse.

"What happened about burial?"

He looked at her blankly.

"He must have been buried," she said.

Burrows turned his head away and made a feeble gesture of appeal to a passing orderly, but was ignored.

"Look at me, Burrows," Julia said. "I want to know. Tell me. You know, don't you?"

He licked his lips. The words came out in a rush. "There weren't nothing to bury. Not afterwards. No bodies. Just a bloody big crater."

So ... that was it. The boy who had grown up with her, the man she loved, the body that had given her so much pleasure, no longer existed. Had gone, for ever. There was nothing left. Just a bloody big crater.

She was halfway down the ward when she remembered and came back. Burrows, seeing her coming, hurriedly closed his eyes. She noted his pallor without pity. Malingering, Sister had said.

"What happened to Mr. Patterson?" she said. "Did he come through all right?"

Burrows was so astonished that he opened his eyes and gaped up at her. "Mr. Patterson copped it months ago."

"*Patterson* did?"

"Drowned, he was. In No Man's Land."

She felt as if she had been dealt a physical blow. She could not believe him. "Are you sure?" she said. How ridiculous. He must be sure. "Months ago – when, exactly?"

He did not know. He could not remember. It might have been months. Or it might not. Weeks, maybe. "It was that pillbox what did it."

She walked away from his bed, without farewell or thanks. He was alive while Geoffrey was dead. What need had he of thanks?

Summoned to Matron's office she found Gabriel standing by Matron's desk. Julia took in the Military Cross ribbon on his chest, the wound stripe on his sleeve. She could not bring herself to look at his face.

"Ah, Miss Purcell," Matron said. "Thank you for coming. I'm sorry, my dear. Captain Mackenzie has bad news to tell you."

"I know it already," Julia said.

Matron and Gabriel exchanged glances. "I'll leave you together," Matron said. The door closed behind her. Very faintly in the distance a bugle sounded the Last Post.

"I'm sorry," Gabriel said.

She said nothing. There was nothing to say.

"How did you hear?"

"From one of the men in the ward."

"We should have thought of that. Frances wanted me to be the one to tell you. She thought it might make it easier."

"Yes." She knew she should feel grateful to Frances. To Gabriel, too, for making the effort to come. She felt nothing.

He looked helplessly round the room. "Can we go somewhere? It's not exactly . . . She said I could take you away for the rest of the day."

"Where do you want to go?"

"I don't know. Into town? I've never been in Rouen before."

"We can go to the cathedral, if you like."

She noticed the limp as soon as he moved, and remembered that he had been wounded. "You're not walking properly yet," she said.

"Habit. You get into the way of it and forget there's no need. Stupid, really."

She left him to look round the cathedral on his own – "Richard the Lionheart's somewhere near the altar" – while she sat at the back and waited. Her thoughts circled round the small dog she remembered lying under the Lionheart's feet. She wondered whether it had been modelled from one of Richard's own dogs; his favourite perhaps. Such immortality, to be remembered seven hundred years on.

"It's certainly impressive," Gabriel said, as he sat down beside her. "Though I still prefer Amiens. For the height, I think. You wonder how those medieval masons ever managed it." He added, "It's the only decent thing in Amiens, the cathedral."

All he knew of Rouen was its connection with Joan of Arc; he wondered whether traces of her time remained. They said little as they wandered through the narrow streets of the old town, but she was comforted by his presence. She realised that he must need comfort too, having lost both brothers ... though it was Antony's loss that would have hurt.

"Joan of Arc marked the end of the Hundred Years' War, more or less," he said, standing in the old market place. "Did you know that?"

They looked at each other, the same thought in both their minds.

"We marched through the site of Agincourt when we first came to France," he said. "Everything was still a big adventure at that time, of course, but I remember thinking even then how damned stupid it all was. 1415, 1815 – because Waterloo couldn't have been far off – and here we were in 1915 ... Who'll be fighting whom over the same ground in a hundred years' time, do you think?"

"It won't be us," Julia said. "We shall be dead by then," and was grateful for the thought.

She took him to the only hotel she knew. A mistake – she had sat with Major Miller in this room less than a week before leaving for Honfleur with Geoffrey. "Are you sure you know what you're doing?" Major Miller had said. She had known exactly what she was doing. She had no regrets, even now.

"He has only been posted as missing," Gabriel said. "There's still a chance he might turn up."

"There isn't," Julia said flatly.

He looked at her face and accepted her statement, without

asking for details. "Have you written to them at home?"

She shook her head. "I didn't know what to say. It seems remote, somehow, Hillcrest, Somerset, all that."

"It is remote. It hasn't altered in any way. You could think you were in 1914 still. Extraordinary, really."

She made a great effort. "Tell me about last summer."

He changed, talking about the summer. She sensed the happiness underlying the sorrow he felt for Geoffrey. Ever since April, during her time in Normandy and the anxious months of the summer's fighting, Gabriel had been at home recovering from the wound received at Arras. Had Frances realised her good fortune, Julia wondered, in having nothing to fear for so long? No wonder she had been able to concentrate on her painting.

"She's doing extraordinarily well," Gabriel said. "I was talking to Denis Bond when he came down to Huish Priory to help choose work for her exhibition. He says her reputation's rising rapidly in the art world. I still find it astonishing, I must admit, though for heaven's sake don't tell Frances I said so. Bond regarded me with the gravest suspicion, I might say."

She tried to smile. "Did he have reason?"

His face lit up. "Not at the moment, no, but it's going to be all right, Julia. In the end I know it will be all right. I've been too impatient in the past, I can see that now, but after the war, provided I'm still alive ..."

The warmth of his emotion began to thaw the ice in her heart. What mattered now was Gabriel's survival; all her hopes and thoughts and prayers must be devoted to willing him through to the war's end.

He put his arm round her when he left her at the hospital. "Chin up," he said.

She went to bed early. From a nearby ward came sounds of singing. The old year was dying – "Should *auld* acquaintance be forgot ..." – the new one coming in. What would 1918 bring? "And *nivair* brought to mind ..." The accents were thick, the words slurred. An orderly too generous with the rum ration perhaps? She dozed, woke, dozed again. She did not know whether she was dreaming or waking.

In the early hours of the morning she remembered Annie, after Bert Hawkins' death. "There's no knowing what might have happened," Annie had said, dry-eyed, calm. "It's all for the best."

So might this be ... but what comfort was there in that?

Major Miller came to see her. She knew he must know about Geoffrey, knew too that if she had wished to confide he would have listened and been sympathetic. She could say nothing. She felt as though she were frozen from the inside out.

The bad chest Major Miller had supposedly diagnosed last winter became a reality this. She was sent to the nurses' convalescent home with instructions not to return until her graveyard cough had vanished. While there – miserable because she had nothing to occupy either her time or her thoughts – the German army burst through the Allied lines in its march to the sea. Julia discharged herself from the home, went to the Transport Sister at Boulogne and spent the rest of her time as a V.A.D. working at Camiers.

She went about like an automaton. At least in those first months, when it sometimes seemed defeat of the Allies was inevitable, she had more than enough to do. It wasn't until the autumn, when the Germans had been beaten back and the volume of work had lessened, that Matron discovered Julia had had no leave for almost two years and insisted she took some now. Julia protested. Everyone knew that it was only a matter of months before the war came to an end. She had signed on for the duration; she would stay for the duration. She was given no choice.

On the day of departure she woke with a sore throat and a

headache. Never had she felt less like travelling. It rained during the crossing; she saw nothing of England until the white cliffs loomed out of the mist above her. In the train she looked out on the sodden landscape of Kent and felt neither elation nor relief at coming home. Reaching London too late to travel on to Taunton she spent the night at one of the V.A.D. hostels in Eccleston Square. By morning she had developed a high fever. The sheets on her bed were wringing wet, her head throbbed unbearably and her whole body ached. She had nursed enough patients with influenza recently to know what was wrong. All her efforts were concentrated on getting back to Hillcrest to her own bed. By the time she reached Paddington she knew it was impossible. She would have to find somewhere in London.

Jamieson had no telephone. The Cartwrights were too far away. Who else was there? Denis Bond, Frances's agent. If she could get hold of Denis ... Her fingers sweated over the pages of the directory.

The girl's voice was bright, efficient. "Mayfield Gallery."

"I must speak to Denis ... Mr. Bond. Please."

"He's not free at the moment." The voice had changed, become wary. "Who is that?"

"Julia Purcell ... I must. Please. At once."

"Ah." Less wary, almost friendly. She must have recognised the name. "Hold on. I'll see ..."

Passengers were coming through the barrier, a trickle at first, then a stream, finally a flood of tired, drab women and khaki-clad men returning to the front. If Denis didn't come soon it would be too late. She tried to remember the girl's name. If only the station were quieter. If only her head would stop banging. She could picture her clearly. Christine, that was it. She would have to ask Christine ...

"Julia," Denis said. She could have wept with relief at the sound of his voice. "This *is* a surprise. Where are you?"

"I'm at Paddington. Only ... I'm ill. Denis, please, wire Frances, tell her I can't ..."

"Don't move," Denis said. "Stay where you are. I'm coming ..." His voice grew fainter, overwhelmed by the other noises in her head. "Are you still there? *Julia* ..."

It had disappeared altogether.

Part Three

1918

Chapter Ten

The ward was hushed. No cheerful banter from the Tommies or lingeringly romantic tunes on the gramophone, no far-off bugles; only the murmur of voices and footsteps echoing between the rows of beds ...

The shadow by her bed turned into flesh and blood as the days passed, turned into Pauline Bond. She smiled down at Julia. "It's all over," she said.

Julia did not understand why Pauline should tell her. She knew it already. It had been over long ago, that day in Bourlon Wood.

"The war," Pauline said. "It's finished at last. They've signed an armistice."

The Bonds took Julia home with them when at last she was discharged. "You'll stay with us until you're fit to travel," Denis said. "I'm not having another morning like the last." It had taken him two hours to find her after her collapse; he still talked about it.

The Bonds cosseted her, tempting her with expensive food and providing a fire in her bedroom. Not until she came downstairs did she realise that they had deprived themselves to do so, food being rationed and coal almost unobtainable.

Frances and Gwen came up to London for the day, bringing a hamper of fruit and vegetables from Hillcrest, messages from Sarah and Annie and letters from the Mackenzies. After the initial excitement and emotion of the reunion there was an awkwardness in the conversation, both Frances and Gwen taking care not to mention Geoffrey's name. Julia would have liked to talk about Geoffrey; she wanted to find out about his last leave, but she could not bring herself to do so, when faced with such obvious reluctance. They had not changed as she had changed; she felt immeasurably older than they. Frances had expected Julia to be strong enough to return to Somerset with them and was obviously disappointed; she gave the impression that she thought Julia could be doing more to pull herself together. Julia was grateful to them for coming, and guiltily relieved to see them go. She had not the strength to cope with visitors, even Frances and Gwen. They seemed so cheerful, so fit, so energetic. She wondered whether she herself would ever have any energy again, or the enthusiasm to do anything with it if she had. She passed her days in idleness of necessity, watching Pauline sew and listening to her talk of the difficulties of living in London during the war.

"You can't have any idea how dreadful it all was. Not enough food. No petrol. Air raids. And such trouble with the servants. They could earn so much more money in munitions, you see." She was using silk for her needlepoint, which was as delicate as any embroidery Julia had done. Julia looked down on her own hands, the fingers scarred and stiff from poisoned cuts during the war, and wondered whether she would ever sew anything fine again.

Any guilt that Julia might feel at accepting so much hospitality was assuaged by the knowledge that Pauline was glad of her company, for Denis was out much of the time. "I hope that means the gallery's doing well," Julia said.

Pauline sewed in silence. Suddenly she burst out, "It's worse than a mistress, that gallery." Such emotion, in someone usually so restrained, took Julia aback. "If I'd only known before I bought it ... He was always determined to have a place of his own place, you know. He told me so, the first time we met. He never made any secret of it. It seemed so sensible, when we got married – and I could afford to buy it for him, after all. I thought it would be a nice little hobby. I thought it would make him happy. I didn't know that it would be like this."

Julia did not know what to say. She had always thought the Bonds such a contented couple, so suitably matched.

Pauline pulled the silk through the canvas. "It's such a *humiliating* emotion, jealousy."

Denis drove Julia to Paddington himself when she returned to Somerset. He found her a corner seat on the train, and bought her chocolates and a magazine, brushing aside her thanks. "I don't suppose you had time to paint in France," he said. Frances would have made the sentence a question; Denis accepted it as fact. "You must let me know when you get going again." He stood outside her compartment looking up at her from the platform as he waited for the train to depart. "Have you ever thought of going in for portraiture? That portrait you did of Frances, hanging in young Mackenzie's room – it's good." The train shuddered and began to move. He kept pace beside it. "I might be able to put the odd commission in your way if you were interested."

She knew he was being kind. She did not want that sort of kindness. "I'll think about it," she said, knowing that she would not.

Hillcrest seemed remote. She felt as if she were looking at it through the wrong end of a telescope. A new maid fresh from school was being trained by Annie in the kitchen, and two lads Julia didn't recognise helped Gwen in the garden. Nothing else had changed. She could scarcely believe that the pattern of life had continued unaltered during all those years she had been away.

The Mackenzies welcomed her as they might have welcomed a bereaved daughter-in-law. Photographs of Geoffrey and Antony were in every room; she had not realised that so many of Geoffrey existed. The detachment she felt at Hillcrest was even more pronounced here. She sat in the drawing-room with Mrs. Mackenzie, reading the telegram and the letters, looking at the scroll from the King. None of it had anything to do with Geoffrey or with her.

Bertha came out onto the Rectory doorstep with Julia, pulling the door to behind her. "Oh, Miss Julia, I'm that sorry." Tears ran down her cheeks. "Such a *nice* lad, Master Geoffrey. Always so kind."

And Julia, who had sat dry-eyed all afternoon, untouched by Mrs. Mackenzie's distress, had to take refuge in the churchyard for an hour before she felt able to face everyone with equanimity back at Hillcrest.

Before the war Julia had run the household with Annie. Now the household ran without her. When she tried to take on at least part of her share of the work, Annie was quick to stop her. "We can manage, love. There's no need for you to be doing that."

"It's all right," Frances said, not once but several times. "Leave everything to us. Sit back and relax. Why don't you start painting if you're looking for something to do?"

Unknown to Frances, she had once picked up her paint-box – and unleashed nightmares long since forgotten. The faces that had haunted her after the Somme came back now, both in her dreams and on the paper under her brush. She could put away her paints; she could not banish the night-mares.

She went down with another bout of flu in the New Year. Frances behaved as though she thought Julia was dying. Though milder than the first attack it took a surprisingly long time to get over. Sarah brought her books up to Julia's room and worked there every afternoon, hunched over the table by the window and glancing over to the bed from time to time with a shy smile, as if glad to see her home. Sarah had been the greatest surprise of her return, an awkward child no longer, but quiet and self-possessed, hoping to go on to study at Oxford the following year. Strangely, Julia felt more comfortable with her than with either Frances or Gwen. Geoffrey had thought her a grand kid, she remembered. She tried to find out details of Geoffrey's last leave, but Sarah's gaze slid away the moment Geoffrey's name was mentioned; muttering something about going to help Annie she disappeared for the rest of the afternoon.

Once Julia was on her feet again, Frances offered to show her the work she had done in Julia's absence. "I'd like to know what you think. You know how much your opinion means to me. It's what I've missed most since you went away." She took the key of the studio off its hook in the scullery and led the way up to the stables. "I've sold quite a few, obviously, but I'd like to know what you think about the ones I've still got. You don't mind my asking, do you? You're still interested?"

It was a blustery March day. The wind ruffled the feathers of the few hens that ventured from the shelter of the barn. Branches of the shrub rose rattled against the wall. The barn smelt as it always did at this time of year, of earth and stored vegetables, parsnips and swedes and turnips, a familiar, homely smell. She had forgotten how steep were the stairs up to Frances's studio; she had to pause at the top to regain her breath.

Frances made them both tea on the primus stove. She talked about Denis. Perhaps she thought that by surrounding Julia with paints and canvas once more she would encourage her to get back to her own work. "Denis would be interested, you know. He's said as much."

"I couldn't possibly let Denis take an interest in me, just because I'm your sister."

Frances stared. "Look – I've known Denis for a long time. I like him very much; we get on well. All the same ... Denis is no philanthropist. If he's offered to help it's not out of the goodness of his heart or because of me. It's because he thinks he'll benefit in the end."

"Maybe," Julia said, unconvinced. "Aren't you going to show me what you've done?"

Frances was nervous. It mattered to her what Julia

thought. For someone so confident – arrogant even – she had always showed surprising humility where her work was concerned. She sat on the floor now, warming her hands round her mug, delaying the moment by further talk – of what she had done in Julia's absence and was doing now, of the paintings that had been sold and to whom. She talked of what she hoped to do in the future and of Denis's plans. When she could delay no longer she brought out her latest drawings and laid them carefully over the floor. Then she fetched the paintings and held them up, one by one, finished and unfinished, watercolour, pastel and oils, leaving them propped against the wall round the room for further viewing. She waited.

"Well?" she said at last.

Julia could think of nothing to say. Not one word.

She should have been prepared. Denis had told her about Frances's work. He had made much of Frances's growing reputation in the art world and had shown Julia the magazine articles. She should have expected . . . but she had not.

"Well?" Frances said again.

Julia looked round the room at an extraordinary outburst of light and colour and form, the summary of Frances's life during the past four years, and for the first time realised the extent of her own failure. What had she to show for those years but a bundle of badly written letters from men she had once nursed, an overwhelming lassitude and a head full of unpaintable pictures that continued to haunt every moment, both sleeping and waking?

The shame she felt at her lack of generosity towards Frances, her bitterness at the terrible waste of those war years so overcame her that she went back to her room and lay all afternoon on her bed staring dry-eyed up at the ceiling. She knew that the loneliness that enveloped her now would be with her for the rest of her life. There was no one who could understand the gulf that existed between herself and the rest of the world.

Except Gabriel . . .

But Gabriel, when he returned in the autumn of 1919, had problems of his own.

Gabriel's leave, so long anticipated, turned into a nightmare within twenty-four hours. He asked Frances to marry him. She turned him down. For ever.

"I can't believe it," she told her sisters. "When I've always *said* . . . Ever since the Slade I've told him. I'd marry him if I could – he knows that. But I can't. Not if I'm going to work."

Gabriel threatened to take up a posting in Army intelligence in Dublin. Unless Frances was prepared to marry him, he would go over to Ireland where the Shinners were trying to overthrow the British Government, murdering police and menacing the Army in their attempts to do so. How would Frances feel about that?

Frances accused him of blackmail.

Julia could scarcely bring herself to speak to her sister. It was Mr. and Mrs. Mackenzie who concerned her quite as much as Gabriel. They had looked forward to his homecoming, believing it signified the end of years of anxiety and the beginning of a new era. Now, thanks to Frances, their hopes and joy had vanished overnight.

Lucy, coming over to Hillcrest in search of Julia, found her in the flower room.

"Thank goodness you're alone. We won't be disturbed, will we? I wanted to have a word with you." There was more colour than usual in her cheeks. She did not look at Julia but played with the flowers that lay on the table waiting to be arranged. She picked up a rose and sniffed it, but absent-mindedly, not caring about its scent. "I don't know how to tell you this. Do you remember the portrait of Frances you gave Gabriel one Christmas, years ago, before the war?"

"Yes, of course. He asked me to paint it for him."

"Do you want it back?"

"Why?" she said blankly.

"Don't take it personally," Lucy begged, abstractedly picking thorns off the rose stem. "He doesn't know what he's doing. He was banging around late last night in his room. When I went to see what was happening I discovered he'd taken the portrait – your painting – down from the wall. He must have been drunk. I can't think of any other explanation, and I do know he stayed downstairs after the rest of us had come up to bed. Anyway, there he was about to go out and burn it."

"*Burn* my painting?"

Lucy nodded. "I couldn't believe it either. You'd have thought Gabriel, of all people, would know you don't go round doing that sort of thing. And can you imagine – a bonfire, in the middle of the night. The whole village would have heard of it by breakfast. I managed to get it away from him, thank goodness, and Bertha smuggled it out of the house before anyone else was up. Bertha's discreet. She won't talk."

"So where is it now?"

"In the hut at the bottom of the garden. You know – where Antony kept his rabbits. It's quite safe – no one ever goes there – but I thought if you wanted it ..."

"It might be better to leave it there for the time being. I'll fetch it later, when Gabriel's gone. I'm terribly sorry, Lucy. About Frances, I mean, not the painting. There are times when I could strangle her. Really."

"You're not blaming Frances, are you?" Lucy sounded astonished. "Why? She's always made it perfectly clear she wouldn't consider marriage. It's Gabriel's fault. He's known how she's felt for years. Why he should suddenly think ...? Mother says he's gone mad. I think he's ... just so *stupid*. I can't understand him, really I can't. Everyone says he's so clever, and then he goes and behaves like an idiot. I suppose he's told you he's going to Ireland?"

"He did mention it. I'd hoped it was one of those things people say in the heat of the moment and don't mean."

"He meant it all right. He's fixed it up already. Father's aged ten years overnight. I can't forgive Gabriel for that."

Gabriel never mentioned the portrait to Julia, not even when he came over to Hillcrest on his last evening. He had been up to the stables to say goodbye to Frances, to Gwen in the greenhouse, to Sarah down in the lower garden. By the time he came striding across the lawn to where Julia waited on the verandah it was already past the Rectory dinner hour.

"You're going to be late," Julia said. "Your mother will be tut-tutting in the hall already."

"I know," he said. "I'm sorry we haven't had time together. I'd hoped we might talk. Are you really all right? No trace of the flu? Fully recovered?"

She thought that he looked far from all right himself. Ireland was the last place he should be going, with its present troubles. "Gabriel, must you –?"

"If you're going to mention Ireland," he said, "don't. People have gone on at me so much over the past few days that I'm sick to death of the place before I even get there."

She walked with him round the side of the house to the front gate. "At least you know what I'd say if you let me."

"I don't want you to misunderstand," he said. "Frances has had nothing to do with my going to Ireland. I was tempted by this job long ago, when Hugh Meredith first mentioned it, but at that time I still hoped that Frances and I ... I knew there was no possibility of Frances coping as an army wife, whereas I really did think she could be happy at Cambridge. She liked it in the old days, and there would always have been Hillcrest to come back to ..."

She did not care about Frances. It was the thought of his parents that upset her. How can you do this to them, she wanted to say, when they've suffered so much already. She knew it was pointless. Every argument she put forward

Lucy would have used already.

He stood in the road, playing with the gate latch. "I must go," he said, but still lingered. "Ironic, isn't it?" he said.

"What is?"

His face was haggard. "The wrong man came home."

There was little conversation at supper. Frances looked like death. Sarah had obviously been crying. Gwen's mention of the *Iliad* – "Gabriel's suggested I do the illustrations for a translation he's making" – trailed into silence. Julia tried to obliterate Gabriel's last words from her mind, words that expressed the thought she had refused to acknowledge ever since his return.

When Frances came to Julia's room that night, Julia did not want to see her. "I'm tired, Frances. Can't it wait till tomorrow."

"Please. It'll only take a minute. Read this letter and tell me what you think."

Recognising the writing, she shook her head. "No. What goes on between you and Gabriel is your affair. I won't have anything to do with it."

"Please." Frances sounded desperate. "He blames me. I want to know whether you do too." She thrust the pages into Julia's hand.

There was nothing personal in the first paragraphs. Gabriel was planning his leave ... the pleasure he took in the prospect was painful to read, knowing the outcome.

"Well?" Frances said.

"Why does he ask you to go to Cambridge with him? He went there before he came home."

"That's where he's asking me to marry him."

Julia stared at her sister. "He doesn't mention marriage."

"It's what he meant, though. To go to Cambridge for good. Married, in other words. I thought the same as you, that he was asking me to go now, look up old friends, have time away from the Rectory, the two of us together. But he

didn't, and when I wrote back and said yes, he thought ...
He took it for granted ... That day we went up on to the
Quantocks he started talking about a honeymoon in
Switzerland. He'd got it all planned. That's what made it all
so dreadful. He was so happy then." She began to cry. "Oh,
Julia, what am I to do? I can't bear to see him so miserable."

What could be said? So much emotion, wasted ... Julia
wanted nothing to do with it. She was worn out. She needed
to be left alone, to get on with her own life.

Julia had refused all invitations from the Cartwrights since
her return from France, at first because she had been too ill,
later because she lacked both the energy and the will to
make the journey. Now Miranda insisted that she should
come. There was a man she wanted Julia to meet, she said,
the son of her mother's closest friend. Miranda, hoping that
something might come of their friendship, wanted Julia's
approval.

Julia slipped back into the household as if she had never
been away. Mr. and Mrs. Cartwright showed a comforting
lack of curiosity about the years since their last meeting.
They gave her news of Aunt Amy, now reunited with Uncle
Henri in Paris. "It was kind of you to write to her, dear,"
Mrs. Cartwright said. "It helped her so much, knowing
everything was all right." Major Miller had been out of
uniform for several months and was working in a hospital
north of London. "Norwich, I think. Somewhere remote, I
know."

"Do give him my regards when you write," Julia said.
"He was kind to me in France. How's his son?" She tried to
work out how old the baby must be. Two and a half. She
felt a pang, even now.

"The apple of his father's eye," Mrs. Cartwright said
complacently. "So my sister tells me. And doted on by all
the women in the family, needless to say."

John Ford, Miranda's friend, was invited to dinner. He

was older than Miranda had led Julia to expect, and quiet. She found conversation with him difficult, and supposed that she must have lost the habit of small talk, if she had ever had it. He was – she was reluctant to admit it, even to herself – dull. Worthy, Annie would say.

"Are you happy?" she asked Miranda, after his departure.

Too quickly Miranda replied, "Yes, of course," adding defensively, "He's shy, you know. He's fun when you get to know him. Really." Later she admitted that he wasn't 'very exciting'. "What can one do? It's no good being choosy these days. There aren't many men around, and I'll be twenty-five next birthday."

Miranda's romance – for it was obvious he was serious – was the only depressing feature about Julia's stay with the Cartwrights. She thought Miranda deserved better, and was sure she herself would never settle for second-best. But she was not an only child, she realised, nor a child of elderly parents.

"I'd always thought we were unlucky losing Mother and Father when we did," she said, telling the other Purcells about it when she got home. "And of course we were, but we were bound to lose them some time. I'd never thought what it would be like not to have brothers or sisters. It must be terrible having no one."

"I could have told you that ages ago," Frances said. "We couldn't have gone on living here, for one thing, unless there'd been the four of us. We need each other. We always have."

It was Julia Frances needed that winter.

Frances had never suffered from the depressions that afflicted Gabriel. This winter however she fell into deep despair. One cause was undoubtedly the break with Gabriel. It had apparently never occurred to her, when refusing his proposal, that he and she could not continue together as before. When his letters to her stopped she was both indignant and frightened. "But nothing's changed," she said, when Julia pointed out that Gabriel would find it easier to make a life of his own without the constant reminder that letters from her would bring. "He's always known I wouldn't marry him. I don't see why we can't carry on writing. I rely on him. He's always been around, long before we fell in love. I can't do without him."

Worse than Gabriel's defection, however, was Frances's loss of faith in herself as a painter. It was not false modesty on her part. Unbelievable as it might seem to Julia or to Gwen, Frances looked at her own work and found it worthless. She continued to go up to the stables every morning, as she had since leaving the Slade, but whether she painted or not no one knew. She never sought Julia's opinion or talked of what she was doing. She only said, with growing frequency, that she was finished. "Life isn't worth living if I can't paint."

Julia did not know what to do. She suggested asking Denis Bond to stay, in the hope that he might be able to help. Frances shook her head. "I talked to him last time I was in London. He refused to take me seriously."

"Why not go abroad for a while?" Julia said at last, not sure whether the suggestion was wise, given Frances's state of mind, but unable to think of anything else. "You used to talk about going abroad to paint when you were at the Slade. Widen your experience, you said. If you were looking at different scenery under a different light you might find it easier to start again. You could afford to go abroad for a couple of months, couldn't you, if you found somewhere cheap to stay."

"I couldn't. Not with Sarah going to Oxford in the autumn."

"We've been saving for Oxford for years. Besides, Mr. Mackenzie's certain she'll get an exhibition. She might even get a scholarship. You worry too much about Sarah. It's your work that's important at the moment."

"Well . . . maybe." She might sound unenthusiastic but at least she had not turned down the idea. "Where could I go?"

"Somewhere with a good light obviously. South, I suppose, at this time of year. How about Provence?" Not Honfleur; anywhere in the world but Honfleur. She could not bear to have Frances bring home paintings of Honfleur.

"A couple of people from the Slade are living in Spain," Frances said slowly.

"That's it, then. Spain. If people you know are there already . . ."

Frances was unconvinced. "I'll think about it," she said.

She was still thinking when news came that Gabriel had been badly injured in an ambush in Dublin.

Chapter Eleven

Within an hour of Lucy bringing the news over to Hillcrest Frances had packed her bag and left for Dublin – Frances, who had never been in a hospital, any hospital, in her life, who sickened at the thought of anything unpleasant and fainted at the sight of blood. Julia, torn between distress on Gabriel's behalf and concern for her sister, tried to stop her. "At least wait for a while, until Mr. Mackenzie's had time to telegraph and find out what's happened."

Frances, half-way up the stairs on her way to pack, stared down at Julia in disbelief. "We know what's happened," she said. "Gabriel's been ambushed. He's likely to die. Hugh Meredith sent that cable to prepare us. What are you suggesting I wait for? The telegram telling us he's dead?"

"You haven't the faintest idea what military hospitals can be like," Julia said desperately. "You don't know how Gabriel is – what sort of state he's in." Forgotten faces swam up in front of her eyes, hideous faces. "He wouldn't want you upset." She stopped, silenced by the scorn on Frances's face.

"You'd go if you were me," Frances said. "Wouldn't you?"

Julia hesitated. Behind Frances, on the half-landing, the grandfather clock tocked steadily on as it had done ever since Julia could remember. "Yes," she said at last.

"Well, then." Frances came down the stairs to give Julia a quick hug. "I know what you're trying to say, and thank you, but I'm going."

The house seemed empty after she had gone. No one knew what to do. Julia took Sarah to the Rectory to see what help they could give the Mackenzies. Sarah, who had hero-worshipped Gabriel for as long as the Purcells could remember, had said scarcely a word since hearing the news. Julia felt desperately sorry for her. Only that morning she had learnt that she had won an exhibition to Oxford. Now happiness at her success would be overlaid, even in memory, by the knowledge of what came after.

At the Rectory they found Mrs. Mackenzie had retired to her bed and Dr. Milne been sent for. "I'm sure she'll be all right," Lucy told Julia, "but it seemed sensible to call him, if only as a precaution. I've cabled the hospital too, and asked them to tell Gabriel about Frances. I thought it might help him if he knew she was coming ..." Her voice tailed off.

Mr. Mackenzie was anxious about Frances. "Arriving in a strange town, knowing no one ... Should I write to the Merediths, do you think? We met them with Gabriel in London, you know, before they went over to Ireland. I'm sure they would be pleased to help; indeed Colonel Meredith said as much in his telegram."

"Mrs. Meredith has to stay in bed all the time," Sarah said. "She's having a baby, Gabriel said, only something's gone wrong. Gabriel's teaching her bridge to help occupy her time." She swallowed. "Was teaching her bridge, I mean."

"I suppose, then, that it would be a mistake ..." Mr. Mackenzie sounded helpless. He looked an old man.

Sarah stayed with him while Lucy walked back with Julia as far as the Rectory gate. "I feel ashamed of myself," Lucy said. "I always thought I was a reasonable person until this happened. I never thought I could feel so bitter ... I keep thinking of Jane Lynch. Four brothers, going all through the war, and not a scratch on one of them. Look at us. Why Gabriel, now, after all we've gone through?"

Julia could give her no answer.

Letters came from Dublin, from the sister at the hospital and the medical officer concerned, as well as one from Hugh

Meredith. They talked about blood transfusions and infection. They said Gabriel had rallied surprisingly, and were hopeful in a way that encouraged the Mackenzies, though not Julia. She had seen too many letters written in similar vein in the past to be deceived now.

Frances's first letter was short. She had arrived. She had found somewhere to stay. The hospital allowed her to sit with Gabriel whenever and for as long as she wanted. He was suffering from concussion, she said, in addition to his other injuries. It was obvious to Julia, reading Frances's few, frightened sentences, that the fact that Gabriel was unconscious had been the worst blow of all. She had travelled to Dublin believing she could will him to live. Now she found she could do nothing but sit by his bed and wait.

Every Easter since before the war the Bonds had driven down to their cottage on the Devon coast, breaking their journey for lunch at Hillcrest. This year the worry over both Gabriel and Frances, the shattering effect of the Good Friday service on minds already distressed, and this morning's activity in preparing the church for Easter had wiped all thought of the Bonds from the Purcells' memory. They gaped when they saw them standing on the doorstep.

Denis's smile vanished at the sight of their faces. "You are expecting us, aren't you?" he said. "I told Frances that unless we heard ... Didn't she get my letter?"

"I'm sorry, I'm sorry," Julia said. "It's my fault. I haven't been forwarding letters."

Denis's eyes went from Gwen to Sarah and back to Julia. "Where is Frances?"

"In Dublin. Someone we know has been hurt there. She had to leave in a hurry."

There was a moment's silence.

"It's Mackenzie, isn't it?" Denis said. "I knew he'd be her undoing in the end. Damn him, damn him, damn him."

"He is *dying*, Denis," Julia protested.

"I'm so sorry for you all," Pauline said quickly. "We'll be off straightaway. Julian, Imogen – back to the car. Hurry, now. Don't worry about us, Julia. We'll get something to eat on the way."

Her words reminded the Purcells of their duty as hosts. "You can't possibly leave now," Julia said. "Come in. Please. Lunch will be a bit late, that's all."

Gwen went up to the stables to fetch more vegetables, Sarah to the kitchen to warn Annie and Lily. Julia took the Bonds into the drawing-room.

Considering his initial reaction, Denis turned out to be surprisingly sympathetic. His questions were both sensible and practical. He asked about the hospital Gabriel was in and the medical attention he was receiving. "He's not got some army sawbones looking after him, I trust."

"He has, as a matter of fact," Julia said, offended by such a description of men she had admired. "There are good ones about, you'll be surprised to hear. We've been told this one's first-rate."

Denis smiled faintly. "Sorry. As long as he really is good . . . How is Frances coping with all this? I wouldn't think the sick-room is her milieu, exactly."

"She's all right," Julia said.

"I could go over to Ireland, you know, if you thought it would help – see what's happening, sort things out, that kind of thing. Give Frances some support."

She was not sure how effective that support would be, remembering the sentiments he had expressed earlier, but she was touched by the offer. "It's kind of you, but I think at the moment . . ."

After a meal where the quality and abundance of vegetables effectively disguised the scarcity of meat, Gwen ushered the others into the drawing-room, leaving Denis and Julia together.

Denis waited until they were alone. "I must apologise for saying what I did about Mackenzie earlier," he said. "It was quite uncalled for."

"I think you're worrying unnecessarily, in any case, if you're afraid of marriage," Julia said. "Frances has been set against that ever since her time at the Slade."

"I know. But do you think that will hold if he's badly hurt? Pity's a formidable emotion. She's never hidden her affection for him, even to me."

"Her work is what matters to her."

"And her family. Don't underestimate her feelings for you all. Does Mackenzie count as family, I wonder. That's the question."

"It takes two to marry," Julia said. "The sort of person Gabriel is I'm quite sure he would never allow Frances to, well, throw herself away, even if she wanted to."

His glance was shrewd. "You know more about his condition than you've said."

She shook her head. "I don't." But for the first time she added up all the information Frances had let drop in her letters, unaware no doubt of its significance, and knew that even if he lived Gabriel could not survive unscathed.

"It's all very upsetting," Denis said. "I was hoping to discuss her next exhibition with her while I was here. Ah, well. Give me her address and I'll drop her a line."

"It would be much better if you didn't. She has enough to worry her at the moment without your mentioning an exhibition."

"I didn't intend to harry her," he protested. "Merely offer sympathy. Still, you probably know best." He sat back and studied Julia. "How about you? Are you painting these days?"

"You're worse than Frances for going on about that."

He smiled. "I've got where I have, let me tell you, because I've never taken no for an answer."

"I'm afraid you'll have to in this case." She stood up. "I think we should join the others." She relented as they went out into the hall. "I am painting a bit, as a matter of fact."

The Bonds did not stay long. They still had far to go and

Pauline was anxious not to impose.

"I meant what I said at lunch," Denis said. "If there's anything I can do ... go to Ireland ... organise a specialist ... anything. And let me know when you think it's safe to write."

Julia had lied when telling Denis that Frances was all right. Frances was obviously far from all right. Her letters to the Mackenzies reporting on Gabriel's progress were short, often not more than a couple of paragraphs, but sensible. The letters Julia received were long, rambling and incoherent, filled with remorse and despair. She blamed herself for Gabriel's situation. If Gabriel died it would be her fault. Tearstains blurred the ink with which she wrote, making whole sections illegible. Julia became increasingly concerned. She considered going over to Ireland herself until Annie pointed out that the hospital was unlikely to welcome a second visitor, and in any case she was needed at home. "'Tis the busiest time in the garden for Miss Gwen. She hasn't time for anything else. There's Miss Sarah going round like a lost lamb and as for the Rectory ... well, you know how Miss Lucy needs you there."

She knew Annie was right. The Mackenzies were barely coping with this latest misfortune. Mrs. Mackenzie's illness was diagnosed as a tired heart by Dr. Milne, who refused to allow her out of bed and prescribed indefinite rest. Mr. Mackenzie had retreated to his study. Gwen needed help, Lucy support, Sarah occupation, Frances encouraging letters from home. Ironically, Julia was in the position she had longed for most after her return from France. She was busy. She was needed. But not like this, she kept thinking; not for such a reason.

The problem of Frances seemed insoluble. "Could we ask the hospital to keep an eye on her?" Annie asked, when she and Julia were discussing the latest guilt-ridden letter while they changed the winter curtains for summer ones. "If you suggested it nicely ... Mr. Gabriel's doctor wrote very kindly to the Rector, Bertha told me. Maybe he could do something."

"It's the sister's job to deal with the relatives, not the doctor's," Julia said. It seemed an idea worth considering, all the same. "I don't know. Perhaps I could. If only he weren't a major. I'd have expected a captain in his position. I'm not sure that I dare write to a major."

"Better write to the sister, then," Annie said.

Julia had doubts about the sister too. Frances was obviously terrified of her, and when Julia looked back to some of the sisters in France ... But in the end it was the memory of Major Miller that persuaded her to approach the medical officer rather than the ward sister. If she could pretend she was writing to Major Miller ...

It was a difficult letter to write all the same. She did not wasn't to sound foolish or over-anxious. She was reluctant to draw attention to Frances if Frances was coping. If, on the other hand, Frances was about to throw herself into the Liffey or under a tram ... She was still not sure she was doing the right thing when she took the letter down to the village to post; she sent up a silent prayer as it fluttered down inside the box.

The reply came sooner than she had expected. Major Elliot was sorry to learn of Julia's worries, though apparently not surprised. Both he and Sister had been similarly concerned, he said, but now considered Frances to be over the worst. He hoped that as a result future letters would give Julia less cause for concern. In an attempt to distract Frances's thoughts, Sister had inveigled her into helping on the ward. For some reason – Major Elliot had no idea what – Frances had begun drawing the men in it, 'an occupation which has turned out to be more therapeutic than anything I could have devised'. There were thirty men there, most of them now expecting to have their portraits done; Major Elliot estimated that Frances would be kept busy for weeks. He reported frankly on Gabriel's progress, offered further help should Julia or the Mackenzies need it and signed himself, 'Yours sincerely, David Elliot.'

It was a pleasant, considerate letter, allaying fears and encouraging hope without building up false expectations. Julia read it through twice before taking it out to the kitchen to show Annie. "He sounds so kind," she said. "And Sister can't be the ogre Frances thinks she is either, if she worried too. Oh . . ." She blew her nose. She felt as if a great weight had been lifted from her shoulders. "You can't help smiling, can you? Frances, back at work . . . She'll be all right if she's able to draw."

She wrote once more to Major Elliot, hoping that gratitude did not make her thanks sound effusive. She did not expect to hear from him again and was both surprised and alarmed when she recognised his writing on a letter less than a week later. His letter contained not bad news as she had feared but the information that Colonel and Mrs. Meredith had promised to take Frances under their wing. He had driven Frances round himself, to meet them. 'Mrs. Meredith has her own problems, I understand, but has always been anxious to help,' he said, adding in a postscript that the Merediths had apparently expected 'Miss Purcell' to be Julia rather than Frances. Why, he wondered.

Julia did not know. Perhaps, she said, the Merediths knew that she had nursed during the war . . .

Frances's letters, though no longer despairing, were subdued. She had assumed that once Gabriel was conscious his recovery would be assured. The realisation that he was still on the dangerously ill list had come as a shock; as had the discovery that the pain he was suffering was impossible to alleviate.

"Poor Frances," Gwen said. "She's always managed to avoid the nasty things in life until now. Still . . . she's not talking about coming home, is she? She's going to stick it out?"

"She hasn't said that she's not. She is funny, though, the way she assumes I know everything. She keeps asking my opinion. Do I think it's sensible for them to make Gabriel sit up when he still gets so giddy and sick? How should I know? I was only a V.A.D."

"I think it's rather touching," Gwen said.

Julia had discovered in France how situations that seemed intolerable at first became commonplace in time. So it was now. They grew used to living on a knife edge, dreading the next letter for the news it might bring. Life had to go on; neither household nor parish activities could be put aside. The eventual discovery that Gabriel would have permanent difficulty in walking seemed almost acceptable after fearing his death for so long. The horror of it, for someone like Gabriel who walked long distances for pleasure and needed such exercise to banish depression, took time to sink in. Even then there was comfort of a sort. "He could have been blinded," Sarah said, and everyone knew that she was thinking of Bill Roberts, the one-time village blacksmith, who had been blinded as well as crippled at Sanctuary Wood; knew too that she was right. Gabriel would have found life insupportable without books and his writing.

Bill Roberts spent his days in a chair in the doorway of his home, taking in as much of the goings-on of village life as a blind man could. Julia sometimes sat with him when Mary, his wife, wanted an hour or two of freedom; on the occasions when Mary took Willy and young Tom to spend the day with relations in Wellington Julia saw to Bill's dressings as well. The shell that had blinded him had changed his personality, making him prone to fits of depression and sudden outbursts of rage. Julia had nothing but admiration for Mary. Four weeks and one brief leave was the only real married life the Roberts had had, yet Julia had never heard

Mary utter one word of complaint. So when Lucy said Mary had been offered a charity holiday by the sea for herself and the boys but was reluctant to leave Bill, Julia volunteered to help.

"I don't like asking it, Miss Julia, when you've troubles enough of your own," Mary said. "Young Jess'll be staying – you remember Jess? – but she's only a girl, and Miss Mackenzie said you being a nurse . . ."

"I'm glad to be able to help," Julia said. "It'll be nice to see Jess again too. I haven't seen her for years."

She remembered Jess as a cheerful, rosy-cheeked child, giggling in corners with Sarah or chattering to Annie in the kitchen at Hillcrest, and was taken aback by the silent, sulky-faced girl Jess had become. Jess was good with Bill, however, treating him with firm good humour as one might a child, accepting no nonsense and patiently encouraging him when he became frustrated. Julia thought life must be lonely with only Bill for company, and suggested to Sarah that she should visit her. "You used to be friends in the old days. Why don't you take her something to read and have a chat?"

"I couldn't," Sarah said, flushing. "She doesn't like me any more."

"Oh, Sarah. Don't be absurd."

"I'm not," Sarah said. "I think it's something to do with her not being able to teach."

One morning Julia arrived later than usual, to find Jess helping two small children make pastry. Bill told her that the children were "our Lizzie's, from over Dunkery way," and that Jess was looking after them for the morning.

"Don't let me interrupt," Julia said, joining Jess after she had dealt with Bill and settled him in his chair. "Sarah said something the other day about your wanting to teach."

Jess's expression changed. "Yes, well. I should'a known 'twas a stupid idea, should'n I?"

Julia was taken aback. "You're dealing with children,

[174]

though, in the nursery."

"Them's babies." Her voice was full of scorn.

"Don't you like babies?"

"I like'em better when they'm older."

Julia nodded to the two children. "This sort of age?"

Jess said nothing.

"Do you look after them often?" Julia said.

"Just mornings. It helps our Lizzie. She's having another." She sounded defensive. "Bill likes little uns around. Gives him something to think about."

The small boy stared back at Julia, floury hair standing on end, absent-mindedly pulling at the sticky grey dough that bound his fingers.

Julia was intrigued. "Do you think I could draw him some time?"

"Can't stop you, can I?" Jess said.

It was scarcely an invitation, but Julia took it as one, and came next day with pencils and paper. She drew Jess too, sitting at the kitchen table teaching the children their letters.

Jess studied the finished drawings in silence. Her expression was blank. Impossible to tell what she was thinking.

"Keep them," Julia offered. "Or give them to Lizzie. Not that they're up to much. I haven't drawn children before. They don't keep very still, do they?"

Jess shrugged, as if indifferent, but she kept the drawings, and when Julia arrived the next day the greeting she gave Julia was noticeably warmer.

Julia stayed on most mornings after that. She drew Jess as well as the children, and Bill too. Having something to do made conversation with Jess easier. By the time Mary returned with the boys, Jess had become almost friendly. She smiled when Julia arrived and talked to her more easily, but Julia never again got her on to the subject of teaching.

Jess and the children were not Julia's only models. Gabriel had asked for drawings of the three Purcells – to remind him of home, he said. Julia worked on a composite picture, the only drawback being that her own portrait had to be a mirror image, while those of her sisters were not. Sarah scoffed at her worries. "Gabriel wouldn't notice a thing like *that*," she said, but then had second thoughts. "I suppose he might, being Gabriel. Well, *I* think it's splendid, anyway."

Julia realised she could not continue to borrow materials from Gwen. She went into Taunton and spent more than she had intended on setting herself up. She consoled herself with the thought that Frances would approve.

"It's ridiculous," she said to Gwen. "I didn't feel like painting at all last year when I had nothing to do, whereas now, when there's no time to fit everything in ..."

"I expect Frances's going away has something to do with it," Gwen said sagely.

Drawings travelled both ways across the Irish Sea. Gabriel persuaded Frances to send back sketches of the nursing staff, thinking that it might help those at home, his parents in particular, if they could put a face to names mentioned in his letters. The portraits provided some surprises. The ward sister who had so terrified Frances on arrival appeared quite human in her portrait, with the suspicion of a twinkle in her eye. Studying it Julia realised that she could equally well have written to the sister as Major Elliot: she would have got help from either. Her correspondence with Major Elliot continued. He had picked up her mention of nursing in France: wondered where she had been stationed, what she had been doing, asked whether she had ever thought of carrying on after the war. His sister had nursed, too, he said, and he had spent much of the war working in casualty clearing stations in Flanders. From sharing similar experiences they moved on to other subjects. He wanted to know more about the Purcells, about Hillcrest, about Julia herself. He made no mention of his own family – Julia assumed he had left them in England – and was reticent about himself. She knew he liked music, for he told her of concerts he attended. He wrote of the pleasures of a day's fishing. Presumably the salmon and trout Gabriel mentioned enjoying were the result of his endeavours. Julia did not realise how much she looked forward to receiving his letters until she ended the correspondence, on the day another of Frances's drawings arrived at the Rectory.

"It's of Major Elliot this time," Lucy told the Purcells when they went over for tea. "It's ... surprising."

"Surprising?" Gwen said. "Why?"

"Well ... how old do you think he is?"

"Old," Sarah said.

"Fiftyish?" Julia said.

"That's what we thought," Lucy said, "but look." She laid the paper on Julia's lap. "There."

Julia looked down on the drawing of a man of similar age to Gabriel, lying back in an armchair with pipe in one hand and a glass of beer in the other. He appeared comfortable and very much at ease, but his eyes were alert and focussed on the artist so that he seemed to be looking directly at Julia. She was conscious of colour flooding up into her face ... and of Sarah's eyes, watching her.

"I don't know why we should have thought he was so much older," Lucy said. "I suppose Frances must have given us that impression somehow. He and Gabriel just missed each other at Cambridge apparently. Here, you'd better read Gabriel's letter."

Julia kept her eyes down. She was dismayed. Had she known Elliot to be Gabriel's contemporary she would never have written to him as she had, or revealed so much of herself. She knew she could not write to him again.

Chapter Twelve

Thoughts of Frances and Gabriel were never far from the Purcells' minds that summer. They wrote, sent parcels – books, drawings, produce from the garden – talked hopefully of their return. There was still worry over Gabriel, but Sister seemed pleased with his progress and he himself wrote cheerfully enough. His request to Julia to send Frances her paints had lessened Julia's concern for her sister considerably, and had amused Gwen and Sarah. "That sister can't be as bad as Frances makes out," Gwen said, "if she's prepared to put up with Frances and her mess all over the place."

There was another worry that persisted, concerning money. The exhibition Sarah had been awarded would not cover her expenses at Oxford. The Purcells had put money by ever since Mr. Mackenzie had mentioned university as a possibility, but Frances in particular had always been determined that Sarah should lack for nothing while studying. Meanwhile in Dublin Frances was having to pay for her food and lodging, no one knew for how long. The months of uncertainty after Mrs. Purcell's death had left their mark on her daughters; they all needed the security of knowing that there was sufficient money in the bank to meet any emergency. When Frances asked Julia to take two paintings to Denis at the Mayfield Gallery, Julia knew that Frances shared their anxiety.

Denis greeted Julia with pleasure. He had heard from Frances, he said, and yes, she had mentioned having paintings to sell. "I suppose she'll stay in Ireland now, until Mackenzie's fit to travel," he said. He sounded resigned. He studied the canvases for a while before naming a figure that

Julia knew, and knew Denis knew she knew, was substantially more than he would have offered in any other circumstance.

They looked at each other.

"Well," Julia said, "if you're sure. She wouldn't want you to ... Thank you very much, anyway. She'll be grateful."

"Nothing to be grateful for," Denis said, adding in doomladen tones, "She'll marry him, you know, in the end." He took Julia out to lunch, said that if only he'd thought of it earlier he would have asked Pauline to join them, and when finally he put her in a taxi to Paddington said, "You'll bite my head off if I ask, so it's not worth my asking, and you'll be too busy anyway, but I suppose you aren't ...?"

"Doing any painting?" Julia finished for him, and laughed. "I am, as a matter of fact. Not much, but I've started again."

A letter was waiting for her on the oak chest in the hall when she got back to Hillcrest. She recognised the writing at once.

She had not expected to hear from Major Elliot again, for it was her turn to write. That she had not done so was entirely due to the portrait that Frances had sent the Mackenzies. She picked up his letter almost reluctantly and took it to read alone in her room.

He thought she would be interested to know that he had taken Frances and Gabriel away for a weekend's fishing. There had been problems, of course, but none that had proved insuperable. He considered the experience had given Gabriel greater confidence in his ability to move about, while two days in the country had changed Frances out of all recognition. He himself had enjoyed the weekend enormously; he feared that hobbies like fishing had made him too solitary. He mentioned, at the bottom of the last page of a long letter, that the Irish rebels had recently taken to stealing mail bags, and assumed her silence meant that either his last letter or hers had been in one of those stolen. He had missed hearing from her, he said.

It was several days before she could bring herself to reply, and when she did she could think of nothing to say. She was reluctant to resume the correspondence, but it seemed rude to leave his letter unanswered when he had been so kind to both Gabriel and Frances. She was reluctant to correspond with someone of Gabriel's age – and unmarried, Gabriel said. Her present life suited her. She had settled down, was reasonably content. She did not want to get emotionally involved ever again.

The problem of money remained.

"I hadn't realised how lucky we've been to have the Mackenzies behind us," Julia said to Gwen. "Not that we've needed their help, thank goodness, but we knew they were there. Now heaven knows what expense they're likely to have with Gabriel. If only we had a better idea about Oxford ... Frances has always been so insistent that Sarah shouldn't have to pinch and save." Frances's insistence had been the only indication Julia had had of the privations Frances herself had endured in London.

"Frances has always worried about Sarah," Gwen said. "I've never thought Sarah needed much worrying over, myself." She added, slowly as if reluctant to suggest the possibility, "Perhaps we should get rid of Waite?"

It was Gwen who had taken Waite on in the first place. She needed full-time help in the garden, she had told her sisters the previous Christmas. Her involvement with book illustration, originating from her work for Gabriel's children's translation of the *Iliad*, meant that she needed more time than the garden allowed her. Waite, an ex-serviceman still suffering from the effects of the war, had turned up on the doorstep shortly afterwards and been taken on without even a reference, being regarded, by Gwen at least, as the answer to a prayer.

"We couldn't dismiss him now," Julia said. "His nerves are so much better than they were, for one thing. And, anyway, it wouldn't be right."

"I can't think of any other way of saving money," Gwen said. "Except ... Frances did always say she'd go out and teach if need be."

"She didn't mean it ... Did she?"

Nothing brought her own inadequacy home to Julia more than discussions about money. Gwen, who made Hillcrest self-sufficient as regards fruit and vegetables, certainly earned her keep. So did Frances with her painting. An Oxford degree meant that Sarah would be able to earn a respectable living in time. Only Julia made no contribution to the family coffers, nor was likely to. If only she had gone to the Slade, she thought now, or taken up a Red Cross scholarship at the end of the war – but she had not.

When she saw an advertisement in the local newspaper for a part-time art teacher at a school only one station down the line from Dunkery St. Michael, she knew it must be meant. Standards for a part-time teacher would surely be lower than for one full-time. She applied – and was summoned for interview by return. She sat in the train from Dunkery, clutching Lucy's best leather handbag and gloves, and wondered at her temerity. How could she expect to bluff her way into a position with no qualifications whatsoever?

Five minutes with the headmistress made it clear that it was availability that mattered rather than qualifications. The previous art mistress had eloped with the science master at the end of the summer term: Miss Bruce was desperate to find a replacement before the start of the school year. Even so she regretted that Julia was not what was required. "I need someone older, Miss Purcell, someone responsible ..."

"I'm well used to responsibility," Julia said, annoyed that the headmistress should doubt it. "My mother died when I was fifteen. I had younger sisters ... and I was frequently left in charge of up to thirty badly wounded men during the war."

"Yes, yes," Miss Bruce said, flustered, "but you must realise how *bad* an elopement looks. I have my *parents* to consider. We have a very *nice* type of girl here. I'm not saying that you ... but I'm sure you'll understand when I say that I had hoped for a ... a widow. Someone elderly. Not *unattractive* exactly, but unlikely to be attracted by, well, to be frank ... a man."

"I lost my fiancé in the war," Julia said. "I think it unlikely that I should be attracted, as you put it."

Miss Bruce's face cleared wonderfully, as if this were the only good news she had heard that day. "If that is so, then of course – not that I'm not sorry about your fiancé, Miss Purcell, of course I am – but from my point of view ..."

"I've got the job," Julia said, on her return to Hillcrest. She felt little elation. "Two days a week. I thought the headmistress was dreadful but I don't suppose I shall have much to do with her, and the art studio's surprisingly well equipped."

"I do wish you wouldn't do it," Sarah said. "I don't mind being short of money, really I don't, so long as I can buy all the books I need. Frances did say we could manage."

"That was before Gabriel was hurt. I'm sure we still can, but I'm not prepared to risk it. Don't worry. It's only two days a week, and I can always hand in my notice at the end of the year if I hate it."

"I don't think Frances will be very pleased," Sarah said.

"Neither do I," Julia admitted, "and because of that you're not going to tell her. Is that understood? Promise?"

Sarah promised, but reluctantly, before cheering up. "It'll be nice for the school, anyway. I'd much rather have you teaching me than Frances."

"You'd be foolish then," Julia said. "She's a better teacher than I could ever be."

They dared not look far into the future. Sister said Gabriel could not be discharged until his wounds had healed. They hoped for his return in time for Christmas, but it was still September when David Elliot wrote to Julia suggesting that Gabriel might return sooner if she were willing to provide the care he needed. Fishing weekends had been stopped by rebel activity in the countryside, Elliot said, and the situation in Dublin itself was deteriorating rapidly. As a result Gabriel was restricted to movement around the hospital and in the Merediths' flat, when he should be exercising further afield if he were to continue to make progress. And in case Julia had doubts, Elliot assured her that Sister considered what was needed to be well within the capability of any V.A.D. with wartime experience in France.

None of them knew how Gabriel would manage the journey. Mackenzies and Purcells alike shivered on Dunkery station as they waited for the train, with apprehension rather than cold. It was a perfect October day, the air clear and crisp, a day to spend ranging over the Quantocks. Julia could not banish that thought.

Mrs. Mackenzie looked thin and frail as she leant on Mr. Mackenzie's arm. She had only recently been allowed out by Dr. Milne. Would Gabriel be shocked by the sight of his parents when he saw them again, looking so much older than they had a year ago, Julia wondered; and how would Gabriel himself look?

Mrs. Mackenzie beckoned to Julia. "If you could stand by the carriage door, my dear, when the train arrives," she said. "You'll know best what help he will need." Her lip trembled. Julia remembered how Mrs. Mackenzie had kept Gabriel in the family circle on his return after the war, banishing the Purcells for that first evening home. We shouldn't be here, she thought guiltily. If she could get hold of Sarah and Gwen and go out to the station yard to allow the Mackenzies the first few minutes alone together ... Too late. The signal had already clanked down. Sarah gave a little cry. "Here it comes ... I can see them!"

Frances was at the window, Gabriel at the door. Jimmy Hancock, the Dunkery porter, stepped forward. "Welcome home, sorr."

"Well, well," Gabriel said. "What a reception." He shook his head imperceptibly at Julia as she stood on the edge of the platform. Slowly and laboriously he negotiated the step, while they watched, holding their breath. Once safely down he gave a smile both triumphant and relieved, tucked his crutches under one arm and held his hand out to Frances. "Let me introduce my wife," he said.

Anyone would have thought, Gabriel said, when he was settled in his mother's upright armchair in the Rectory drawing-room, that he had come home in his coffin and not on his feet. "It's worse than an Irish wake, all this weeping. First, you lot, and then, when we've got that over, the servants ..."

There was so much to tell, so much everyone wanted to know, that it was difficult to know where to start. When? Where?

"A week ago. In the hospital chapel."

"I don't know how you could. To get married, without a word to any of us ..."

"We wanted to see the surprise on your faces," Gabriel said. "It was worth it, I can assure you. I suppose we ought to have waited, but it seemed right, somehow, after all those months in hospital to get married there. Everyone who had ever had anything to do with us came ... I don't know what it is about females, one really needs a life-jacket when they're around. Hugh managed to remain dry-eyed, which was just as well as he was best man. David Elliot gave Frances away. Sister baked the cake. It was a very family sort of wedding, wasn't it, darling, even if it wasn't our own family."

"And then ...? What happened then? Did Frances ...?"

"We stayed in the Merediths' flat. Hugh moved out into the Castle – Mary had come back here to have the baby –"

"Hector, they're calling him," Frances interrupted. "Can you imagine it? Fancy christening a child Hector. It's the sort of name you'd expect Gabriel to choose."

"– so we had the flat to ourselves," Gabriel finished. "Which was a relief, I can tell you, after I'd been living in a goldfish bowl for so many weeks. Sister came in every day, that was all, to make sure Frances was treating me properly."

His stamina, alas, did not match up to his high spirits; the walk from the Rectory to Hillcrest later that afternoon left him so exhausted that he made little protest when Julia suggested he should go to bed once dinner was over. She went up with him, offering help on the stairs which he refused. "They say I should go on improving for a while yet, but only if I work at it."

Despite Sister's warnings, Julia was shocked by the extent of his injuries. "I'm glad I didn't have to do this six months ago," she said. "I'm amazed you survived."

"There were times," Gabriel said, drily, "when I wished I hadn't." He sat up gingerly when she had finished, and reached for his pyjama jacket. "It's only thanks to David Elliot that I'm here." He watched her as he did up the buttons, his smile mocking. "Are you two still writing?"

She busied herself with clearing away. "Sometimes."

"You'll like him, you know. You're very similar in many ways."

"I wouldn't have thought so. Are you all right? Can you get to bed on your own?"

"Yes, of course. Everything takes ten times as long as it used to, that's all. I said we'd invite him to stay – David, I mean. He should be back in England soon. He's hoping to get a hospital appointment in London but it depends on whether the Army'll let him go. They made him stay on after the war to help with rehabilitation ..."

"Is that where he comes from – London? He's never mentioned his family."

"He hasn't one. There were two sisters, apparently, but something happened to them during the war. I'm not sure what."

"Nobody else?"

"Not as far as I know."

She was silent, trying to imagine what it must be like to have no one. No sisters. No Mackenzies. No one who cared.

Frances was waiting in Julia's room. "Is everything all right? Do you mind doing it? It seems an awful lot to ask, only Gabriel was getting desperate in that hospital. He kept saying it was time he stopped being an invalid and got on with his life."

They talked quietly in the dusk, not of what had happened but only of the two families. There was a sense of contentment about Frances that Julia had not seen before.

"How do you think the Mackenzies really feel about Gabriel and me?"

"If Gabriel's happy, they'll be happy. You know that."

"I suppose so. You don't think Mr. Mackenzie was hurt, not being asked to marry us?"

"I'm certain he felt you'd done the right thing."

"It was Gabriel who insisted ... though I was relieved, I must admit, when I thought about it afterwards. Imagine having to face everyone if we'd got married here – all the village gossips gathered round the church door."

"You'll have to face them some time. Tomorrow, presumably, at morning service?"

Frances nodded. "Mr. Mackenzie's said he'd say something – pray for us, no doubt. I don't know that I shall have the courage to go. Gabriel's determined to be there – he wants to see the old ducks' faces. 'Throwing himself away on that extraordinary Purcell girl ... ' – I can hear them now." She gave Julia a rueful smile. "I must get back to him.

[186]

I just wanted to talk for a bit, and, well, thank you for everything."

Julia watched her slide off the bed, search for her shoes and put them on. She knew that it was no business of hers but suddenly she needed the truth. "Did you really want to marry him, Frances? You didn't do it because you were sorry for him?"

"Oh, Julia. You always think people are nicer than they are. I married him because I couldn't carry on without him. It was as simple as that." She stopped at the door. "You've got things the wrong way round. I think that was why Gabriel married me. He was sorry for me."

Julia had always intended to tell Frances about her teaching while Frances was in Dublin, but for some reason had never done so. Now it was forced on her without warning when Frances suggested a joint expedition into Taunton.

"Not tomorrow," Julia said. "I work on Thursdays."

"You work?"

"Teach. Two days a week. At St. Hilda's." Why did she have to sound so defensive? "You know – the girls' school."

Frances gaped. "*Teach*?"

"I meant to tell you but I – I didn't get round to it somehow. It seemed sensible ... teaching."

"Why?"

"Oh, you know, Sarah going to Oxford, your being away, not knowing ... Insurance, really. Money in the bank. That sort of thing."

"I'm ... speechless," Frances said. "I don't know what to say. Why didn't you *ask* me?"

Julia felt anger rising. She was painfully aware of Sarah's anguished expression on the other side of the room. "Ask you," she said. "What for? Permission? I'm twenty-five, for goodness sake. Can't I decide what to do with my own life?"

Frances had gone white. "Not permission, no, of course

[187]

not. Ask me what I thought – that's what I meant. I'd never have agreed. You don't like it, that's obvious, and when I think of all you've gone through, well, I'd rather you didn't do it, that's all."

Julia stood up. "That's all I need ... your pity."

She was shaking by the time she reached her room. What was it about Frances that made her so angry – sitting there, deciding what her sisters should or should not do, laying down the law as if they were children still, their mother only recently dead.

She breakfasted early on teaching days. Only Annie and Lily were up when she left the next morning and on her return from St. Hilda's she found Gabriel alone on the verandah, stretched out on the chaise-longue with a rug over his legs, a book lying open on his stomach and his eyes closed. "If you give Annie a shout," he said, without moving, "she promised to make tea the moment you came home. I'm parched."

Julia came back from the kitchen to sit on the flagstones beside the chaise-longue. She picked up his book, read the title and made a face. "Where is everyone?"

He opened his eyes. "At the Rectory."

She glanced across the verandah. Two places had been laid on the table for tea. "So ..." she said. "We're being Uncle Gabriel today, are we?"

"It's one of my many talents, being avuncular," he said. "I'm surprised you hadn't realised that by now. Come on, Julia. Don't be angry with Frances. She doesn't mean half she says – you should know that. She's upset about your working. So am I. We both feel you've done enough. I suspect you knew exactly what our reaction would be or you'd have written and told us about it long ago. Which would have been the sensible thing to do, I might add. Frances couldn't have done anything to stop you from Dublin, and she'd have grown used to the idea by the time she came home. Then we wouldn't have had that little to-do we had last night."

"So it's my fault, is it? I always do everything wrong. Leave us alone, Gabriel. This has nothing to do with you."

"But it has. Did it not occur to you that in marrying Frances I took on her responsibilities as well? Sarah included. I presume it's Sarah and Oxford that has pushed you into this?"

She stared. "I don't see why you should take on our responsibilities."

"It is customary."

"We wouldn't expect it."

"No," he said. "You wouldn't. You're all as obstinate as each other. Family pride . . ." He stopped as Lily came out with the teapot and water jug, and waited until she had returned to the house. "I wish you'd hand in your notice," he said gently. "I'm sure we can manage between us."

She shook her head. "I must stay for a year." But she was touched by his concern, the more so when his own future was so uncertain.

He watched her pour out the tea. "You don't like teaching, do you? It was written all over your face last night. That was what upset Frances. She wouldn't mind if she thought you enjoyed it. What's wrong?"

She was silent for a moment, trying to sort things out in her own mind. "I think I feel I'm a cheat. I shouldn't be there. I haven't any qualifications . . . I'm not much good as a painter . . . and I'm a rotten teacher. I think that's the worst part. I can't even keep order."

She had said nothing at Hillcrest about her days at St. Hilda's. They had to be endured for Sarah's sake; there was no point in discussing them. But Gabriel had also taught. She found now, as she had found in the past, that shared experiences gave both sympathy and understanding.

Frances gave Gabriel a quick glance when she returned with the others, as if seeking reassurance. Then she came over and sat down beside Julia. "My paintings arrived from

[189]

Dublin this morning," she said. "Will you come up to the stables in the morning, and tell me what you think?"

Julia had awaited the arrival of Frances's paintings with curiosity. She sensed that Frances was not dissatisfied with the summer's work, though she said little. Gabriel had been non-committal when asked for his opinion. "Wait and see," he told Julia. "I'll be interested to know what you think."

"I don't know what Denis will do about an exhibition," Frances said, as she took Julia up to the stables. She was sure that he would hate all she had done. He had told her the previous year that people wanted to forget the war; these paintings would only remind them. She did not sound unduly concerned – "If I'm stuck in a military hospital, there's not much else I can paint, is there?" – and was more worried about facing him as a married woman. "It wasn't exactly an enthusiastic letter he wrote when I told him I'd done it."

"He was expecting it," Julia said. She looked at the stairs up to the studio with new eyes. "How does Gabriel manage with these?"

"I don't know," Frances said, "but he does. It's amazing what he can do when he's determined." She unlocked the studio door and let Julia in. "You don't have to say anything if you don't want to," she said.

The canvases were already round the wall, on the easel and propped up along the length of the bed – a surprisingly large number, considering Frances's lack of paints during her first days in Ireland and her pre-occupation with Gabriel all the time. Julia went in, glanced round – and stopped. Frances saw her face. She looked stricken herself. "Oh, Julia, I'm sorry. I should have thought. Would you rather not? You don't have to if you don't want."

Julia took a deep breath. "It's all right. Of course I want. It just ... brought things back, that's all."

"I'll leave you," Frances said. "Then you can do what you like. Stay. Go. Or just sit. We can talk later."

She shut the door quietly behind her. Her footsteps sounded down the stairs and on the hard earth floor of the barn. A hen squawked and flapped as she passed under the window. Julia was alone.

There was something different about Frances's work, something indefinable. Or was it the familiarity of the hospital setting that made it seem so? There were other scenes besides the hospital scenes – a small garden painted through the changing months of summer, landscapes, presumably from the weekends away, several interiors, and a portrait of Mary Meredith, arms resting on the curve of her unborn child as she gazed unseeing into the distance. It was a portrait of the archetypal mother, dreaming of her child and its future, painted with vision, tenderness and love.

She found herself returning to one particular canvas, a painting – not large – of an unremarkable, hospital room. The single bed had been stripped of its bedclothes. A meagre pile of possessions – clothes, some letters, a wallet – rested on the mattress. The room was like none that she had ever worked in, and yet it seemed to her that in this small area of canvas Frances had distilled and put down in paint all the emotions she herself had experienced while working in France but never been able to express.

She remembered how long ago, before the war, Gabriel had referred to Frances's talent as genius. She had taken for granted then that his feelings for Frances had influenced his judgment. Now she wondered whether his love had not given him deeper insight than those with greater knowledge. For the first time she saw Frances's art as something quite apart from Frances herself and beyond Frances's control. The acceptance of that knowledge released something in herself. It liberated her from the burden of comparison. It set her free.

Chapter Thirteen

Julia closed her eyes briefly as she sat back in the train. She could never understand why a day's teaching, surely so much easier than a day's nursing, should so exhaust her. If only, she sometimes thought, she could feel that she had inspired even one child . . .

She glimpsed the car in the yard as the train came under the bridge into Dunkery station and was curious. When she came through the gate it was still there. Its driver came forward to meet her. She recognised him at once.

"We haven't met," he said, holding out his hand. "I'm David Elliot. Hello."

She had known that sometime they would meet, but his arrival was so unexpected that she could think of nothing to say. "I'm Julia Purcell," she said at last.

"I know. I couldn't mistake you. You're very like Frances. Besides, Gabriel gave me the drawing you did of you and your sister."

"What are you doing here?"

He smiled. "Meeting you. Gwen suggested it and I thought it was a good idea to meet each other away from the others."

"I didn't know you were coming to England."

"I didn't say anything because I wasn't sure of my plans. Leave can be uncertain in Ireland. And then when I was coming down this way it seemed a pity not to call in to check up on Gabriel and see how you were coping with nursing duties once more."

"Gabriel isn't here. He and Frances have gone over to the Merediths for Hector's christening. They don't expect to be home till late."

"So your sister said. If I'd known I'd have come down a day earlier. I could have driven them myself and saved them the expense."

She was conscious of Jimmy Hancock's face pressed against the glass of the booking-office window. "I think we'd better go. People will talk if we stand here much longer."

She watched him surreptitiously as he drove back to Huish Priory. She knew the face from Frances's drawings, but not the man behind it, despite the letters that had passed between them. He was taller than she had expected, and older; more serious than Frances had shown him in her portrait. He had looked at ease then, but not so now. The realisation that he was as nervous as she both surprised Julia and calmed her.

"Will you be able to stay overnight?" she said. "We could put you up. Frances and Gabriel would hate to miss you."

"Thank you, but I'm already installed in Gabriel's room at the Rectory. Mrs. Mackenzie insisted. She wants me to see Gabriel – professionally, I mean. How do you think he is? Has he found it hard to adjust?"

She considered. "I'm not sure. He's always been light-hearted about things that matter – *particularly* about things that matter – so it's difficult to tell. Sometimes I think it's worse for us, having to watch him take half an hour and more to get from Hillcrest to the Rectory when he'd have done it in a couple of minutes in the old days. He's surprisingly cheerful, really, just a lot quieter than he used to be. Has he told you he's writing a book?"

"What sort of book?"

"A thriller. Based on classical mythology." She smiled at the raised eyebrows. "I know. He said all the thrillers he'd read in hospital were so awful he was sure he could do better, so he's set out to prove it – only, being Gabriel, he has to be different."

Gwen had tea ready for them when they arrived at Hill-crest and a message from Mrs. Mackenzie to say that dinner would be at the Rectory. "It's given her a tremendous fillip, David arriving like this," Gwen told Julia when they were alone. "She says she's so thankful she can show him how grateful she is. She's taken charge completely. Lucy's not being allowed to do a thing."

Mrs. Mackenzie certainly took charge of the conversation at dinner that evening, subjecting David to a positive interrogation. She discovered over the soup that he had been born in India of medical missionaries, remaining there until sent back to England at the age of six with his sister to be educated. During the fish course she found out about Helen, the half-sister who had brought the two of them up and by the time the meat was on the table knew the name of his school, college and medical school. Lucy rolled her eyes at Julia. "Really, Mother. Do give the poor man a chance to eat."

Mrs. Mackenzie paid no attention. "Tell me about your parents, Major Elliot. Are they still in India?"

"They died when I was eight. Cholera, I think, though I'm not that sure I was ever told." Sensing their shock he said, almost apologetically, "Small boys can be pretty callous; I don't remember being particularly upset. I hadn't seen them for two years, remember, and Helen continued to bring us up. Our life didn't change."

Sounds of activity in the hall heralded the arrival of the travellers. Frances burst in, followed more slowly by Gabriel.

"*David*! What a wonderful surprise! I couldn't believe it when Annie said ..."

In the excitement of welcoming them back, sorting out what they would eat, and then hearing details of the Meredith christening, David's private life was forgotten. In the drawing-room later Lucy came over to where Gabriel was sitting with Julia. "Mother's impossible. Wouldn't you have thought she could have waited before checking his credentials?"

It was almost like old times. With eyes closed Julia could imagine herself back to the days before the war. Talk, laughter, Lucy playing ... she opened her eyes and saw David at the piano, turning over the pages of music for Lucy, but his gaze was on the photograph of Geoffrey before him.

"I don't know why I should be playing when you're so much better than me," Lucy said. "Gabriel says you're a wonderful pianist. Have a look through the music and see if there's anything you'd like to play."

He picked out a fat volume. "Beethoven's seventh symphony, adapted for four hands. I didn't know you could get such a thing. Shall we try it?"

"I knew he'd fit in," Gabriel said to Julia. He looked complacent. Exhausted too, by the trip to the Merediths, but he had refused her earlier offer to take him back to Hillcrest. "Don't be ridiculous. I'm not a child," he had said. "Just look at Mother," he said now. "I haven't seen her so lively for years. We'll have to invite him again."

The Beethoven came to a sudden and discordant end. "Sorry," Lucy said. "My fault. I'm afraid I'm not up to your standard. Accompanying the church choir is more my line."

"I enjoyed it," David said. "We must try again when there's no one around."

"Gabriel wrote of concerts in Sister's flat," Mr. Mackenzie said. "Won't you give us one here?"

David took Lucy's place at the piano, refused the offer of music, and sat silent for a moment before raising his hands to the keys. Julia watched his face as he played, still, absorbed. His eyes were half closed; he was in a world of his own. He was different from anyone she had known, she thought, so quiet, so reserved, more serious than the letters had led her to expect. He would be difficult to get to know well. She thought the effort required would be worthwhile.

There was no sign of David at Hillcrest next morning. "He'll have been cornered by Mother," Gabriel said. "She'll want to know his opinion on the situation in India, quite forgetting that he hasn't set foot on the continent for thirty years. Or perhaps she's impressing on him the wonderful service he's performed for mankind by saving my life."

"Well, I'm sorry, but I can't wait any longer," Julia said. "It's our week for doing the church flowers."

The sound of the organ reached out across the churchyard, cascades of notes seeming to burst through the walls of the building. David turned his head as she went in. "Hello," he said. "Lucy said you'd be coming." He played the piece to its end, while Julia sat in a pew and listened. "Wonderful," he said, finishing with an impressive series of chords. "I can't remember when I was last let loose on a church organ." He came down from the chancel and sat beside her. "I'm glad you've come," he said. "I wanted to apologise for last night. I'm afraid I monopolised the conversation rather. Though it was difficult not to, with Mrs. Mackenzie asking so many questions."

"Don't worry. We were interested. You've never told me anything about your sisters, you know, beyond saying that one of them nursed. What happened to them? Gabriel said something about the war . . ."

"Helen – my half-sister – was killed in a Zeppelin raid. And then Rowena died at Wimereux in 1918. She caught some fever or other while she was nursing – you'll know the sort of thing. I was sent for, but it was too late."

"I'm sorry," she said. "Were you and she close?"

He nodded. "Helen was years older than us, so, yes, we were. There was only a year between us and we'd had to cope with so much together, from the time we'd come back from India. And we had a common interest in medicine. She used to help me chop up frogs on the washstand when we were small. She wasn't beyond chopping up the odd one or two herself, as a matter of fact."

Julia was intrigued by the picture conjured up. "Didn't Helen mind? I can just imagine what Annie would have said if we'd started chopping things up."

"Helen was determined I should finish up in Harley Street. I think she felt that blood over the washstand was a small price to pay."

"You don't mind my asking about your sisters, do you? There seems to be so much I don't know about you, in spite of your letters."

"I'd have told you before if I'd known you were interested. One doesn't want to seem to be looking for sympathy, that's all."

She felt at ease with him this morning as she had not the previous day. Perhaps the shared confidences helped. He filled the enamel jug for her from the tap outside the church and then sat back in a pew, watching her arrange the flowers while he talked of his plans for the future – "Hopes, rather. I'm afraid there's nothing so definite as plans." A doctor with whom he had worked in France was starting a surgical unit in London and thought there might be an opening. "At St. Luke's – you've probably heard of it. It's a teaching hospital, so I'd have a chance to do some research. It would be marvellous experience, but I daren't hope too much at this stage."

"What about Harley Street?"

"That's in the future," he said. "I shall get there in the end. I must. I owe it to Helen."

He admired the finished arrangements – "I wouldn't know where to start" – helped her clear up the debris and walked back with her to Hillcrest. He stopped at the gate. "Could we have some time on our own while I'm here, just the two of us? Go somewhere, perhaps. I've always envied people in large families, but I begin to see that life can be overcrowded."

She felt momentary panic. "I think Frances and Gabriel expect you to spend time with them."

He gave her a quizzical look. "Not every minute. They're more worldly than that. They know we've been writing."

She remembered Gabriel's complacent expression the previous evening. "Well, all right, if you want. Yes. Why not?"

She took him up on the Quantocks. The ground was sodden and heavy underfoot. Mist hovered over the dead bracken and cloud hid the surrounding hills. She was sad that it should be November and the hills not at their best for his first visit; it mattered to her that he should appreciate them. He admitted to preferring the challenge of trout streams to the pleasures of long-distance walking, but he followed where she led happily enough, and they reconnoitred possible places to bring Gabriel in the spring, where accessible slopes were within reach of a car. "I've never heard him complain," Julia said, "but he loves the Quantocks so much that he must miss them dreadfully. I see him sometimes in the churchyard, looking across ..."

David left Huish Priory after nearly a week's stay at the Rectory, on one of Julia's days at St. Hilda's. She refused his offer to drive her to the school, terrified that Miss Bruce might see them together, but let him take her into Dunkery station on his way back to London.

They said goodbye in the station yard. She wondered what she would do if he kissed her. "Thank you for the lift," she said. "It's been nice meeting you." How ridiculously formal she sounded. "I hope things work out in London."

"You sound as if we're saying farewell," he said. "We're stilll going to write to each other, aren't we?"

"Is that what you want?"

"Of course. I shall be back in Ireland on Monday. Write to me there." He leant forward and kissed her on the cheek.

Jimmy Hancock winked as she went through the gate onto the platform. "It's a grand morning, Miss."

She looked out on the Quantocks as the train rattled along

the line to St. Hilda's. She hadn't wanted David to kiss her. How illogical then to be disappointed by the peck she had received. She did not know what she wanted. She liked and admired him. Watching him deal with Gabriel professionally she had been impressed. But ... I'm getting too old for emotion, she told herself. I'm content as I am. I'd rather things stayed as they are. It's easier that way.

There was another obstacle to further involvement. She would have to tell him about Geoffrey.

David returned to England the following February, spending his last days in uniform at the army hospital in Woolwich before joining the surgical unit at St. Luke's as assistant surgeon. His free time at Woolwich was never long enough to let him escape to Somerset; he suggested Julia should come to London instead. She hesitated. Eventually, and against her better judgment, she went.

Her fears were groundless. When she left Somerset she had been relieved that her teaching at St. Hilda's set a limit to her visit; by the time she had to return she would have stayed longer had she been able.

He had planned her visit with care, introducing her to music – "nothing too highbrow to start with. We'll break you in gradually," – by taking her to *The Beggar's Opera* at the Lyric, and an afternoon concert at the Queen's Hall – Berlioz, Delius and Beethoven's Emperor piano concerto. "It's a pity we couldn't get to a piano beforehand," he said. "You'd enjoy it more if you had some idea what the composer was trying to do."

They did some sightseeing – "We only went to art galleries when I came up to London before the war," she confessed – took the boat to Greenwich, and spent several hours at the Tower of London because she wanted to see if it was as impressive as she had remembered from her childhood. One morning David drove her to Richmond to visit Miranda Ford and see her god-daughter for the first time. Miranda was impressed. "Wouldn't it be wonderful if you and David ...? I do so hope ..."

Julia would not hope, nor look into the future. She was content with the present, enjoying her time with David, but enjoying herself too when he was working, wandering round galleries and museums on her own.

She stayed with the Bonds, and was both surprised and disappointed by Denis's antipathy to David when the latter came round to dinner. David's ignorance about everything to do with art so shocked Denis that he could find little else to discuss. "Clever chap," he observed, after David's departure, "but he's not going to do much to encourage *your* work, is he?"

Denis's reaction was one disappointment of her stay. The other concerned David himself. She persuaded him to take her to a tea dance the afternoon they came back from Greenwich, sensing his disinclination but not understanding it until she was on the floor. Then, with his arms around her and the orchestra sweeping into the tumbling notes of *Charmaine*, she discovered that he was barely able to dance. She felt extraordinarily deflated, far more than the occasion warranted. "There was never time to learn," David explained apologetically. "Helen always thought dancing a bit frippery anyway."

On the last day of her visit David took Julia down to Kent to meet Margaret Wood, the ward sister who had so terrified Frances during her first weeks in Ireland, now back in England on leave. "I promised her I'd introduce you," he said. "She's been wanting to meet you for a long time. I hope you like her. She means a lot to me." They had known each other before their time in Ireland, having worked together in France where Margaret had been his theatre sister. "She helped me enormously after Rowena died. We'd both been wounded in an attack on our clearing station during the Retreat – not serious, but what with that and the business with Rowena, and Helen before that, I was in quite a bad way. She arranged for me to come and stay with her brother and family for a couple of weeks on their farm before I went back to France. They were desperately short of help, so I lent a hand with the harvest. Just what I needed, as it turned out. Hard physical labour doesn't give one time to brood."

Margaret was staying at a cottage on her brother's farm, which she used when on leave. She welcomed Julia warmly, exclaiming over her likeness to Frances. No one could have been less like the dragon Frances had described in her early letters – though it was true that Frances had come to appreciate her later. Margaret herself wanted to know all about Frances now, how Gabriel was coping and Julia too. "I hope you didn't mind our asking you to help, but quite apart from the political situation Gabriel needed to get away from the hospital. It was the only way he could become independent."

"He's become almost too independent. He's talking of Cambridge already. Both Frances and I think it's ridiculous so soon."

"He can't go until I've given approval," David said. He was lying back in his chair, legs stretched out to the fire. He seemed very much at home, both with Margaret and the cottage. He knew where things were kept, when lunch came got out the glasses, saw to the wine and carved the beef. Julia wondered whether Margaret had replaced Helen in his life, and said as much when helping her clear away after the meal. Margaret gave her a sharp look. "I trust not," she said. "A very dominant female, Helen, I've always thought."

Julia was amused, knowing Frances's opinion of Margaret herself. "It's very strange talking to you," she said. "You must know so much about us all but I've no idea what. What did Frances tell you?"

"Very little. She was too scared to open her mouth, at least in the early days. I learnt most from Gabriel. It seemed to help him to talk when he was coming to terms with his situation and it was easier, I suppose, to do so to me rather than to Frances. I wasn't involved, as she was. David told me a certain amount, too, though he's not one for confidences." She patted Julia's shoulder. "You've been good for David, my dear. I thought the war had swallowed up his ambition. There was a time when I was afraid he'd bury himself in the Medical Corps for the rest of his days. It would have been a terrible waste of his talent. It's thanks to you he's got going again. I'm very happy about St. Luke's."

Julia felt she was getting credit where none was due. David's position at St. Luke's had nothing to do with her.

Margaret smiled. "I wouldn't be so sure."

It was a happy day. Julia felt welcomed, comfortable and at ease. She listened to David and Margaret discussing past cases, and joined in reminiscences of medical life in France. She felt the same companionship that she had experienced then and had never thought to enjoy again, and was sorry when David declined Margaret's invitation to stay on for supper. "There's something I want to show Julia on the way back," he said. "We can't see it in the dark."

Margaret came out into the road to wave them goodbye. "I'm so glad to have met you at last," she told Julia. "I'm sure we'll be seeing more of each other in the future."

David waited until they had rounded the bend down the hill. "That went off even better than I had hoped," he said.

Julia had an uneasy feeling that approval had been sought, and given.

He turned off the London road on reaching the outer suburbs and drove slowly, looking from left to right as if uncertain of the route. He parked near a mainline station by a railway embankment and switched off the engine. She waited. "You'll think me very stupid, no doubt," he said, "but I want to show you something that meant a lot to me when I was a boy."

They left the car and walked along the pavement under the railway arch. Pleasant stone-built houses set in large gardens stood back from the road beyond the bridge. He stopped at the first. "That's it," he said.

She was puzzled. "What is?"

"What I wanted to show you. That house. It fascinated me for years – all my schooldays, in fact. I still dream about it. I used to pass it every term in the train going to and from school. I can still remember how excited I got as the train drew near, wondering what would be happening this time, what everyone would be doing. I used to pray that the signal would be up so that we would have to stop on the bridge. There was always so much going on, you see, and so many children about. We were very quiet at home. Helen didn't like having people in. All my friends were at school. I had none in the holidays."

They walked along the pavement by the hedge. The laurel was untrimmed, the garden unkempt. No light showed in any window, although the afternoon was drawing to a close.

"There were always so many boys around. Playing cricket or football, or climbing trees. Even pinching raspberries one summer. I've often wondered what happened to them all. Dead, I suppose, most of them."

"Perhaps they moved away," she said. "They'll have grown up. Had families of their own."

"Maybe." He sounded as if he thought it unlikely. "I bicycled over here from home one summer. I planned it all very carefully. When I got to the end of the road – up there, by that tree – I jabbed my back tyre with a nail I'd brought specially. It was quite flat by the time I'd reached here, of course. I knew it would be. I knocked on the door, said I'd got a puncture and could I have some water to mend it. They invited me in and called a couple of older boys in from the garden to help. The mother hovered over us all the time and when it was done said they'd be having tea in half an hour and why didn't I stay, so I was taken out into the garden to play cricket and be introduced to all the rest. I was in such a daze I didn't take in a single name. After a while a maid brought out the tea and we all sat around ... It was like being in Paradise."

He did not take his eyes off the garden. She was sure he could see the scene still.

"Were they all one family?"

"Cousins, as far as I could make out, and friends up the road."

"Did you go back often?"

"Never. No one suggested it. And when I got home that evening I realised what a fool I'd been. I couldn't go near them ever again. They'd recognise me if they saw me hanging about and wonder what I was doing. So, just as I'd got entrée of a sort, I'd lost it. This is the first time I've been back. I've never told anyone about it, either, except you."

Mist curled up from the ground. An elderly maid appeared at the window of the room overlooking the drive and tugged the curtains together. A train rattled to a halt on the bridge. People stood up in the lighted carriages and began to move towards the doors. A child pressed its face against the window, staring down at the garden. The train gave a mournful whistle and edged towards the station.

"A knell for my childhood," David said.

She watched him as he stood on the pavement, gazing at the old, neglected house, and saw in him the lonely school-boy he had once been, searching for family and home.

Chapter Fourteen

"*Well?*" Frances said, alone with Julia for the first time after Julia's return.

"Well?"

"Didn't anything happen?"

"What did you expect to happen?"

Frances looked confused. "I thought ... I'm sorry. I know it's none of my business."

It might be none of her business, but Julia, lying awake that night, knew that she needed advice and that Frances was the one to give it.

"Are you busy?" she asked Frances at breakfast next morning. "Could we chat some time?"

"Come up to the stables," Frances said instantly.

She had coffee ready when Julia arrived and a tin of Annie's biscuits. They discussed Frances's work for a while and Denis's plans for her forthcoming exhibition. "What about you and St. Hilda's?" Frances said. "I know you're used to it now but you still don't like it much, do you? We've managed all right without using your money. Why don't you hand in your notice? You'll have done a full year by the time you leave in the summer – that must be enough."

"Miss Bruce will expect me to stay longer than that."

"Oh, Julia," Frances said, exasperated. "Don't be so ... so scrupulous. Besides, what about David?"

"What about David?"

Frances hesitated. "Hasn't he mentioned marriage?"

"No."

Frances's face was almost ludicrous in its disappointment.

"But he's going to, isn't he?"

" I don't know," Julia said, well knowing that David would have proposed during their last evening together had she given him the slightest encouragement. She looked directly at Frances. "You'd like him to, wouldn't you?"

Frances hedged. "It's nothing to do with me. You never said what you felt about Gabriel and me, and I'm sure you would have liked to, lots of times, so I wouldn't presume to try and influence you. You and David seem so well suited, that's all." She added, "It would be nice for Gabriel and me if you did."

"It isn't as simple as you think," Julia said. "That's what I wanted to talk to you about. I don't know what to do. It all goes back to the war, and Geoffrey and me."

"David knows about Geoffrey," Frances said. "I told him. He used to take me out to lunch in Dublin and ask questions about us and Hillcrest and the Mackenzies. I think he was envious, not having any family himself. I told him about Geoffrey then."

"Not everything about Geoffrey," Julia said.

"What do you mean?" She stared at Julia. Realisation came slowly, followed by incredulity. "You and Geoffrey ...?"

"Yes."

"You *can't* mean ...?"

"I do."

"I don't believe it. *Geoffrey*, of all people."

"For goodness' sake, Frances. Why not Geoffrey?"

"I'm sorry, I'm sorry. Just surprised, that's all."

Julia bit back her irritation at Frances's misunderstanding of Geoffrey. "The thing is, what do I tell David?"

"Nothing," Frances said instantly. "It's in the past. It has nothing to do with him. You don't have to tell him anything."

"No," Julia agreed. "I suppose you're right. It would be stupid. And unnecessary."

What was stupid, she thought afterwards, was asking Frances in the first place, if she had no intention of taking her advice. For a while she considered it, knowing that she could not do it. It would be dishonest not to tell him. She would feel she was cheating, by pretending to be what she was not.

He came down to Huish Priory for a couple of days between leaving the Army and joining the surgical unit at St. Luke's. He met Sarah, home from Oxford, for the first time. Sarah was cool towards him. Julia was piqued. "Don't you like him?"

"I want things to stay as they are," Sarah said.

Julia sensed David's determination. They were going to Minehead for the day, he told her. "And no, Gabriel and Frances aren't coming with us. We can take them to the Quantocks tomorrow if Gabriel wants a day out."

He refused Annie's offer of a picnic, saying that they would lunch at a hotel. Annie was offended. "It's a strange do when people sit indoors at the seaside," Julia heard her tell Sarah.

She sat beside him in the car as they drove along the edge of the Quantocks, rehearsing what she might say. When should she tell him? Over lunch? Or after?

The town was quiet, with scarcely a soul about. It was too early in the year for visitors. The tide was far out. David insisted they bare their feet and walk down to meet it. "I remember Helen taking us down to Camber Sands once. We must have been quite young because Rowena kept falling over and soaking herself. She had to sit in wet clothes in the train going home. Helen never took us again. The next time I saw the sea must have been when I crossed over to France."

They walked slowly up the beach. He left a trail of footprints in the sand, pigeon-toed, splay-footed, deep footprints far apart. She laughed at him. "I thought you were a great doctor and here you are, no more than a child."

"And why not? And this child is very hungry, let me tell you. It must be all that fresh air."

He took her to one of the hotels on the front. She protested. Her skirt was damp, its hem bedraggled, her hair coming loose – she was in no state to go into a first-class hotel. He did not care. "Sweep in with an air," he said, "and no one will notice."

He became serious over lunch, talking about his appointment at St. Luke's, the work he would be doing and what he hoped to achieve. He revealed more of himself than he had in the past. She had thought him confident in his work, however diffident he might be socially. Now she discovered that he harboured professional fears too. "Four years in casualty clearing stations – yes, of course it's been marvellous experience, I couldn't hope for better, but it was very rough and ready. Speed was what mattered not technique. I must have got into terrible slip-shod habits over there. I've had all this clinical experience, and yet I'm not properly trained. I've simply got to get the Fellowship. In normal times I wouldn't have got the post without it. It's only because of my experience in France ..."

He apologised when they retired to the lounge for coffee. "I've talked too much about my work. I'm sorry. I know I get carried away."

"It's all right. I'm interested." It was his absorption in his work that had attracted her in the first place.

"You can't imagine what it's meant to me, finding someone I can talk to, who understands what I'm talking about and is interested ..."

The minutes, hours, were ticking by. She had said nothing about Geoffrey. She knew that at any moment he might propose. For a moment she considered keeping silent. Did she really have to tell him? She knew, after a minute's rebellion, that she must.

"Why don't we walk up North Hill?" she said. Rather

than tell him face to face it would surely be easier to do so while they were walking together. "We need exercise after all that food ... and the views from the top are splendid."

Today the view was too indistinct to be splendid. There was no sign of the Welsh coast though the Quantocks were clearly defined, a long, low ridge, tawny still in their winter covering, lying like an animal waiting to pounce.

"Gabriel told me about a walk you all once did on the Quantocks. You stayed out all night, he said. It sounded tremendous." His voice was wistful. "I do envy you, all growing up together. I used to listen to Gabriel and Frances talking in the hospital and think what fun you must have had. My childhood was very serious, looking back. I never went anywhere except on my bicycle and always on my own."

She could have no easier opening. "It was wonderful, that walk. I don't think any of us ever forgot it. We climbed up near Bagborough and walked the length of the ridge along to the sea. We spent the night in a farmer's barn. Gabriel had done that sort of thing before but the rest of us hadn't. It was magical, really magical. In the morning we had breakfast out in the open by the side of a stream." She remembered the smell of fried mushrooms and bacon, the sound of water trickling over the stones and of bees in the clematis on the wall – and Geoffrey smiling at her across the table. For a brief moment she saw him as he had been then, young and eager. A schoolboy. "Afterwards we walked down to the beach. The others did, at least. Geoffrey and I stayed behind in the woods." Sunlight and shadow; the smell of pine needles; seagulls crying beyond the trees. The sound of seagulls was with her now. "David," she said, "there's something I should have told you before, about Geoffrey and me."

"There's no need," he said. "I know. I've always known. Frances told me long ago."

"She couldn't have told you everything."

He held her hand in both of his. "It doesn't matter," he said. "I'm sorry you've been unhappy, but it's all over. I'll make you happy again. I promise you you'll be happy. What matters now isn't the past. It's us, you and me, our future together. I love you, Julia. I want to marry you."

They were astonished when they arrived back at the Rectory to discover that their engagement had been expected. Champagne was already on ice, and a celebratory dinner being prepared in the kitchen.

"But how did you guess?" Julia said.

Mr. Mackenzie smiled. "I think we have known for some time."

She looked round the dinner table that evening, at the careworn faces of Mr. and Mrs. Mackenzie, who had had so little joy in their lives in recent years, at Frances and Gabriel who regarded David almost as a brother, at David himself, smiling across at her, both confident and proud. She had made them all happy. Of course she had no doubts.

"Now you really will have to hand in your notice at that place," Frances said, triumphant as if Julia's engagement was worth it for that alone.

Mrs. Mackenzie wanted to know about wedding plans; Mr. Mackenzie where they would live.

"We'll find a flat somewhere," David said. "I'd like somewhere in the Harley Street area, but it depends where Julia would prefer." He looked anxiously at Julia as he spoke, as if fearing she might ridicule the idea of Harley Street.

"Of course I'm happy with Harley Street, if that's what you want," she said, having only the vaguest idea of its whereabouts.

She handed in her notice at St. Hilda's the next day she went in. Within an hour she had been summoned to the headmistress's office. Miss Bruce held up Julia's letter between two fingers, as if it were contagious. "Would you kindly explain *this*, Miss Purcell. I was under the impression that you were a permanent member of our staff."

"I don't think we discussed how long I should stay, Miss Bruce. I shall have been here a year by the time I leave, and I'm giving you more than a term's notice. That's all that's required."

"Perhaps you would be good enough to tell me exactly *why* you are leaving, Miss Purcell."

She knows, Julia thought. Or suspects. She's trying to make me feel guilty. "I'm getting married," she said, and took pleasure in saying it.

"I see." The headmistress's mouth was a thin line. "May I ask what became of the fiancé, Miss Purcell?" The tone became vicious. "The fiancé lost in the war? Did he ever exist?"

Julia could bear the conversation no longer. She stood up. "If you're going to accuse me of lying, Miss Bruce, I shall leave today instead of at the end of next term. It might be more sensible if I left this term in any case. You don't want a *liar* teaching your nice girls, do you?"

She was still trembling when she reached the art room, to find her next class already assembled and larking about. She clapped her hands. "*Quiet!*" she said. "We'll have a different sort of art lesson today. I'm going to draw one of you. Dorothy, go and sit in that chair over there. Make yourself comfortable; you'll be sitting for some time. I'll show the rest of you how to set about drawing a portrait, then you can try to do one yourselves."

For the first time that she could remember she could have heard a pin drop.

The flat she and David found was near enough to Harley Street to satisfy David, who did not seem to mind its distance from St. Luke's. "It's important to be in the right area from the start. I give us ten years to save up enough . . ."

Julia wandered round the empty rooms, looked out of the sitting-room window to the mirror image of their house across the road and wondered how easily she would adjust to city life. Now that the decision to marry had been made she was impatient. She felt as if she were hovering between two worlds. She wanted to start on her new life.

David left the choice of carpets and curtaining to her. The furniture they chose together. Tact was necessary. Had David had his way the flat would have been furnished with heavy black oak, presumably in imitation of the home Helen had provided. Julia, anxious not to offend, tried to make him understand. "You want to be careful in a flat. You need light. Oak makes everything so dark. You can't step out into sunlight from the third floor."

She was less successful when they came to buying the bed. Double beds were out of fashion, the salesman said, and quoted research that had proved them to be both unhealthy and unhygienic. His discovery the David was a doctor provided further reason. "Think about it, sir. Late nights, emergency calls in the early hours – it's hardly fair on the wife, is it, disturbing her nights? Whereas with single beds ..."

"Don't you think single beds seem ... strange, somehow?" Julia said, when they came out into the street after succumbing to the salesman's pressure.

"He obviously knew what he was talking about. I'm sure he's right about a good night's sleep. I'm a rotten sleeper; I wouldn't want to keep you awake."

"Are you? Why? Because of the war?"

"Lord, no. It goes back to when I was a boy. I used to work through the night, studying for exams. At university too. It becomes a habit in the end; you can't sleep when you want to."

She brought up the subject of beds again when David saw her off at Paddington. "We could always go back and say we've changed out minds. I'm sure they'd understand. Not that it would matter if they didn't."

"But we haven't changed our minds," he said.

It had never occurred to Julia that the engagement would widen her social life – little had changed for Frances and Gabriel who lived very quietly at Hillcrest – and she was surprised when she and David received invitations to houses in the district. The two of them dined at Clay Court with the Taskers; lunched with Colonel Sherwood, who prosed on at such length about the medical services in the South African campaign that she nearly fell asleep and even David grew glassy-eyed, and were entertained by the Donnes at the Manor. She had hoped Hester might be there too, but Hester was now living in the Home Counties, having made an eminently suitable marriage to the son of a baronet, and rarely came back to Huish Priory.

Julia worried that David would find such occasions tedious but they were so different from anything he had previously encountered that he was entertained rather than bored. She noticed that he was always more at ease with the men than with their wives; it took her time to realise what a monastic life he had led, despite having had two sisters – away at school, university, medical school and finally in the Medical Corps during the war. She grew to know him better not from what he told her – confidences like those in the hotel at Minehead were rare – but from dropped remarks and little incidents.

Life was full; she was happy. She made curtains and took them up to London; the flat looked more like home immediately. She camped in one room, entertained Pauline Bond to morning coffee when there were only orange boxes to sit on, and gave Miranda tea on her shopping expeditions to London. Frances admired Julia's future home on her way through to Cambridge to sort out the details of Gabriel's return. "It'll be useful having you here," she told Julia. "A halfway house between Cambridge and home." Gwen brought up plants and planted out window-boxes. "You will impress on David the need to water them every day, won't you?" she said, before returning to Hillcrest. Julia was uncomfortably aware of the plants' likely fate. "He's got a lot on his mind, Gwen. Don't you think it would be better to wait until I'm living here too?"

Once the furniture had arrived and David moved in, visiting London became more difficult. For herself, Julia would not have cared. One of the beds could have been shunted into another room – another point in favour of single beds, presumably – making everything perfectly proper, but the Mackenzies would have been upset even by that, and Julia could not bear to hurt them. She suspected, though she did not try to find out, that David himself might have been shocked. She came up the day he moved in to see him settled and make sure that the flat was in good order. He went through the rooms with a bemused look on his face. "I've never had a place of my own before. You've made it into a real home." He had few personal possessions, most having been lost when the Zeppelin destroyed his home – a few photographs, some books, the beginnings of a record collection. Julia's heart ached for him, watching him unpack. She determined to make up to him for all that he had lost.

Having been deprived of Gabriel's wedding, the Mackenzies were determined to make the most of Julia's. They insisted that the reception should be held at the Rectory. Julia waited for Frances to object but Frances said nothing. Julia suspected that she had been silenced by Gabriel.

"How could we do anything else?" Mrs. Mackenzie replied to Julia's protests. "We owe Gabriel's life to David."

"You must allow us the pleasure, my dear," Mr. Mackenzie said, when Julia brought up the subject with him, at the end of a discussion about money and the family trust. "It gives us such happiness to see you happy once more." He looked at the photograph of Geoffrey on his desk. "I was touched that David should ask my permission. I told him that you had passed out of my hands long ago. But it was because of the past, too, he said."

There was a long silence. Geoffrey's face looked out of its silver frame at them both. She could not see in it the Geoffrey she had known. It was the photograph of a subaltern, any subaltern.

"I never appreciated him when he was alive," Mr. Mackenzie said. "I wasn't fair to him, I see that now. Never a day goes by when I don't reproach myself ..."

She dreamt of Geoffrey that night. In the months after his death she had dreamt of him often, without once seeing his face. Now, as then, he kept his head turned away. She wanted his blessing on her marriage. She begged him, pleaded with him. Could they not still be friends, she asked. He sat hunched up, his back to her, and said not a word.

When she woke she was crying.

Life had taken on a momentum of its own. She could not have stopped or delayed it even if she had wished to do so. The time to voice doubts was long past. She was no more than a spectator, looking down on bride and groom and guest alike. Faces moved in front of her as if in a dream. The Cartwrights, with Miranda and John, John looking more than ever middle-aged. Mrs. Cartwright pressing a jeweller's box into Julia's hand – "Yes, yes, dear, I know there's the tea-set, but I wanted you to have a little something for yourself, just from me. It seems so long since that first time we took you and Miranda out to lunch ... do you remember? Oh, and I almost forgot – Tom Miller said to be sure to give you his best wishes." Annie, wearing a new hat bought at great cost for the occasion. Bertha, crying. Oh, please, Bertha, don't cry. Where were the absent faces? Margaret Wood, back in Ireland; Hester Donne ... why hadn't she invited Hester? She smiled at those she scarcely knew, or knew not at all – Professor Wilkie and his wife, medical friends and colleagues, the distant cousins from Hereford-shire – smiled and talked and laughed, but it was a stranger who did so, not the Julia Purcell she knew.

Gabriel was standing at the bottom of the stairs when she went into the Rectory to change. His arm held her close. "All right?"

"I'm sorry. Stupid ... Yes, of course I'm all right."

She heard David moving about in Gabriel's old bedroom as she changed in Lucy's room. She remembered how his hand had shaken in the church when he pushed on the ring. She had realised then that he was as nervous as she. Would he be nervous tonight?

Lucy and Frances fussed over her. "Don't forget your bouquet. Sarah's waiting in the hall to catch it. Are you ready? Yes, of course, you look all right. You look lovely. Do hurry – David's been ready for ages. Everyone's wait-ing."

She dropped her bouquet over the banisters as she came down the stairs. Sarah's triumph was muted. "I wish you weren't leaving us," she said. The Mackenzies kissed her. How could she express what she felt for the Mackenzies? The crowd parted as David led her out to the drive and helped her into the car. Sarah appeared at the car window. "Don't go." Julia felt panic rising. What was she doing, leaving home and family, the life she knew ...?

David sat beside her in the driving seat. He smiled. "Well, Mrs. Elliot," he said, "shall we go?"

Of course. She was Julia Purcell no longer. She was Mrs. Elliot. A new name. A new person. A new life.

Part Four

1930

Chapter Fifteen

Plump, well dressed, teetering dangerously on the edge of the pavement, the figure waved frantically at Julia from the other side of Piccadilly. Julia looked surreptitiously around to see if the wave could be intended for anyone else ...

"Julia! *Julia Purcell*!"

That voice. It couldn't be. It must be. It was – Hester Donne.

"So stupid of me not to remember your name," Hester exclaimed, when at last she reached safety on Julia's side of the street, apparently unaware of the shouts and hoots of drivers enraged by her zigzag dash between their cars. "Elliot – yes, of course. Oh, Julia, how *wonderful* to see you again. It must be years ... Let's look. You haven't changed a bit."

The same could not be said of Hester who had put on a couple of stone since their last meeting, and now looked positively matronly. A sophisticated matron, however, immaculately made-up with rather more rouge than Julia would have dared use, her hair the new length under the fetching straw cloche and her clothes the latest cut, but underneath the sophistication she was as affectionate and bubbly as Julia remembered. And as commanding.

"We must have coffee together. I know just the place. It's quiet. We can talk. Yes, of course you can manage it. Forget the Summer Exhibition – you've got all summer to see it. My milliner will have to wait too. We can't say goodbye as soon as we've met – I want to hear what you've been doing with yourself all this time."

The low spirits that had unaccountably hung over Julia for

days now began to lift. "As long as I leave in time to collect Andrew ..."

In the restaurant Hester insisted on a table by the window, brushed crumbs off the cloth with a gloved hand – "Dear, dear, I hope the place isn't going downhill" – and ordered coffee and cream cakes. Once settled, she put her elbows on the table, clasped her hands under her chin and said, "*Now*. Tell me everything. I've quite lost touch with Huish Priory these days. What are you all doing? Is Frances still painting? You don't have to answer – of course she is. What about you? Whose portrait are you doing now?"

"Oh, I gave all that up as soon as I married," Julia said. "Though I do help Andrew occasionally. He's surprisingly good at drawing for a five-year-old." She added quickly, "I don't think I'm saying that because I'm his mother. Frances considers he's got promise, too."

Hester had always been a good listener. She let Julia talk about both children and asked to see the snapshots Julia had with her, exclaiming over Rowena's Purcell looks.

"The Purcell character, too, I'm afraid," Julia said. "Gabriel says that she's as bossy as Frances, even at eight."

Hester giggled. "I don't see any of your family in Andrew. Perhaps he takes after your husband?"

"I don't think so. They're both dark. That's about all."

"Tell me about your husband," Hester said. "A doctor, isn't he?"

So Julia told her about David's progress at St. Luke's, where he was now Associate Surgeon, the research project which absorbed not only his time but most of his interest and the increasing private practice which he hoped to take to Harley Street the following year. Hester was so impressed by mention of Harley Street that Julia scarcely dared admit she regarded such a move with dread. "I hate the thought of living in one of those houses. They're so big. So difficult to run. And expensive. I like where we are. It's so light and airy and convenient. It looks out on the square gardens as well. The house is almost a garden itself, in fact. Gwen comes up from Hillcrest every so often to organise the window-boxes and see to the climbing plants. You can't see the house in summer for greenery."

"But, Julia," Hester said, her mind still on the move, "all the best people go to Harley Street. There'll be royalty at the door before you know where you are. You couldn't turn that down."

That she envied Julia was obvious, not only for the possibility of Harley Street but also for producing a son at the second attempt. "I had to have four tries before I managed the tenth baronet," she said, "and though I wouldn't admit it to anyone but you, Julia, I really don't like children very much. Thank goodness for Nanny, I always say."

Julia would have hated to hand Rowena and Andrew over to a nanny but the life Hester led was obviously very different from Julia's, occupying as she did much the same social position as Lady Donne had done in the old days in Huish Priory. Hester would be more conscientious than her mother, Julia thought, and a great deal more entertaining. She laughed at Hester's accounts of terrible happenings at Conservative fêtes and charity bazaars, of ceremonial scissors that couldn't cut, curtains that stuck over plaques and marquees in danger of collapse, and remembered how in France Hester had apparently shattered thermometers at a glance (*how* many had it been in the end?), lost equipment, broken splints ...

"That's enough of me," Hester said at last, and waved an imperious hand at the waitress to order a further supply of cream cakes. "Tell me about everyone else. How's Gabriel these days?'

"Busy," Julia said. "A don at Cambridge still. He writes, too. His books are very successful."

"I know," Hester said. "I've read all of them. Don't look so surprised. I can read, you know." She pursed her lips up in amusement. "Though I do agree – they're not my usual read. And sometimes, when I see a review, I do wonder. I mean, the critics go on at such length about his use of legends and the philosophy underlying it all – I don't know what they're talking about. I just think his books are a jolly good read."

"Gabriel says his books are like icebergs," Julia said. "They're written on different levels so you can go down as far as you want. That's why they're so popular in academic circles, according to Frances. They give people the chance to show off their superior knowledge. She's quite funny about it."

"He always was clever, wasn't he?" Hester said – wistfully, Julia thought. "I used to be terrified in the old days that he'd find out how stupid I was. I hardly dared open my mouth when he was about."

Julia was amazed, remembering how she had always envied Hester her self-possession and confidence. She was about to say as much when Hester suddenly asked, "Do you ever look back to the old days?"

Julia hesitated. "Before the war, do you mean?"

"Later than that. To the war. To when we were in France."

"No," Julia said, after a moment's pause. "Do you?"

Hester nodded. The wistfulness was unmistakeable now. "Those were the best years of my life. It sounds ridiculous, I know, but they were. Oh, life's very amusing these days and I do enjoy it, don't think I don't, but sometimes I do wonder what it's about. Opening fêtes and hospital wings, judging bonny babies – what do they matter, when you come down to it? Whereas everything did matter in France. Do you know, Julia, it's the only time in my life when I felt what I did was really important. Do you know what I mean?'

"Yes. Yes, I do."

"I could disappear off the face of the earth today and no one would notice. Well, they'd notice, of course, but the children would be as happy with Nanny as with me – happier, probably – and as for Hugo, Bellingham would carry on whether I was there or not and that's all he cares about." She stopped, made a deprecatory gesture. "I expect you think I'm being very stupid."

Julia shook her head. She was surprised, even dismayed. Who would have imagined Hester harboured such thoughts?

"I tried discussing it once with Mother," Hester said. "She used to lead the same sort of life when she was my age. I thought she might have felt like I do. She didn't understand what I was talking about. She never has. She didn't understand my going to France either. She thought I should help in her nursing-home because of all the nice young officers who passed through it. She didn't know how I could bear all the dreadful sights I had to see in France. They were dreadful, I'm not saying they weren't, but we had a lot of laughs, didn't we?" She recalled some of them with such clarity that Julia began to laugh with her, and then remembered incidents of her own that she had forgotten long ago.

"Do you remember that time you came over with Geoffrey Mackenzie?" Hester said. "Wasn't he funny about field cards? I did what he said, you know. I sent them off to everyone I could think of. I got hundreds of letters back, from all sorts of people – great aunts who hadn't seen me since I was a baby, for instance." She put her hand out towards the éclair that remained on the plate. "Do you . . .?" Julia shook her head. "I did like Geoffrey," Hester said. "He was so comical in a droll sort of a way." Cream squished out over her fingers as she bit into the choux paste. "You were in love with him, weren't you? Of course you were. You'd only got to see the two of you together to know that."

Julia stopped laughing. "Yes," she said, and changing the subject abruptly began to talk about Crawford, whom Hester had met and who was now running her own nursing-home in the West Riding. "Very efficiently, I believe. She always was practical, of course. And determined to be independent, even in those days ..."

They exchanged addresses and telephone numbers at parting. "You're sure you won't stay on for lunch?" Hester said. "I'm so late for my milliner as it is, another couple of hours won't matter."

Julia refused. She knew she must hurry or Andrew would be waiting on the doorstep. "Come and have lunch with me next time you're in town," she said. "It would be a pity to lose touch this time."

"I will, I will." She kissed Julia in the middle of Piccadilly, dabbed at the lipstick she had put on Julia's cheek and said, "Next time, I promise. It's been *lovely* seeing you again. I feel twenty years younger."

The euphoria Julia felt as a result of their meeting did not last long.

That afternoon she took Andrew to see the school he was to join in the autumn. The visit left her immeasurably depressed, by the school itself and by Andrew's reaction to it, as well as by David's lack of sympathy when she talked about it at dinner that evening.

"You can't expect him to like it at first," he said. "He'll get used to it. He's growing up. You can't keep him a baby forever."

"I know. I don't want to. It's just that I'd be happier if I thought it was the right place for him. There wasn't a single picture on the walls, not even in the art room. They don't use paint in art lessons, apparently. They say it's too messy." She saw again the rows of subdued little boys sweltering in thick flannel suits in unventilated classrooms while the sun beat down outside, and nervous masters bowing down under the headmaster's icy gaze. "I don't know what there was about the place," she said. "I thought it was dreadful. Uncaring. Regimented, somehow."

"You're not used to boys' schools, that's all. Of course

it's regimented. Boys need discipline. You can't have them looking at pictures when they should be concentrating on their sums. It's a good school. It gets results. Andrew's not going there to learn to paint. He can do that at home."

She remembered Andrew's convulsive grip on her hand throughout the afternoon, and the desperate way in which he had begged afterwards to be allowed to stay at his kindergarten for one more term. "You don't think it would be sensible to postpone it a year? He's only just five, after all, and he's so quiet. I don't know how he'll fit in."

"He'll have to learn to fit in some time. You'll be surprised how quickly he settles down. Look at Tony Mackenzie. Frances and Gabriel didn't have any trouble with him. I can't understand why you're so worried. We've all had to go through it. It's not as if he'll be boarding. I'd had to leave my parents and come all the way to England by his age."

You were a year older, Julia was tempted to say but did not. Nor did she point out that Tony Mackenzie and Andrew could hardly be less alike, despite being cousins. She wondered why she worried so much more over Andrew than she had over Rowena. Was she being overprotective? Or was it due to the children's different personalities? Rowena had always been able to stand up for herself. Girls were survivors – one had only to look at the Purcell and Mackenzie families to see that. Perhaps it was only selfishness on her part that made her want to delay Andrew's start and keep him close to her for a little while longer. "Life will seem very strange with both children at school," she said. "What shall I do with myself?"

"You'll find plenty to do. For one thing, this autumn ..." He checked himself, considered for a moment and then smiled. "I shouldn't be telling you this. The invitation's not official yet, so don't breathe a word to anyone until we've had confirmation at St. Luke's, but if it will cheer you up ... Wilkie's been asked to give a paper at McGill University in October. He wants me to go with him. It's as much my research project as his, of course, but it's an honour, even so."

"Oh David, how wonderful." Her pleasure on his behalf, knowing how much both the research and Professor Wilkie's good opinion mattered to him, for a moment distracted her thoughts from Andrew.

He stretched out his hand. "Ever since Wilkie mentioned the possibility I've been thinking ... Why don't you come too? You'd have to entertain yourself during the symposium itself, but we could go away afterwards together. Take a holiday, just the two of us. Do you know that we haven't been away on our own since Rowena was born?"

"We never seem to get further than Hillcrest, do we?" she said. "You're always too busy. A holiday would be wonderful. I'm terribly ignorant though. Where is McGill?"

"Montreal. Eastern Canada."

The smile went from her face. "*Canada*?"

"It's the best time of year to see that part of North America, according to Wilkie. He's been there before. He says the autumn colouring is unbelievable."

She pulled her hand away. "But David, how could we go so far? What about the children?"

It was obvious from his expression that he had not given thought to the children. "We could take them to Hillcrest," he said after a moment. "You know how they love it, and Gwen and Annie would be delighted to look after them."

"We couldn't take Andrew away from school so soon after he's started. It wouldn't be fair on him ... and I doubt whether the school would allow it."

"Well then ... we'll ask Frances to come and take over here. Andrew would be thrilled. You know how he dotes on her."

"She wouldn't leave Gabriel."

"She goes back to Hillcrest without him."

"Only for her work. And not often."

"She'd leave Gabriel if you asked her ... He wouldn't

[226]

mind moving back into college. He's done it before. It's not as if we're going to make a habit of leaving the children."

"But, David, how long does it take to cross the Atlantic? We'd be away weeks."

"No more than three. I can't spare the time to be away longer. As for the crossing, I thought that would be part of the holiday. You know you could do with a break."

One objection after another rushed into her mind. "What about the cost? You said we should start looking for a place in Harley Street this winter. We can't afford to do that if we go away now."

"My expenses will be paid. I know we'll have to pay yours, but it seems ridiculous to turn down such an opportunity. I thought you'd be pleased." He sounded like a disappointed child. "Don't you want to see Canada?"

"It's the children. I'd come if it weren't for the children." She believed it. If only she could make him believe it too. "You're doing so well, David. There'll be plenty of other invitations later on. I'll come with you then. It won't matter leaving the children when they're older and more sensible. It's just now that it's impossible, particularly for Andrew ... You do understand, don't you?"

His face was expressionless. "Yes, of course."

The silence was broken when Nellie came in with the coffee. "I think we'll have it in the drawing-room please, Nellie," Julia said. She looked across at David. "Will you play for me tonight?"

Some of the happiest times of their marriage were those evenings spent listening to music, either at concerts or at home. But this evening the music failed to soothe.

She never told David of her meeting with Hester. She could have entertained him with Hester's tales of life in the Home Counties; made him smile at her description of Hester devouring Julia's cream cakes as well as her own while she lamented her increasing girth, but she did not. She suspected guilt was the reason for her silence. She had never before breathed a word of her feelings about Harley Street to anyone. She felt she had let David down by revealing them to Hester now.

She went up to Harley Street the next morning when Andrew was at kindergarten, and walked slowly up one side and down the other, studying each house in turn, wondering which 'one' might become theirs and trying to face up to the future that she could see lying ahead.

It was a strange, troubled summer. The meeting with Hester had unsettled her, resurrecting memories Julia had thought buried for ever. She tried not to think ... but a snatch of an old tune played on a mouth organ at the street corner, a waft of fish coming off a stall in the market, the sound of a gull over the river and she was back, in a past so vivid that it might have taken place yesterday. She began dreaming, always the same dream, of herself floating down the St. Lawrence between flame-coloured banks, happy, filled with eager anticipation, impatient to start on her new life. But she could never identify the shadowy figure standing on the deck beside her and when she woke she always remembered that the prospects of that new life had died before Geoffrey himself.

Only the afternoons could distract her. She savoured the times she spent with Andrew, knowing they would not return, helping him with his attempts to draw the ducks round the Serpentine, easing the tantrums that came from frustration when the birds waddled away. "Why don't you draw flowers, like Aunt Gwen? They stay still. Leave ducks until you're a bit older."

"But I want to do them *now*."

She taught him to swim, watching him gain confidence slowly until he could launch himself into the water without hesitation and paddle in circles, chin held high and a smile of triumph on his face. "When can I show Daddy? I want Daddy to see."

The summer was as hot as the one in which she and David had married. She looked back with longing to happier, earlier days, when David had needed all the support and encouragement she could give him and Rowena and Andrew had been totally dependent. Now growing success meant that David could manage very well without her and the children were rapidly developing lives of their own. What would she do with herself in a cavernous Harley Street house?

She and David were growing apart. She seemed powerless to prevent it. Every night he returned late from the hospital, bringing work home that kept him up into the middle of the night. She could not remember when they had last been out to a concert or to the theatre. The silences between them became interminable. Nothing more had been said about Canada; he had rebuffed her attempt to return to the subject. "It's all right. I understand. Don't let's talk about it."

Canada, Andrew's schooling, Harley Street, the future . . . soon there would be nothing left for them to discuss. What would happen to them then?

"Do you remember Donald McInnis?" David said. "You met him, I think. In practice up in Edinburgh. We were in France together. He wants me to have a look at a patient of his."

"Will you go?" Julia said.

"If only Edinburgh weren't so far. Wilkie and I are still very involved with the McGill paper. Yet it sounds an interesting case."

"If you travelled by sleeper," Julia suggested, "you'd only miss the one day down here."

"You wouldn't object?"

"David, when have I ever objected to your work?"

"Well . . ." He sounded sheepish. "Donald did suggest my going up on Friday and staying over the weekend. He thought we could get in some fishing."

[229]

"It sounds a good idea," Julia said. "It'll give you a break. You've been overworking for months. You might start sleeping better after a couple of days' fishing. And it would be nice if you could bring back a salmon for us."

She went to see him off at King's Cross on the night of his departure, racked with guilt because of the relief she felt at the prospect of being without him for a weekend. What was happening to her . . . to them?

"There's no need to wait till the train goes," he said, once they had found his sleeper. "I'm all right. I'll catch up on some reading."

"Well, if you're happy . . ."

He gave her a chaste kiss. "You're sure you don't mind my staying on until Sunday? Monday evening, in fact. I'll go straight to the hospital from the train in the morning."

"I might take the children down to Hillcrest while you're away. Just for the weekend. Yes, I think I'll do that. We'll catch the first train tomorrow."

She sat in the taxi taking her home and wondered why she had not thought of Somerset until now. She shut her eyes and imagined herself walking round Hillcrest in the twilight, breathing in the scents of evening, feeling the dampness of dew on her skin. It's London, she thought, August in London, that's making me feel so dreadful. I shall be all right once I'm back in the country.

Chapter Sixteen

They nearly missed the train next morning. The children, wildly excited at the thought of Hillcrest, rushed round the house gathering up all the items they wanted Julia to pack. "It's only two days," she told them, but she might as well have been talking to the deaf. Then, when they were about to step into the taxi taking them to the station Andrew remembered his drawings and refused to leave without them. "Aunt Gwen always asks me," he said, feet planted solidly on the front door step. "I want to show her my ducks."

In the rush and confusion – the drawings had been put away in the nursery on the top floor – Julia forgot to send a telegram, so that there was no Gwen to meet them at Taunton; they had to change on to the Minehead train and take a taxi from Dunkery St. Michael instead. Not that the children minded; they adored train journeys and poured out all the details of this one to Jimmy Hancock while waiting for Mr. Evans to arrive with his car. "Bright little nippers," Jimmy said. "Shot up, haven't they, since last time they came." They bounced from one side of he car to the other, while Julia waited for Mr. Evans to complain on behalf of the springs. "Here's the common . . . Uncle Antony's geese . . . the cricket field . . ." They held their breath as the car went up and down the bridge over the stream, shouted to Bill Roberts, and scrambled and pushed to be first out at the end of their journey.

"I hear voices," Andrew said, struggling with Rowena over the gate latch, and coming second in the rush to the garden. Julia heard his shriek of delight – "*Aunt Fran!*" – and came round the corner of the house in time to see

Frances scoop him up into her arms.

"What a lovely surprise," Frances said, laughing over his head at Julia. "I had no idea you were coming. Is David with you?"

Julia shook her head. "He's in Edinburgh. What are you two doing here? I thought you were in Devon – don't get up, Gabriel."

But Gabriel had already pulled himself on to his feet. He came forward from the table where he was sitting with Gwen, kissed Julia, ruffled Andrew's hair and suggested that Rowena should tell Annie of the family's arrival. "What fun. Have you had anything to eat?"

"I'm not hungry," Julia said, "but if Annie could give the children something in the kitchen ... I'm sorry I didn't let you know we were coming, Gwen. I only decided last night."

"It doesn't matter. You know we're always happy to see you."

Like Hillcrest, Gwen never changed. She still wore her hair long, coiled over her ears, and if she took note of fashion it was invariably a year or two late. "Don't look," she said now, seeing Julia's eyes fall on the safety pin that held up the hem of her skirt – not discreetly on the inside of the garment where anyone else would have put it, but visibly, on the outside. "I keep meaning to mend it, but I forget in the evening, or else I'm too tired. How long are you staying? Will David come later? What's he doing so far north?"

Julia lay back in a deckchair and listened to herself explaining about David and Edinburgh, telling them of her dislike of London when the summer was so hot " ... so here we are. What about you two? I thought you'd taken Denis's cottage for the summer."

"We should have been there a couple of days ago," Frances said, "but we decided to drop Tony off at the Merediths. Gabriel needs peace and quiet to get on with his

[232]

book and you know what life's like when Tony's around. And then when we got here we realised Gabriel's parents needed help."

"I'm afraid they're very frail these days," Gabriel said. "Lucy decided a breath of sea air would do them both good, so I took the three of them down to Budleigh Salterton yesterday for a fortnight. Much more sensible for me to drive them than let them struggle on the train. I'm thinking of changing careers and becoming a chauffeur. I'd have fetched you from Taunton if I'd known." He was amused, as well as complacent; he enjoyed being the family driver. The purchase of a specially adapted car had revolutionised his life. Nowadays he had more mobility out of doors than in. More important, the car had made him feel a useful member of society once more.

Julia took pleasure in being useful herself later that afternoon. "Give me a hand with the raspberries," Gwen said, "and you can take some jam back with you." So she helped Gwen pick and listened to her talk of Tony Mackenzie. "Frances and Gabriel don't understand him, you know. They haven't the faintest idea how to handle him. He's just an ordinary schoolboy. With rather more energy than most, I agree, but we never have any trouble when he comes to stay here. We'd have liked to have had him this summer while Frances and Gabriel are in Devon, but Frances insisted he went over to the Merediths. She says that we spoil him."

"It's probably easier if he goes to the Merediths," Julia said, trying to soothe the ruffled feelings. "He'll have Hector to play with there, and Mary will be able to keep them both occupied on the farm." Her sympathies were with Frances rather than Gwen; she found Tony's high spirits wearing when she had him to stay, though she thought the restrictions imposed by London surroundings partly to blame.

She felt more cheerful after an afternoon's work in the garden, tired from physical effort rather than mental strain.

Perhaps I need a holiday as well as David, she thought. If only we could stay here longer.

"Must we go home on Monday?" Andrew said, face flushed from his bath, his hair unnaturally tidy, when Julia tucked him up in bed in Sarah's old bedroom and kissed him goodnight. "I want to stay with Aunt Fran."

"He is an attractive child," Frances said at supper that night. "So different from Tony. I can't think why Gabriel and I should have produced such a terror."

"Tony's not nearly as bad as you make out," Julia protested. "I wish Andrew had some of his confidence. I don't know how he'll cope with his new school."

Gabriel pooh-poohed Julia's fears, although he was more sympathetic than David had been. It was all very well for David and Gabriel, Julia thought. Neither had minded school; by all accounts Gabriel had actually enjoyed it. Not everyone felt the same. She could not bear to think of a child of hers dreading the start of every term, or hating so many months of each year of his youth.

"You'll find life very strange without Andrew," Gabriel said. "Frances couldn't wait to get rid of Tony, but I suspect you're very different. What will you do with all that spare time?"

"She can go to the Slade," Frances said.

Julia stared. "*The Slade*? What on earth are you talking about?"

"I think you should go to the Slade," Frances repeated. "Attend art classes. Get back into the way of working. A couple of days a week, that's all you need to give you a bit of self-discipline."

Julia did not know whether to be angry or amused. "I do hand it to you, Frances," she said. "After all these years ... You never stop trying, do you?"

"No, but seriously," Frances said, "can you give me one reason why not?"

"I'm too old."

"Rubbish. It's not age that matters but whether you're any good. You know what we've always said. If you've got talent then it's your *duty* to use it."

"Well, I haven't. Not enough. I might feel differently if I were like you, but I'm not so I don't."

"Just as well I didn't compare myself to Cézanne then," Frances said tartly, "or I'd never have got started."

"That's different," Julia said automatically. Of course it was. Wasn't it?

It was years since she had done any serious painting, having given it up soon after her wedding. Painting had been part of the old life that she threw off when she got married, its abandonment made easier by David's description of it as a nice little hobby. If that was all it could be, she had thought when he said it, better to put it aside altogether. And she had done so, at least until Andrew showed talent of his own, when she had begun, just occasionally, to draw herself.

"David would never agree," she said now.

"If that's really so," Gabriel said, "and if David's your only reason for not going, then someone will have to have a word with him. I'll do it myself."

"No," Julia said. "Please, Gabriel, don't. Let me think about it."

Gwen, looking from one to the other, was quick to change the subject. "I suppose you couldn't go down and see Bill Roberts while you're here? He isn't too good at the moment, and Mary's always grateful for your visits."

No more was said about the Slade. At the end of the meal Frances offered to check on the children. "You look tired," she said to Julia. "Stay where you are. I don't mind going. I might even draw them if they're already asleep." Gwen, muttering something about shutting up the greenhouses, disappeared through the French windows.

"It's getting dark," Julia said. "I'll fetch in the lamps."

"Not yet," Gabriel said. "I like this light. It has a touch of the mysterious about it. It's easier to talk in the twilight." He sat back, cupping his brandy glass in the palm of his hand as he watched her. "What's wrong, Julia?"

Her first reaction was anger with herself, that she had not realised the feeble excuses Frances and then Gwen had produced for leaving were no more than a ploy to leave Gabriel and her together.

"Nothing's wrong," she said.

"I don't believe it."

"It's true, all the same."

"David in Edinburgh, you down here ..."

"I told you this afternoon. Donald McInnis is an old friend from the war. He wanted David to look at one of his patients. An interesting case, he said. You know David. He couldn't turn down an interesting case if he tried."

"So he decided to stay on? Away from you and the children – that doesn't sound like David."

"He needs a holiday – we all do – but he says he can't spare the time, the way the practice is growing and then the McGill paper on top of everything else. Both Wilkie and he say the symposium's come a bit early. They could have done with another couple of months to collate the results. And he drives himself too hard. You say that yourself. He's been worse than usual this summer, and he always finishes up the same way, unable to sleep and not wanting to eat ... He'll be getting an ulcer if he's not careful. Edinburgh seemed a good idea. He's always able to relax when he's fishing. A couple of days seemed better than nothing."

"So that's all it is? Overwork. Everything else is all right."

"Why shouldn't it be? I don't know what makes you think ..."

"Well, then, I'll tell you. Your face. There's been a closed look about it all day. I can't describe it, but I'll tell you the last time I saw it – when I came back from Germany after the war. Do you remember? You were just beginning to get over everything – Geoffrey, flu, working in France – and then I came along and made that stupid remark about the wrong man."

She stared at him without words. Then she burst into tears.

It was difficult to know which was the most shocked.

"Oh, God, Julia, I'm sorry. I'm so sorry. What an insensitive brute ... Here. Take this." He thrust a handkerchief, ghostly white in the half-light, across the table, while she made a desperate effort to quench the tears that now they had started to flow seemed impossible to stop. He pulled himself over to the sideboard, busied himself there for a while and came back to the table. "Drink this," he said.

"What is it?"

"Brandy. It'll make you feel better."

She took too big a gulp. It caught at the back of her throat, made her choke. She felt its warmth begin to go through her. "I'm sorry," she said. "I don't know what happened."

"No need to apologise. It happens to all of us from time to time. Now, take your time ..."

She did not want to tell him. She did not know what there was to tell. Almost without her being aware of it the words came out, one by one, while Gabriel listened, probed, asked the occasional question without making any comment or passing judgment. When she reached the end she was ashamed. "It seems wicked to be so miserable. What have I got to be miserable about?" If this was what Gabriel suffered during his black moods, she thought, why hadn't she been kinder to him? "I think, is this all there is to life, and then, when I look at you ..."

"Why me?" Gabriel said. "I have so much. And what I haven't, well, that's something I've come to terms with."

Yes. As far as he was concerned the success of his marriage had compensated for all else that he had lost. Though even now Julia would sometimes look at him and wonder whether the real tragedy of the war was not epitomised by him, rather than by Geoffrey or Antony. All the enthusiasm she remembered from his work in the East End, the determination to make the world a better place – all gone, forever ... And here she was crying about nothing. She wiped her face, blew her nose. "Do you ever go to the Settlement these days?" she asked.

If he was surprised by the change of subject he did not show it. "I'm afraid the building's too much of a rabbit warren to be easy for someone like me. I keep in touch, that's all. Something else I've had to come to terms with."

"I suppose so."

"I wonder if that's not part of your trouble. What can't you accept, do you think?"

She shook her head. "I don't know."

"When did all this start?" he said. "You seemed cheerful enough when we saw you at Easter."

She had never asked herself when. Why, but not when. And now, thinking back, she could pinpoint the moment precisely – the first morning of the summer term, as Andrew had paused on the top step outside his kindergarten and called back to her – "What are we doing this afternoon, Mummy?" The knowledge had hit her then, like a physical blow, that her afternoons with him were numbered. In the autumn he would start full-time school, would grow up, become noisy and irrepressible, full of silly schoolboy jokes, like Tony Mackenzie. Andrew would go, as Rowena had gone; as David, too, had gone, now that he was successful. And then, not long after the beginning of term, she had met Hester Donne, unhappy too under that superficial brightness, who had resurrected memories best left buried, and from then on despair had fed on despair.

Gabriel sat silent for a while. "Have you told David about any of this?" he said, at last.

"I tried once. He suggested we had another baby."

"Oh dear. I'm afraid David has a very basic view of life. It

[238]

must come from being medical. Not that there's anything wrong with having a baby. Indeed I can see it would solve your problem quite nicely, the way you feel about babies, but it would only postpone the problem. Presumably you had the sense to see that. So, you let it go, did you? Never mentioned it to him again? Stiff British upper lip and all that? You've never been much good at pushing yourself, have you? I've sometimes wondered how much Frances was to blame for that."

"Frances has nothing to do with all this," Julia said.

"No, of course not. On the other hand there are times when I think you should give Frances the deference due to an elder sister." His tone was suddenly light. "I thought she talked a lot of sense this evening when she mentioned the Slade. Here you are, wondering about the purpose of your existence, not knowing what to do with yourself – I would have thought the answer was obvious."

"I've hardly done any painting for nearly ten years, Gabriel, and I wasn't brilliant, even then. Mine's a very minor talent, best left alone."

"I can't believe I'm hearing such sentiments from one of the Purcell family," Gabriel said. "I remember Frances arguing about the parable of the talents – she couldn't have been more than seventeen at the time, and not exactly religious, I'd have thought, and yet there she was quoting chunks of the Bible at Father as if he'd never heard them before. I was highly amused. I've always taken it for granted that that parable was the guiding light at Hillcrest, and yet here you are, making excuses ..."

"Oh, I know," she said, bitterly. "I've made a mess of everything, haven't I? Painting. Marriage. Even Geoffrey, when you think about it."

"Geoffrey?" he said, quickly. "What do you mean – Geoffrey?"

"I didn't mean ... Forget it."

"I certainly won't. What exactly did you mean?"

She had told him everything else; why not that? "Geoffrey didn't care about me towards the end."

"Oh? It's not the impression I got. What makes you think that?"

"I think he said something to Frances on his last leave. She talked about him coming back, but once he was home she never mentioned him. He must have told her."

"Did you ask her about it?"

"That wasn't the only thing. He stopped writing to me. I hadn't heard from him for weeks before he was killed. Months, almost."

"I don't think he wrote at all that autumn. Mother complained to me about it, as if she thought I could do something. I never heard from him myself after his friend was killed, and that must have been . . . August, was it? No later than September, anyway."

She stared "He told you about Patterson?"

"Not much. No details. He was taking it badly, as far as I could tell, but there was nothing I could do. The three of you planned to go to Canada after the war, he said."

She was astonished that Geoffrey should have told Gabriel so much. "Yes."

"I don't imagine this trip of David's can have helped you then in your present state, bringing back all the might-have-beens. Does David know about Geoffrey and Canada?"

She shook her head.

"Or your feelings about Harley Street? Have you told him about them?"

"How could I, when it was what Helen wanted for him. He'd feel he was letting her down if he didn't finish up in there."

"Helen has nothing to do with Harley Street," Gabriel said. "He's doing it for you."

She could not believe it. "He told once me he owed it to Helen."

"Well, possibly. Gratitude. That sort of thing. After all it

[240]

was she who held up Harley Street as the prize when he started out. By the time Frances and I met him it wasn't part of his plans, I assure you. I don't know whether he was physically exhausted by the war or whether it killed his ambition, as it did with the rest of us – but I do know that when Frances and I were in Ireland he had every intention of staying on in the Medical Corps. Margaret Wood was very concerned. She used to go on about the waste of his gifts while she was doing my dressings. He was quite somebody in Dublin, you know. Hospital staff prostrated themselves when he appeared. Really. Even Margaret indulged in a fair bit of knee bending when she was in uniform and he was around. Then you and he began writing, and in no time at all he was talking of leaving the Army and coming to London. He and I discussed our possible futures over a weekend fishing trip, I remember, and I'm certain he never mentioned Harley Street then. That came later, after he'd met you."

She did not know whether he was speaking the truth or saying it to help her.

"We've been talking about your feelings all evening," Gabriel said, "We haven't mentioned David's. What does he think about all this?"

"He doesn't know. He's so wrapped up in his work he doesn't notice ..."

"I wouldn't be so sure." His face was no more than a blur across the table, as he said slowly, "I've sometimes wondered whether David's compulsion to overwork has any connection with Geoffrey. I'm only guessing – he's never said anything to me – but it has struck me that someone like David would find it hard to cope with the thought of comparison. It must be difficult to have to compete with the dead, don't you think? No chance of proving yourself better. Or even equal."

"I hadn't thought ..."

And at that moment Annie came in to clear the table, tut-tutting when she found them alone in the dark. "Really,

Miss Julia. Didn't you have sense to ring for the lamps? I thought you'd have been in the drawing-room long since."

Lamplight, when it came, made the room suddenly, cruelly, bright. As if at a signal, Gwen reappeared from the garden, Frances came in from the hall.

Julia pleaded tiredness and went up to bed.

Tired she might be, but sleep took a long time to come. She listened to the church clock mark the hours, went over and over the conversation with Gabriel, tried not to think of David ... Geoffrey ... David ... The room was already beginning to lighten by the time she fell asleep; when she woke the sun was shining on the far wall.

When she went into Sarah's room she found it empty and the children's nightclothes lying on the floor. Rowena's voice came from the kitchen, talking to Annie. In the dining-room Frances and Andrew were playing a drawing game at the breakfast table. Frances looked up. "We thought we'd let you sleep on," she said, as she gathered up the drawings and gave them to Andrew. "Go and show them to Annie. Then you can see if Waite has arrived." She watched him run out of the room. "He'll finish up at the Slade, mark my words."

"I'm afraid David wouldn't be very happy about that," Julia said.

Frances made no comment. "The coffee's still hot," she said. "Annie made me a second pot. Do you want a cup?"

Julia accepted the coffee, helped herself to toast and then wondered why, when she had so little appetite. "You should have woken me," she said. "What time are you leaving?"

"We're not. We'll stay as long as you're here. It seemed stupid to go rushing off to Devon when we haven't seen each other for months."

"I'm sorry about that. It's this symposium. It's hard enough getting David away at the best of times ..."

"So Gabriel said." Frances poured coffee for herself, fiddled with the coffee pot, her cup, a spoon. "Gabriel also

said you'd got some very strange ideas about Geoffrey."
And as Julia opened her mouth to protest, "Don't mind him
telling me. You know he'd never dream of repeating anything you'd said in confidence, but he was upset. He didn't
know why you should think what you did. He wondered
what I thought and when I said of course Geoffrey cared for
you he said I should have a word ..."

"I don't know why I said what I did last night," Julia
said shortly, "I must have been tired. There's no need for us
to talk about it. The past is past. Forgotten."

"You haven't forgotten," Frances pointed out.

"Well, then, it doesn't matter any more."

"It must matter, or you wouldn't have said anything to
Gabriel. It was my letters, he said, that made you think what
you did. You must be crazy, Julia. There was never anyone
but you, as far as Geoffrey was concerned."

"But you never said anything about that last leave."

"No."

"Why not?"

Frances took a long time to answer. "All sort of reasons."

"What reasons?"

"Well ... I didn't know what to say, if you really want to
know. It was as simple as that."

"It doesn't seem simple to me."

"Look," Frances said. "It was a long time ago. You've
said that yourself. Geoffrey loved you. I'm as sure of that as
I'm sure of anything. Isn't that enough?"

"No. Not now we've started. *Why* didn't you know what
to say?"

Frances hesitated, then gave in. "Because he was in such a
terrible state. I thought he was mad, quite honestly. He was
jumpy. He'd got the shakes. He couldn't concentrate. He sat
staring into space half the time. And he was so rude. He'd
offended half the village within a couple of days of being
home. It was as if he didn't care what people thought any
more. He kept spouting *The Ancient Mariner* at me, too. All

the grisly bits – I'm sure he only did it because he knew I'm stupid about blood and all that. So curious, when he'd always hated poetry. It was criminal, sending him back to the front in his state. I tried to get him to go and see someone at the Red Cross Hospital in Taunton, but he wouldn't. He wouldn't even talk to Dr. Milne. I had to go myself in the end."

Julia stared. "To Dr. Milne? What for?"

"I thought he'd be able to help. I thought if he saw what Geoffrey was like he'd write to the authorities and make sure Geoffrey stayed in England. I thought he'd be able to do *something*. He couldn't. Or wouldn't. I don't know whether you'd have done any better, but you know how bad I am with people. I just put his back up. He was vile about Geoffrey, really vile. I was *glad* when he broke his neck out hunting after the war. It served him right. Except I'd have chosen something more lingering."

"Oh, Frances," Julia said.

"The funny thing was, he was all right with Sarah. Geoffrey, I mean. He was happy with her. They spent a lot of time together, that leave, larking about like a couple of schoolchildren. He was helping her collect chestnuts, I seem to remember; she won a prize for them later."

Yes, Julia thought. 'A grand kid,' she remembered he'd called Sarah.

"I did all I could to keep him home," Frances said. "You must believe me. Say you believe me."

Julia realised to her surprise that Frances felt guilty . . . "I believe you."

"And the other? You and him – you believe that too?"

"I'd like to," Julia said.

"But you don't?"

"I don't know." She had not realised that the pain was still so strong. "If only he'd written to me, Frances, just occasionally, I could believe it. He hadn't written for months, only field cards, and you know what field cards are like. They don't tell you anything. Just ticks."

"But that's what I'm saying. He wasn't capable of string-ing even a couple of sentences together himself. At least he sent field cards; he was doing what he could to keep in touch."

It had never occurred to Julia to consider Geoffrey's cor-respondence, or lack of it, from that point of view.

"I can prove that I'm right, if you really want proof," Frances said, slowly.

"How?"

Frances hesitated, as if already regretting her offer. "I painted him that leave," she said. "I asked him to sit for me. He didn't want to – I was surprised he came, in fact. It was the only way I could think of helping him. I thought if I was painting and he was just sitting there, he might feel able to talk. It didn't work, of course. I only made things worse. I've never forgiven myself for that."

"I can't think how you could make things worse," Julia said.

"Well, I did. He wanted to see what I was doing. Every-one does, don't they, and you know how it is – you don't know what you've done until you stand back and look at it. It was like that. I was shocked myself, but Geoffrey – I don't think he had any idea how bad he was until he saw ... He was devastated."

It was too much, too unexpected, all this detail of the past suddenly confronting her. She could not take it in.

"Frances, what is it you're trying to tell me?"

"That Geoffrey was shell-shocked. Neurasthenic. What-ever it is they call it these days. If things had gone wrong between the two of you it was for that reason, nothing else. Not that I think anything had gone wrong, not from the way he talked about you."

"Why didn't you say anything about him in your letters?"

"What could I say? 'Geoffrey's splendid, in fine form, keeps us in fits with his jokes'? I wasn't going to tell lies like that, but how could I tell you the truth? It seemed better to say nothing. I thought the others ... didn't Sarah mention him?"

"No. The Mackenzies did, but none of you."

"I'm surprised at that."

"So," Julia said. "You painted him?"

"Yes."

"What happened to it?"

Frances sounded wary, as if sensing the next question. "I didn't finish it. I couldn't."

"But you've still got it?"

"Yes."

"Where?"

"It's up in the stables. Put away."

"I want to see it."

Frances shook her head. "No. I swear it's all true, everything I've said. Can't we leave it at that?"

"It's not that I don't believe you," Julia said carefully. "I have to see for myself, that's all."

They sat looking at each across the table. "I suppose," Frances said at last, "if you insist ..."

"I do."

"All right. I'll take you up after breakfast."

Why wait till then, Julia thought. She was exhausted, emotionally drained, by this overturning of her idea of the past. Let's get it over with. "Take me now."

They walked up to the stables without speaking. An ordinary summer day, no different from any other August day, the sun shining, casting shadows from the walnut tree and the magnolia over the grass towards the stables.

Frances stopped at the barn door. "Wait here," she said.

Julia waited, while Frances went up to her studio. She heard the sound of doors opening, drawers being pulled out. November, she thought. Late autumn. Winter, almost. A south-westerly blowing through the bare branches of the trees in the copse. Rain, probably, spattering down onto the rough winter grass, scattering any fallen leaves that still remained. And Geoffrey, coming up the path on his way to be painted.

Frances came down the steps. Her face was pale. For the first time Julia realised that this was upsetting for her too.

"It's on the easel," Frances said. "Julia, please. Won't you think again? You shouldn't, really you shouldn't."

"I must."

"Do you want me . . .?"

Julia shook her head. "I'm better alone."

She watched Frances walk down the path and disappear into the house. I could go after her. I don't have to see it. I'm frightened.

She took a deep breath and went very slowly up the stairs to the studio.

Chapter Seventeen

She had no idea where she was going. She was scarcely aware of what she was doing. She only knew that she had to escape – from the stables, from Hillcrest, from the village, more than anything else from the faces the portrait had summoned up, those faces long forgotten that had haunted her so mercilessly twelve, thirteen, fourteen years ago.

She came to her senses up on the Quantocks, as she frantically clambered up the meadow below the beeches on the skyline. Her legs ached, she had a pain in her side, her breath hurt with each gasp. Her shoes, not meant for such walking, slipped on the coarse grass. If she could reach the shelter of those beeches . . .

She tried to regain her breath as she rested in their shade, her eyes shut against the pictures she wanted to hide from her sight. Voices sounded in the distance. She looked up to see a party of walkers, ten or eleven of them, talking and joking together, young, energetic, jolly. They smiled at her without curiosity as they came up to her. They were looking for the Triscombe Stone, they said. Did she know . . . ?

"It's down there." She shaded her face from their eyes as she pointed. "You can see it from here."

"Is that it?" one of the women asked, the disappointment clear in her voice. "We were looking for something bigger than that."

"Just the right weather for walking today," said the leader. "Not too hot."

Julia watched them go, noting the stout shoes, the maps they carried and the knapsacks on their backs. It was an expedition they were on, not a morning stroll. They stopped when they reached the stone, pulled off their knapsacks and brought out packets of food. The leader glanced back towards Julia, as if wondering whether to invite her to join them.

She got up quickly and walked away in the opposite direction. She did not want people. She wanted to be alone. She left the path, scrambled through bracken and gorse until she came to the head of a combe. She slipped and slid down its steep side until she came to a hollow in which she could stay, hidden from the ridge above. She was safe. No one would find her. She was alone with her thoughts, back in the stables.

She had not recognised him. That was the terrible part. For seconds – minutes, even – she had seen nothing of Geoffrey in the painting Frances had left on the easel. If she had ever doubted what Frances had told her she could do so no longer. Every line in that portrait vouched for the truth of her words.

And yet, and yet . . .

She shivered, despite the sun, clutching her knees to her chest. Now, at last, everything slipped into place, all the clues that she had ignored in the past or not seen. Of course he had been shell-shocked, but not only shell-shocked. There was more to it than that.

Patterson's death. It was Patterson's death in the summer that had pulled Geoffrey apart.

She should have known. She had seen on the wards how the loss of a close friend could break a man as no physical injury could do. Why had it not occurred to her when the Somerset man told her of Patterson's end? Drowned, he had said. Was Patterson one of those men Geoffrey had talked of in his last letter, who had died out in No Man's Land beyond rescue by those safe in the trenches?

He had told Gabriel of Patterson. He had not been able to tell her. Why not? Perhaps Patterson and she were too tied up in Geoffrey's mind with the future – had he thought their future in Canada would have to be abandoned with Patterson's death, and did not know how to tell her? Or perhaps, as Frances had suggested, he was so badly affected he could do no more than concentrate on his own survival. She had seen that too in France.

She would never know the details of Geoffrey's last weeks. She could only surmise. But she knew enough to understand that he had never stopped loving her, that his love had lasted till the end. She put her head down on her knees and wept, shedding all the tears that she had never allowed herself to shed until now, tears for herself as well as for him, for the good times and the bad, for their unfulfilled dreams of the future and the children that might have been.

She stayed up on the Quantocks for the rest of the day, alone with her thoughts, gazing unseeing at the farmland laid out below, scarcely aware of the hours passing. Only when the sun moved away from the combe, leaving her in the cool shade of evening, did she become conscious of time. She saw the shadows that lay across the fields in the valley, the sky beyond Minehead slowly turning to deep rose, and got awkwardly to her feet, her body stiff from sitting so long in the same place. Her legs were unsteady, as if she had been ill for a long time, as she started down the combe.

She saw the car parked by the Huish Priory road as soon as she came out onto the common, recognised it at once but thought that she must be mistaken. Then she saw David sitting in the driving seat. He looked up and saw her at almost the same time. He got out and waited.

"Hello," he said.

She stopped. "What are you doing here?"

"Waiting for you."

"I thought you were in Scotland."

"I decided I'd rather be in Somerset."

"Haven't you been fishing?"

He shook his head. "There wasn't time. I came back on

the sleeper last night, and drove down this morning."

She said nothing. She had been so involved with thoughts of Geoffrey all day that she found it difficult to cope with David's unexpected appearance.

He opened the car door for her. "You look as if you could do with a rest."

She wondered whether tearstains were still visible. She saw his suitcase on the back seat, beside a pile of medical journals. "How did you know where to find me?"

"Gabriel was sure you'd go up to the Quantocks. He said you'd come back this way whichever route you'd taken."

He had seen Gabriel. What had Gabriel told him? "Have you been waiting here long?"

"Long enough." He smiled at her briefly. "Not a bad thing. I had plenty of time to think."

It was the first indication that there was more to his arrival than he had said. She tried to untangle her thoughts as she watched him turn the car. "You're going the wrong way," she said, as they set off. "This takes us on to the Minehead road."

"We're going to Minehead," he said. "I've booked us in at a hotel for the night. The children are happy at Hillcrest – they want to stay for the rest of the holidays, they tell me – so it seems stupid not to take the opportunity to get away."

"But, David, I can't possibly stay in a hotel," she protested. "Look at me. I haven't the right clothes."

"Frances thought of that. She packed for you. Don't worry. Relax."

He sounded so confident that she sat back in her seat, too tired to protest further. She watched him surreptitiously, wondering what he might be thinking, and why he should have made the long journey from Scotland for so short a time. He frowned slightly as he drove into the evening sun. She saw grey hairs that she had not noticed before, and realised, with a shock, that he was twice the age now that Geoffrey had been at Honfleur. What would each have thought of the other, she wondered. She could not guess. Geoffrey had still been developing when she knew him; David already mature at their first meeting. Gabriel's words the previous evening came back to her. She could not believe that David had ever been disturbed by thoughts of Geoffrey.

The hotel seemed vaguely familiar. She looked round the reception area and through the arch towards the dining-room. "Wasn't this where we came the day we got engaged?"

"We had lunch here, yes," David said. "That's why I chose it."

Their bedroom looked out over a small garden. Salvias clashed with geraniums in the flower beds. "I asked for a sea view," David said, "but I suppose it was too much to hope for in the middle of August. At such short notice, anyway."

She was so tired that it was a relief to let him take charge. He made her lie down while he unpacked and then ran her a bath. He made no comment on the state of her shoes or her stockings but remarked on the dress that Frances had packed. "I haven't seen it before, have I?"

Julia sat up to look at it. "It's not mine. Frances must have put in one of hers. I only brought old things down for the weekend."

"Will it fit, do you think?"

"We always used to share our clothes in the old days, when she was at the Slade. It made us feel we'd got a bigger wardrobe than we really had."

When she came to change she discovered that Frances had had the foresight to put in evening shoes, as well as some jewellery. As a result Julia was able to follow the head waiter into the dining-room with more confidence than she might otherwise have felt.

She was surprised to realise that she was hungry. Breakfast seemed a long time ago. David only picked at his food, and was apologetic when he saw Julia watching. "I'm all right, really. Yes, I know I've been overdoing things lately but it's

[252]

difficult not to." He distracted her attention from his lack of appetite by talking about the Edinburgh case. "Disappointingly straightforward," he said. "I did wonder whether Donald was using it as an excuse to get me up to Scotland for some fishing. It's years since we've been fishing together."

"It seems a pity you didn't stay," Julia said.

"Other things are more important. As a matter of fact, Gabriel did suggest the four of us might arrange a weekend together on the Exe. He and I could fish, you two could do what you wanted. Paint, I suppose."

She was grateful that Gabriel should suggest such a possibility when she knew that he was anxious to finish his book. She wondered what else had been discussed at Hillcrest. David was reluctant to say. He told her instead that Frances had shown him the portrait that Julia had painted of her for Gabriel before the war. Julia was astonished.

"What made her do that? She hates that portrait. She won't show it to anybody. She refuses to let Gabriel have it up. It's a rotten likeness, she says."

"Gabriel didn't seem to think so. I was impressed by it, I must say. How old were you when you did it?"

"Oh, I don't know. Sixteen – seventeen, perhaps."

"It seems a pity you've never carried on. Have you ever thought of taking it up again now that you'll have more time?"

She gave him a sharp look. "You've been talking to Frances."

"Oh, no, I assure you," he said wryly. "It's Frances who has been talking to me. I don't know whether she was trying to make me feel guilty or not, but she certainly succeeded. I've been blind, haven't I? I know you were teaching when we first met but I never got the impression that you enjoyed it. I don't think it ever occurred to me that painting might be important to you."

"It's never mattered to me as it has to Frances," she

admitted. Yet at one time, she remembered, she had been frantic to study in Paris.

"Why don't we invite the Bonds round to dinner one evening?" David said. "Frances tells me he's always been interested in you. He might be able to give some advice. At least it would be worth talking things over with him."

She was touched that he should make such a suggestion. Denis and he had never taken to each other; for years the only contact between the two families had been between Pauline and herself. "Frances suggested my going back to the Slade, just for a couple of lessons a week, to get my eye in," she said. "I thought you wouldn't want me to do it. It's not the sort of thing people expect of the wife of a prominent surgeon – being an art student."

"That wouldn't worry me. Though – I have to admit it – I don't think I could be as long-suffering as Gabriel."

"I'm sure that wouldn't be necessary. Frances has always *had* to paint. I've only wanted to. There's a big difference. I would like to start again, as a matter of fact, but it seems absurd, really, becoming a student at my age. It's not as if I shall ever make any sort of mark. Another difference between Frances and me."

"One that you mind?"

She considered. "I did once. I don't any more." She knew that Frances's success had been achieved at great cost, not only to Frances over the years, but also to Gabriel. She would not have wanted success for herself on such terms.

"It's what happens when you reach our age," David said. "You begin to realise your own limitations. I know now that I'll never get my name into the medical text books."

She was surprised. She had not thought him ambitious in that way. "You never told me that's what you wanted."

"Not wanted exactly – took for granted, I think. I always assumed I'd be another Harvey or Hunter when I grew up – I thought that's what happened to doctors. I did realise I'd been over-ambitious by the time I got to medical school. I hoped then I'd finish up naming some condition. Bright's disease, Pott's fracture – you know the sort of thing. Only I could never work out what Elliot's problem might be."

"You're not disappointed, are you? How can you be, when you've done so well."

"A little, maybe. And there are compensations. But it's the same with you. You have to accept that the Tate won't hang your paintings as they have done with Frances. Does that matter, if you give pleasure to others and get satisfaction yourself?"

She had not thought of her painting in that light before. "I suppose not."

After dinner David suggested going for a walk. Julia, light-headed as a result of emotion, the long day and the effects of the wine she had drunk, was reluctant. Besides, Frances's shoes, not as good a fit as the dress, were beginning to pinch. "Let's wait till tomorrow."

"Darling," David said, gently, "don't you think we should talk?"

She looked at him quickly. "I suppose so."

The Esplanade was thronged with visitors taking their evening stroll, the retired, widows with attendant daughters in tow, courting couples, children who should have been in bed. A few red streaks still lingered in the sky. Lights clustered at intervals along the coast. The tide was almost up, lapping softly over the sand and then sinking back with a hiss.

They walked for a while in silence. Julia began to shiver, despite the warm evening. She did not know what David wanted to talk about; she did not know what she should say.

"Do you remember when we first started writing to each other?" he said at last. "You wrote me such splendid letters. You were so honest and direct. So caring, too. I felt I could say anything to you. I didn't know it could be like that. I fell in love with you long before we met."

She was silent.

"Do you remember?"

"Yes."

"You felt like that too, didn't you?"

She had thought him married, she recalled. Once she had known he was not, she had been afraid, reluctant to become involved again. Yet in the end his letters had won her over. "Yes," she said.

"It's not been like that for a long time, has it?"

She shook her head.

"What's been happening to us, Julia?"

How could she explain the summer to him? "I don't know."

"I've been desperate," he said. "I've seen you growing further and further away. I haven't known how to prevent it."

"You've been working too hard."

"What else could I do? It's easy to pretend everything's all right if you're up to your eyes in work."

"Oh, David. What does that solve?"

"Nothing. I know."

The shoes were too tight. She began to limp. "Could we sit down?"

They found a seat among some flower beds. A toy windmill stood in one corner. The sails remained still. David leant forwards, arms on his knees. "I began to think there must be somebody else," he muttered.

She could not believe it.

"Is there?"

"No, of course not. Whatever made you think . . .?"

"There didn't seem to be any other reason."

"Why didn't you tell that's what you were thinking?"

"I was afraid, in case it was true."

"It isn't. The idea's ridiculous."

"That's what Gabriel told me." He gave her a shamefaced smile. "I'm sorry."

"No, no, I'm the one who should be sorry. If I'd known ... if you'd told me ..."

"Yes, well."

They sat without talking. A spaniel, overweight, smelling of salt, lumbered towards them, wagging its tail.

"What else did Gabriel say?" Julia asked.

"He told me not to be such a fool." He paused for a moment, as if debating whether to tell her the rest. "He said, 'For God's sake, go and talk to the girl.'"

She smiled, in spite of herself. "That sounds like Gabriel."

"I'm not very good at talking, am I? Not about emotion, at least. It wasn't something we went in for at home. That doesn't mean I don't feel ... I thought you realised. I thought you knew how I felt. You're all I've got, Julia. Nothing else matters but you and the children."

She looked at him, shy, introverted, not so very different from her, and felt a ridiculous urge to burst into tears. She knew that he meant what he said, knew too that his work mattered as much. She did not mind. It was his dedication and skill that had attracted her so strongly when they first met. She was happy to support and sustain him. It was the fear that he no longer needed her support that had added to her unhappiness this summer. "I know," she said.

They walked slowly back to the hotel. Seagulls were screeching over scraps someone had thrown onto the beach. It's been my fault, Julia thought. I've been so tied up in my own misery, I shut David out.

"I remember in Dublin," David said, "Margaret Wood once telling me that she thought Gabriel owed much of his character to you Purcells. She considered that growing up with the four of you had made him quite human. She made it plain she didn't think anyone had done that for me."

"But you had two sisters."

"Sisters aren't the same thing, according to Margaret. Too reverential. Not that I imagine she was reverential towards her own brothers. Margaret's got no illusions about men;

[257]

she's had too much to do with them. I know what she means. Gabriel's much better at understanding people than I am."

They had reached the hotel. She was exhausted. It had been a long day. She had used up too much emotion. She was filled with remorse for David's misunderstanding, seeing the reason for it. It was Geoffrey who had been the other man, ever since that meeting with Hester.

As David stopped for a last look out over the Channel she knew what she must do. "David, why don't I come with you to Canada, after all? It isn't too late, is it? Would you be able to change to a double cabin?"

He turned round. She sensed incredulity, relief, delight. "You said we couldn't leave the children."

She remembered the concern Gabriel and Frances had shown during the weekend. "We'll ask Frances to take charge. You were right. She'd be glad to do it. And Andrew would be thrilled." Even the difficulties of starting a new school would be tolerable if Frances was waiting to meet him at the end of the day.

"I don't know," he said. "You've been so very against the idea. I don't want to push you into it."

"You wouldn't."

"You'd have to find something to do with yourself during the symposium," he said.

"I'll take my watercolours. It'll help prepare me for the Slade. You know how Professor Wilkie went on about the fall colours – there must be trees in Montreal that I could paint."

"A mountain, too, I believe. And afterwards? We'll find somewhere to stay for a few days?"

She nodded. She was apprehensive. How painful would it be, visiting the country that had meant so much, being reminded of past dreams? She knew that she must go. She remembered the dreadful finality of that moment when as a child at her mother's funeral she had dropped her handful of earth onto the coffin. Her farewell to Geoffrey had been said up on the Quantocks. Visiting Canada was the only way left to her of scattering earth over his grave. It was something that had to be done.

For the first time for months she began to feel faint stirrings of hope. She and David had been given the chance to start again. There would be time, during the ocean crossings and in Canada, for all the talking that should have been done years ago. Perhaps she would be able to explain to him why she had felt as she did about Canada, even tell him something of Geoffrey ... and help lay his own ghosts, if ghosts there were. Dimly she sensed that the eagerness with which she had embraced a new life at the time of her marriage had masked her inability to come to terms with the old; that a strong future could only be built on the foundations of the past.

There could be no miracle solution to her difficulties, she knew that. It would take time to break down the barriers that had grown up over the years, and patience to bring back confidence and understanding, but the effort would be worthwhile. It was what she wanted. She knew now that David wanted it too.

THE SILENT SHORE
Ruth Elwin Harris

"We don't want to live in Taunton. We want to stay here. Hillcrest is our home. It's the only home we've ever had... Don't you see – it's all we've got left..."

The Silent Shore is the first book in the Quantocks Quartet, an entralling saga, following the fortunes of the four Purcell sisters – and their neighbours, the Mackenzie family – from the death of Mrs Purcell in 1910, through happier times (epitomised by the idyllic outing to the Quantocks) to the dark days of the Great War and its aftermath. Each book is told from a different viewpoint; this is the story of the youngest sister, Sarah...

"A winner... Vivid, solid, absorbingly interesting for its people, places, feelings... Memorable."
The Guardian

THE BECKONING HILLS
Ruth Elwin Harris

"Gabriel, I must go. It's the most important thing that's happened in my life... You've got to help me."

The Beckoning Hills is the second book in the Quantocks Quartet, an entralling saga, following the fortunes of the four Purcell sisters and their neighbours, the Mackenzies, from 1910 through the years of the Great War to 1920. Each book is told from a different viewpoint. This is the story of the eldest sister, Frances, and tells of her eventful years at art school and of her stormy relationship with Gabriel Mackenzie.

"A family saga with all the necessary ingredients to enthrall teenage readers."
The Times Literary Supplement

THE DARK CARD

Amy Ehrlich

*On the night table were a pile of chips,
a few bills and some other jewellery...
And there was also a gun...*

Alone in the family house near Atlantic
City, Laura is struggling to come to terms
with her mother's recent death when she
meets Billy, a blackjack dealer in one of the
casinos on A.C.'s infamous Boardwalk.
Soon she finds herself drawn into the
flashy, alluring, high-risk world of the
gambling tables, where the dark card is
queen and nothing is as it seems.

"Extremely carefully crafted and a com-
pulsive read."
School Librarian

DAUGHTER OF THE WIND

Suzanne Fisher Staples

"Shabanu, you are as wild as the wind. You must learn to obey."

Shabanu and her family live in Pakistan's Cholistan Desert. She is a free-spirited girl in a society which denies women the right to be independent. At twelve years old, Shabanu is already betrothed and her sister Phulan, a year older, is about to be married. Then, tragedy strikes...

"Outstanding... An enthralling and well-sustained plot, featuring dust storms and desert rangers, casually vindictive oppression, murder and tribal skulduggery."
The Independent

"A small miracle ... touching and powerful."
The New York Times

DOUBLE VISION

Diana Hendry

"People would do a lot better if they could see double like me... I mean seeing things two ways – with the head and the heart. Reason and imagination."

It's the 1950s and, for fifteen-year-old Eliza Bishop, life in a small, North West coastal town is unbearably claustrophobic. But for her small, fearful sister Lily, the seaside setting affords unlimited scope to her imaginative mind. Through these two very different pairs of eyes a memorable range of characters, events and emotions is brought into vision.

"Succeeds totally where very few books do, as a novel which bestrides the two worlds of adult and children's fiction with total success in both... The stuff of which the very best fiction is wrought."
Susan Hill, The Sunday Times

"Full of acute observation and humour."
Geoffrey Trease,
The Times Educational Supplement

MORE WALKER PAPERBACKS

For You to Enjoy

☐ 0-7445-1313-8   *The Silent Shore*
by Ruth Elwin Harris   £2.99

☐ 0-7445-1356-1   *The Beckoning Hills*
by Ruth Elwin Harris   £2.99

☐ 0-7445-3021-0   *The Dark Card*
by Amy Ehrlich   £2.99

☐ 0-7445-2067-3   *Daughter of the Wind*
by Suzanne Fisher Staples   £2.99

☐ 0-7445-2044-4   *Double Vision*
by Diana Hendry   £2.99

☐ 0-7445-1435-5   *Sweet Whispers,
Brother Rush*
by Virginia Hamilton   £2.99

☐ 0-7445-1488-6   *The Charlie Barber
Treatment*
by Carole Lloyd   £2.99

☐ 0-7445-1449-5   *So Much To Tell You*
by John Marsden   £2.99

**Walker Paperbacks are available from most booksellers. They are also available
by post: just tick the titles you want, fill in the form below and send it to
Walker Books Ltd, PO Box 11, Falmouth, Cornwall TR10 9EN.**

Please send a cheque or postal order and allow the following for postage and packing:
UK & BFPO – £1.00 for first book, plus 50p for second book and
plus 30p for each additional book to a maximum charge of £3.00.
Overseas and Eire Customers – £2.00 for first book, plus £1.00 for second book,
plus 50p per copy for each additional book.
Prices are correct at time of going to press, but are subject to change without notice.

Name _____

Address _____

_____